THE BOY WHO FELL THROUGH THE SKY

Book One

PETER NORTH

Copyright © 2018 by Peter North

All rights reserved.

No part of this book may be reproduced in any form or by any electronic or mechanical means, including information storage and retrieval systems, without written permission from the author, except for the use of brief quotations in a book review.

❦ Created with Vellum

For Louisette

CONTENTS

1. The Ghost Hunters — 1
2. Falling Into Finkley Field — 20
3. The Black Diamond — 33
4. The Attack — 42
5. The Dark Tower — 49
6. The Great Oak — 52
7. The Morning Of The Ceremony — 65
8. Verko — 74
9. The Ceremony Of The Ring — 77
10. The Book Of Writing That Cannot Be Unwritten — 87
11. Krukill — 96
12. The Tomb — 99
13. Vrix — 112
14. The Falls Of Rhandoror — 115
15. The Escape — 122
16. The Fire — 126
17. The Unfillable Lake — 138
18. The Orgils — 160
19. The Atta Desert — 171
20. The Crystal Coffins — 188
21. Stirianus's Oasis — 193
22. Beyond The Oasis — 214

Afterword — 239
About the Author — 241

The Ghost Hunters

Ghost hunting on a Monday morning might not be everybody's dream job mused Finn Gibson, whilst he stalked through a mist so thick it tugged at his cheeks.

A blue-grey shadow loomed.

His skin prickled. Then he relaxed. It was only a gorse bush.

Setting his elf-like chin, he stalked on, steadily making his way along a lumpy track that was weaving an erratic route over a lonely moor. He got to imagining evil spirits were oozing out of the soil and the gorse bush had ripped up its own roots and fled before something truly terrible happened. However, before he had trodden many more steps, a perky breeze peeled back the foggy shroud and sunlight flashed across the heather, picking out a broken down white house. It wasn't much more than a half-mile distant. Not far beyond it the moor ended, truncated by cliffs, and further out lay only sea. Finn shot a quick glance behind. His parents were close. Jane and Keith Gibson —*professional* ghost hunters. Well, at least their monthly magazine was covering expenses . . . almost.

His mother had her eyes pinned on him. Finn grinned at her, knowing it was a privilege to be allowed on the hunt, then he again became engrossed in what lay ahead. Jane swapped a proud look with her husband, who was a tall man with angular features and red hair. On this particular Monday morning they were hunting a special ghost. Something it had done ten years ago had changed their lives, forever.

The breeze died to nothing and no one spoke, so the only sounds were their gravelly footsteps as they scrunched along the ancient track. Then, when Finn came to within fifty paces of the white house, he got the urge to halt. With his heart thumping faster now, he stood quite still and stared. Something about it was bad. Creepy bad.

His parents caught up with him.

Keeping close together now, they walked straight past this dwelling of the dead. Finn thought he heard the house groan, as if it was calling out to him. He glanced sideways, shivered and hugged himself. Then they went as close to the lip of the cliff as they dared and gawped over the five hundred foot drop. A squall raced toward them, howling and tossing steel-grey waves into frothing white horses. When it hit, they braced themselves against the violence of the air and, for a while, watched the sea rage. Then, alternately pushing against and being pushed by the wind, they staggered around the haunted ruin. Half its roof had fallen in. They peered inside through its smashed windows before trying its paint-less door. It swung open. But, as soon as they had entered, it crashed shut behind them. Dust fell from cracks in the ceiling. Then the wind calmed to nothing, as if a warning had been unheeded.

Ignored, even.

Finn's chestnut eyes gawped at the missing floorboards, glass shards strewn everywhere and a staircase, half-missing.

Jane's nose twitched at the boggy reek of decay, "It's worse."

"Ten years worse." Keith said.

"Is this where it happened?" Finn said.

Keith tousled his son's untidy blonde thatch then jerked his thumb at a green door with a panel missing, "No, down in the cellar." He offered Finn his torch.

Finn went to the door and shone it through where the panel had been. He stared along its beam wondering what lurked down there, just out of sight. He didn't want to go first.

"Come on." His dad said and yanked the door open.

Finn's stomach sank, then he smiled when his dad held his hand out and winked at him. He passed the torch over then creaked down dusty steps after him, his mother followed. The cellar was cool and dank, then the odours became more refined and, just in one spot, Finn distinctly caught a whiff of old books. When they shuffled further in though, his senses were met by an odour of rotten sacks and rats.

Finn studied wherever the torch led whilst his mother draped her arm around him and explained ritualistic symbols on the walls.

She gave him a squeeze, "That's fake."

"How would I know?"

"It's back to front."

"How can a pentacle be back to front?"

"Look how the words read." Jane watched approvingly as her son went to the pentacle and worked it out.

Then her husband trained his torch on something else and flinched, "Well, whoever drew *that* knew what they were doing."

Jane peered at the hieroglyphics and shivered, *"A Breach to the Underworld!"*

"There's not many know how to do that." Keith said.

"It looks like its drawn in blood." Finn said.

"Won't work unless it's human." Jane said and reached out to touch it but fractions away she recoiled her hand, "Maybe . . . maybe we should call the gang—get some advice."

Finn looked from one to the other, "When can I *really* hunt ghosts—come at night, I mean?" His voice had derelict house echo all over it.

"Soon." His mother said absently.

They didn't find anything else that might be a worry so quit the house and headed back across the heath.

"Ghosts are weird." Keith said. "They always have an attitude. Why don't they just turn up for a friendly chat from time to time? Why is there always something *dark* going on? More to the point, what did the one we're after do with Angus and Susie?"

Jane studied her husband's profile. He was cool, bright and made her laugh. It had been enough for her. At first. Then he got into ghost hunting and it became exciting. That clinched it. Sometimes people went missing. Ten years ago their best friends, Angus and Susie Finkley, disappeared forever whilst hunting this particular ghost on the night of a blue moon. So, they had a score to settle. Her leather jacket crinkled as she fished a packet of Pall Mall's from her handbag, sparked one up and passed it to Keith. She lit one for herself, drew on it and blew out a thin stream of smoke. Tomorrow, a blue moon was coming. The biggest for ten years.

"You shouldn't smoke." Finn said.

His breaking voice tugged at her heart. She dumped the cigarette and screwed it out with her foot.

They spent the rest of the day on a beach, fishing for crabs in rock pools and sheltering from the weather behind a red and white striped wind break. That evening they had baked trout for supper in the hostelry where they were staying.

"Caught them myself from the stream behind the pub." Ben, the landlord said.

After the meal Jane chatted with Shirley, Ben's wife, whilst Finn watched his dad beat Ben at darts and pool. Then Ben coached Finn at bar skittles and he thrashed his dad. When the evening drew to a close the Gibsons retired content.

Happy, even.

∼

THE FOLLOWING NIGHT, WAY OUT OVER MOON-DRENCHED HEATHLAND, Jane and Keith Gibson were ensconced in the haunted house, sitting together on the dusty floor of the cellar. They had been staring at the Breach To The Underworld for so long their behinds were getting sore.

'The Breach' was formed from a secret and complicated sequence of ancient Egyptian glyphs painted in human blood on the deepest cellar wall. The glyphs were arranged in the shape of a door and it was becoming boring just sitting there watching and waiting for a ghost to come through it. Neither of them had ever seen a 'Breach' open up and they didn't quite believe it was going to happen.

However, they had known two people who swore to them they had witnessed it—Angus and Susie Finkley. Angus had drawn out the peculiar alignment of the glyphs for them, then got them to memorise it before destroying his diagram. He warned them that the black magic contained within the glyphs was so dangerous that the sequence must never be made public. He also told them that if a 'Breach' was going to open, it would probably happen at midnight and it was their job to catch whatever came through it.

It didn't happen.

"Maybe British Summertime might affect it." Jane suggested.

Keith nodded and they waited on.

They both got the shivers exactly on the stroke of one a.m. Something was wrong—the presiding glyph at the highest point of the Breach To The Underworld had begun to drip blood.

Jane's heart thumped. She grabbed Keith's hand, "*That's not supposed to happen!*"

"What the . . . ? The wall should go transparent."

They got to their feet.

"Listen!" He said.

Nothing.

Then Jane distinctly heard faint scraping coming from behind the wall and leaned in. As soon as she did so a small hand came through it like it was shooting out of a still pool and grabbed her wrist. She screamed and thrashed and kicked her foot up to brace herself against the wall but it had no substance and her leg went straight through it. Whoever or whatever had grabbed her had tremendous strength and dragged her forward. She melted into the wall—all of her but the ankle that Keith was desperately clinging onto.

"Jane!"

Now the presiding glyph was spurting blood. For long moments Keith pulled and pulled but the thing that had seized Jane was too strong for him and he could either let her go or follow her into the underworld.

Jane's muffled screams were killing him

He sucked in a deep gulp of dank cellar air and a spurt of blood splashed into his mouth. Immediately, he felt his muscles go mushy, his mind dimmed, and Jane's leg slipped out of his grasp.

"No!" He gasped.

He pulled himself up and stood panting, his bulging eyes staring at the wall.

Suddenly, two small arms shot out of it and yanked him off balance. He fell forwards screaming and kicked out madly with his Doc Martins in an attempt to gain a purchase but, like Jane, he was dragged forwards by something with supernatural strength and disappeared into the dirty cellar wall.

Once he was gone, all the spilled blood gathered together like blobs of mercury then fled back into the wall and the glyphs, the pentacle and other symbols faded to nothing, leaving the cellar looking completely undisturbed.

∼

Soon after one a.m., Finn was woken up by owls hooting. It gave him a hollow feeling in his belly. He was tucked up in his cosy single bed, the pub had gone quiet but he could hear the stream gurgling outside. The owls hooted again and his eyes shot to the window. Moonlight seeped past the edges of the curtains. He thought about his parents out ghost hunting in the crumbling white house by the cliff and slipped out of bed. A floorboard creaked. Gingerly, he teased the curtains open wide enough for his head and peeped out. Two owls, perched together on a wooden fence, stared at him, all silver in the moonlight. The smallest hooted mournfully. He looked up. The moon was big, full and bright but didn't seem particularly blue to him.

Next morning, he woke up hungry, jumped out of bed, slapped on jeans and a T shirt and knocked on his parent's door, no answer. He tried the handle. Locked.

Damn, I want to know if they caught a ghost.

Clopping down the stairs he went to the dining room. Empty. Rain lashed the windows. He went to one and wiped the condensation off. Their noisy Ford Capri with the blue stripe down the bonnet was missing from the car park. He smelled something cooking and stomped to the kitchen.

"Where's mum and dad gone, Shirley?"

Shirley's kitchen overlooked the car park. She looked out and frowned, "I'll just take this fried egg sandwich to Ben and ask."

Finn liked Shirley, she kept slipping him packets of crisps. He went back to the dining room, sat at a table and waited. Homemade marmalade filled a white pot. He poked his finger in and sampled it, then, grinning, he scooped up a big dollop. Footsteps.

It was Ben, "Did you not see them earlier?"

"I just got up."

Ben looked puzzled. He took a bite out of his chunky sandwich and munched, egg yoke and ketchup dripped onto the plate he carried. He went away and jogged upstairs, down again a minute later then had a hushed conversation with Shirley. Finn heard the ting of a telephone receiver being lifted then the barroom door closed and their voices became even more muffled.

An hour and some later, a pale blue police car turned up but Finn didn't notice it. He was in the lounge by then, engrossed in a game of hangman with Abbie, Ben and Shirley's daughter. The doorbell rang and his head shot around—voices said cheery hello's. *Not mum and dad.* He turned back to the game. Shortly afterwards, when Ben and Shirley came into the lounge, their usual cheery smiles were absent.

"There's somebody here to see you." Shirley said.

The policeman looked Finn up and down, lingered on his impish face then took off his helmet and sat.

"Could you make the constable a cup of tea, dear?" Shirley said. Abbie stood, brushed her skirt flat and went out. Ben left to check the barrels in the cellar. "This is Constable Bill." Shirley told Finn.

Finn nodded hello. Nobody said anything else until Abbie returned with a white cup and saucer and gave it to Bill. He stirred it and took a quick sip, "Perfect." He settled himself deeper into the armchair.

"Would you like some crisps?" Shirley said. Finn nodded. When she left Bill took a long slurp of tea and scrutinised him further. Finn felt his muscles tense up.

"Finn Gibson—that your name?"

Finn nodded again.

Bill pursed his lips and took another slurp. When Shirley returned with cheese and onion crisps Finn popped the bag.

Suddenly Bill sat forwards, *"Where did your parents go last night?"* Finn flinched, fumbled the bag of crisps and a few spilled out, he spilled more trying to catch them. *Dad told me not to tell.* His chin twisted this way and that as he struggled with what to say. Constable Bill's eyebrows knotted, "Now you be telling me everything!"

"What have they done!"

"It's not what they've done, lad it's where they are that concerns me!"

Finn stared at Bill, Bill stared at Finn.

"Friends! They went to see friends."

"And what might these friends be called?"

"Erm . . . Angus and Susie."

"Surnames?"

"Dad just said Angus and Susie!"

Later that day Constable Bill Braddock found the Gibson's car hidden behind gorse bushes close to a stretch of unmarked road a mile and a half from a derelict house said to be haunted. It was also a suicide spot. They all left their cars somewhere around there. He wasn't a ghost fearing man and gave the house a good look over. He checked the cellar. Empty. Nothing but paint-flaked walls. No trace of Keith or Jane. He drove back to the pub and phoned his superintendent from a red telephone box on the pavement then got back into the police car and sat there staring blankly through the windscreen for over ten minutes. Every so often he shook his head and dug his fingers into his palms. Finally, he shrugged, extricated his bulky frame from the car and went to face Finn. Unknown to Bill, Finn had been watching him through the lounge window, he didn't know why but when Bill left the telephone box he began to feel incredibly lonely. He watched until he got back into his car.

"Abbie?"

Abbie looked up from her book, "Sorry, I was miles away, I—"

"Something's wrong."

Abbie caught the deep frown on his face and came to see what he was looking at, she saw Bill sat in the police car staring into space, "You wait here, I'll go see if mum's finished baking the scones."

Finn checked the clock, three-eighteen pm, the scones would have been ready ages ago. A while later he heard the doorbell. Voices. Subdued. This time, Constable Bill came into the lounge alone. He sat in an armchair, took his helmet off and rubbed his eyes.

"Where's my mum and dad?"

Bill sighed. He levelled his eyes on Finn, "I don't know."

Finn swallowed, "The ghost's taken them, hasn't it?"

"Beg your pardon?"

"The ghost in the house on the cliff, the one that stole the Finkleys."

Bill frowned and leaned forwards in his chair, "And what would you be knowing about these Finkley's then?"

"Maggie and Tom Finkley are my best friends."

Bill puffed his cheeks out and rubbed his chin. He remembered it like he remembered everyone who had jumped off the cliff. Angus and Susie Finkley, pushing ten years ago, no bodies found, the local newspapers had latched onto the ghost aspect. They always did. It made the nationals. It was quite possible the Gibsons were going to make the nationals too.

Finn watched him take his policeman's pad out of his top pocket, check the clock and scribble something with his pencil. He was feeling more and more agitated, and lonely, indescribably lonely.

"Did you ever meet this Angus and Susie whose surnames you don't know?"

Finn dashed out of the room, "Abbie! Shirley!"

He ran through the bar—it was empty and towels were over the beer pumps—into the dining room—a couple with three giggling children were having cream teas—into the kitchen, Shirley and Abbie were there, whispering to each other. Constable Bill wandered in a while later.

"I just rung the station again, the superintendent wants me back."

Finn glowered at him, Shirley half smiled half frowned.

"We'll watch out for Finn."

Bill went out. Half way to the police car he stopped and turned to look at the pub. Tranquil, nothing out of place, he sighed, shook his head then went to the car.

Finn heard it start, "I don't like policemen."

"Would you like a scone?" Shirley said.

Finn nodded.

When the family had paid and left Shirley went to the roadside and brought in the board advertising 'Cream Teas' then locked the door.

"Dad won't like that." Abbie said.

"Can't be helped."

They sat with Finn, neither knew quite what to say. "Bill's a good man," Shirley said at last, "he'll do his best."

Finn's eyes opened the widest they'd ever seen, *"What's happened!"*

"We're not sure—there's people out looking for your mum and dad, that's all we know."

Finn lowered his eyes and scrunched his jeans in his hands, "The ghost's taken them."

Abbie and Shirley looked at each other uncomprehendingly. Finn stuffed the last of his scone into his mouth, "Can you let me out?" He said with his mouth full.

Shirley frowned, "Now, I know I'm not your mum, but she'd want me to ask where you're going."

"The telephone box."

"You can use ours."

"It's private."

"Abbie will go with you."

Finn frowned.

"I'll wait outside." Abbie said.

"Ok."

They went to the big red box, Finn heaved the door open, got inside and stuffed some coins in. He stood so that Abbie couldn't see the number he was dialling. A businesslike middle aged voice answered.

"Hello, Hattie Finkley speaking."

"H—Hattie? It's Finn. Is Tom or Maggie there?"

"Finn! I didn't expect to hear from you this week. How do you like Cornwall?"

"It's ok." He said quietly. "Are they there?"

"Maggie's here, we just got in."

Finn heard muffled voices and a yelp of excitement.

"Finn! We've been to a castle! It was huge and we went in the dungeons!"

"Maggie?"

Her voice went quiet, "Is something the matter?"

"*The ghost's taken my mum and dad too!*"

Finn heard the receiver drop and Maggie shouting, "Tom! Tom! Come quick!" She came back on the line, "Tom's gone upstairs, I'm going to get Aunt Hattie."

"No!"

But she was gone, the beeps sounded and Finn pushed another coin in, Abbie knocked on the door. Are you ok? She mouthed. Finn pointed to the receiver and forced a smile, after a while he heard Hattie's voice, it was authoritative.

"Finn?"

"Hello."

"Do you have the telephone number of where you are staying?"

He banged on the glass for Abbie, "What's the telephone number of the pub?" Abbie told him and he dictated it to Hattie.

"Now Finn, just what exactly is going on?"

"Mum and dad have gone missing. *It was the ghost!*"

There was quite a pause. "I see. Who are you with?"

"Abbie, she lives at the pub, she's really nice."

"Good. Give me the name of the pub." He told her. "Thank you. Now what I want you to do is to go back to that public house and please, please, whatever you do, don't go out on your own, just wait until I call. It'll be this evening. It might be late."

"Ok."

"And Finn?"

"Yes?"

"We love you."

The phone went dead. He fumbled it back into its cradle, wiped his eyes, pushed the door open and heard an insistent throbbing engine. A yellow RAF helicopter appeared a hundred feet above the car park. The trees surrounding it swayed in the blow from its rotors. A man in uniform sat in the open doorway, hanging onto a strap. He waved. Abbie waved back. Finn didn't. In three-seconds it was gone.

"They're going to look for my mum and dad, aren't they?"

Abbie hugged herself. She nodded. Her mouth was tightly pinched, "Let's go inside, we can help mum get the evening meal together."

"It's got them." Finn whispered. "I know it has."

Just then a couple of red Land Rovers chugged past followed by Bill's police car, behind that was Ben's silver Volvo Estate. He pulled it into the car park and got out.

"Give us a hand, Abbs." Bill called out. Finn went to help too. "Not the whiskey, Finn, here, grab this box of crisps." He glanced at Abbie, "Mum not baking today?"

"She took the sign in."

"Oh?"

"She'll explain."

It was a Wednesday, the local village darts team had an away match so the pub was quiet that evening. Finn stayed in the lounge and watched all the news programmes and Ben and Shirley made sure that either one of them or Abbie were with him constantly. Constable Bill turned up just in time for the nine o'clock news, he stood behind Finn's chair and listened.

'News has just come in about a couple missing at an undisclosed location on the North Cornish coast. No names have been released but we do know a full scale search by air, sea and land is underway. At least two helicopters are involved. In Bristol this morning a sub post office was robbed, the police are searching for . . .'

Bill walked further into the room, "Mind if I switch the TV off?" He didn't wait for an answer.

"Should I stay?" Abbie asked.

"Please." Bill pulled up a chair so he was directly opposite Finn, "That newscaster was largely accurate, we also have your parents car but so far no clues as to where they are. How are you?" Finn's eyes brimmed up but he didn't answer. "Well, I'm about worn in, lad, so, I'll be off to get some sleep. There's a big team out there searching and they'll go at it all night, everyone's doing their best."

Shirley came in, "There's a phone call for you." Bill made to get up. "No, not you, it's for Finn."

Finn jumped up, Shirley led him to the cubby hole which did for the pub's office, a receiver was laying off the hook on a busy desk. She pushed the sliding door shut, Bill had followed, he put a finger to his lips and pressed his ear to the door.

Finn picked up the receiver, "Hello?"

"Finn, it's Hattie, have you been following the news?"

"Yes."

"Very well. Are you being looked after?"

"Yes."

"Good. If anything happens phone me immediately but if events don't change I'm coming to pick you up at the weekend, do you understand?"

"Yes. Thank you. Can I—"

"Tom's here, he'd like a word with you."

"Finn!"

"Tom! *It's happened to me too!*"

"We're coming to get you."

"I know, but—"

"They might find them, you shouldn't—"

"Hang on, I think someone's listening—"

He yanked the door back but Bill was already turning the corner at the end of the corridor. When he picked the phone up again the connection had gone dead. He replaced it in its cradle and scrunched his fists up, then shrugged and tried phoning back but kept getting an engaged tone. He returned to the TV lounge, Bill was gone but Abbie was still there.

"I'm going to my room."

"OK."

He tramped up the stairs and stood for a while outside his parents door. He checked the handle. Locked. He decided he didn't want to see inside just yet and went to his own room. Just after midnight an owl hooted, he was still wide awake. *This time last night mum and dad were with the ghost, what's it done to them—doing to them?* He dozed off eventually but in the middle of the night he woke up.

"Mum?"

The door opened. "Hey," Abbie said, "you need to sleep."

"What are you doing here?"

"I'm sitting in the corridor reading. Mum, dad and me are taking it in turns."

"OK, thanks." After she closed the door he fell back onto his pillow and fought tears back.

Next morning, Bill was interviewing him again.

"I want to go there."

"Where?"

"The house."

"Which house?"

Finn got up, walked straight past him and along a corridor into the bar. Ben wasn't around but he heard clanking so he climbed onto a stool and peered over the counter. The hatch to the cellar was propped open.

"Ben?"

An echoey voice floated back "Who's that, I wonder?"

"It's me."

"Hang on, just changing a barrel." Thirty seconds later Ben's head popped up in the hatchway, "Hello, *Me*."

Finn grinned, it was the first time he'd cracked a smile since the disappearance, "Will you take me to the haunted house?"

Bill was right behind him, "I'll ask the superintendent."

Finn nearly jumped out of his skin, Bill caught him as he wobbled off his stool, he struggled free.

"Stop creeping up on me!" Bill didn't answer. "Sorry, but if you don't believe in ghosts you can't help."

"How do you mean?"

"My mum and dad didn't jump off that cliff!"

"Come on, let's have a cup of tea and you can tell me all about them." He held out his hand. Finn looked at it for a long moment then shrugged and shook it. "Does that mean we're friends?"

"Kind of." Finn said.

They went back into the lounge. Bill listened and made notes for a long time whilst Finn told stories about his mum and dad. Finn was very quiet after he left, and for the next few days spent most of his time staring out of windows. Bill called round several times before the weekend gathering more information and giving fruitless updates. His superintendent had said no to Finn visiting the haunted house, but, knowing the searches there were completed, he took him there in secret on his day off. Finn and Bill hoicked their legs over the police tape and scrambled over every inch of it. The glyphs and pentacle and the backward writing were gone from the cellars. When Finn mentioned them Bill frowned and said he hadn't seen any when he checked over the building that first day. Finn knew he wouldn't have missed them, being a policeman, maybe he was lying, maybe he wasn't, he didn't press for more. They went outside, sat together by the cliff, and spent a long time staring at the sea in silence.

On the Sunday after the disappearance, Hattie Finkley's little green Morris Minor 1000 saloon putted into the pub car park. She was alone. Constable Bill interviewed her.

"So you'll be Angus Finkley's sister?"

Hattie was rotund with rosy cheeks. Her hair was gathered up into a bob fashioned from plaits. She wore a neat dress suit and polished brown brogues. From behind her glasses clear blue eyes held Bill's.

"I am."

"The sister of the Angus Finkley who was married to Susie Finkley and who both disappeared exactly the same way as Finn's parents?"

"I am she."

"You're going to have a problem with Social Services."

"How so, constable?"

"Bill, please." Hattie didn't answer. "Well, the thing is, you might be wanting to look after Finn but they might be wanting him to be living somewhere where he isn't closely connected to a similar event. So to speak."

Hattie studied Bill. He shifted in his seat. "Finn will give Social Services far more problems than any they send my way."

"How so?" Bill echoed.

Hattie gave him a big smile, "Just you wait and see."

She had brought all the paperwork she needed to prove who she was and where she lived. She confirmed Bill's research that Finn had no relatives and after an hour he was satisfied it was safe to let Finn go with her.

"Social Services have an appointment booked to collect Finn from here tomorrow, they are intending to take him to a temporary home. It totally slipped my mind to let them know you were coming today, but, I will be obliged to tell them where he is."

"You are a very intelligent man, Constable Braddock. If you are ever in my area please feel free to drop by, and I don't extend that invitation lightly. Now, where has Finn got to?"

"He'll be with the publicans."

It was quite the most emotional goodbye Ben, Shirley and Abbie had ever had with a guest. When Hattie attempted to settle up Finn's bill Ben refused point blank to take any payment. When she insisted he brought her a model of a lifeboat with a slot in it.

"You're welcome to put a donation in here, but I'll not be taking any money off you, Mrs Finkley."

Shirley looked proudly at her husband. Abbie squeezed his hand. They gave Finn a postcard of the pub and a photo of themselves sat by the stream. At the car Finn hugged all of them in turn including Constable Bill Braddock, "I'm really sorry I caused so much trouble."

Shirley wiped her eyes, "Just you get in that car before I have to fight Mrs Finkley to keep you."

Hattie fired up the little green Morris and they puttered out of the car park turning left for Warwickshire. The boot and the back seat were full of Finn's and his parents suitcases and bits and pieces. He got a last glimpse of everyone waving at him over the top of them.

"Where's your mum and dad's car?"

"The police took it apart."

"Hmm."

"It wasn't Bill."

"I don't suppose it was, dear." Hattie was silent for a minute or so. Finn let his mind wander to what the ghost might be up to with his mum and dad. "Maggie and Tom were hopping mad when I told them there was no room for them."

"Where's Harry? I thought you'd all come in his car."

"He's in London, arguing with the admiralty."

"He always looks so stern."

"It comes in useful. It was him who got the army involved in the search. He's friends with a brigadier who is friends with a major-general."

Finn looked at Aunt Hattie. She was hanging onto the steering wheel like it would fall off if she didn't, "Does he believe in ghosts?"

Hattie guffawed so much she had to slow right down even though they were already going slow. "No, dear." She said, once she got control of herself. "Harry is a very practical man."

"Do you believe in ghosts?"

Hattie's eyes opened very wide, "I believe in all sorts of things that even *you* don't believe in."

"Tell me!"

"No Finn, I won't—when you're older perhaps. Now, you have a very big story to tell me, and I want to hear everything."

"Everything?"

"Everything."

Finn was silent for a while, "We were walking through a mist along a rough old track . . ."

Hattie didn't like motorways so it was country roads all the way. Hours later they crossed the border into Warwickshire and fifteen miles further on turned into an unsigned farm track full of potholes. It was dusk. Hattie pushed her face as close to the windscreen as she could whilst steering. The car grumbled and bumped under trees for a couple of minutes then, coming around a bend at the brow of a hill, their way was blocked by a gate. Finn jumped out, checked for cows, unhitched the chain and hefted it open. The road beyond was good. Once Hattie was through he shut the gate and ran off the track along a shortcut. Twenty-seconds later he saw Hattie's cottage nestled with its back against a wood. Two small figures stood in the doorway silhouetted by the hall light.

"Tom! Maggie!" Finn yelled and belted across the meadow.

They cheered him on as he raced their Aunt Hattie who pipped the Morris's horn with their secret call sign. She let Finn win just like she always let Tom and Maggie win.

Finn hugged them fiercely.

"Oh Finn." Maggie said quietly.

"Hello, mate." Tom said

"Hi guys, I—" He couldn't form any more words and hung his head. They led him inside. Hattie stayed out of the way until he was more composed then brought in tea, jam and crumpets.

"Now Finn, you'll be in your usual bed in the attic room. Tom and Maggie can help you get your things up the ladder. I'll be in the kitchen if you need me. Supper will be late."

"Thank you. Thank you for rescuing me."

"Can Finn come and live with us?" Maggie said.

"I'll discuss it with your Uncle Harry, dear. Finn would like to stay with us but there was a very nice policeman I met in Cornwall who warned me the authorities may take a dim view of it."

Tom snorted, "Yeah but that's Cornwall, Uncle Harry can fix it."

"His influence only goes so far, dear. Now I must get on with supper."

After she left Tom smirked, "Don't worry, mate Uncle Harry can fix anything."

The next morning was sunny and they were in the garden. Tom and Maggie taught him a game they'd invented. It involved imagining a castle and everything in it. Finn thought about inventing a ghost but cancelled that thought. Two days later Harry got back from London. He wore tweeds and had a bushy moustache. His hair was silver above blue-grey eyes. He took Finn to one side. "Rum business, young Finn, rum business. The search is still on. I've done what I can but it's looking bleak."

Finn had his eyes lowered, "Thank you, thank you for trying." He looked up. "I felt they were gone. I felt it the day after . . . when I saw the policeman making a phone call. He tried hard too."

Harry fussed with his tie then searched for his pipe, "Well, we don't know quite yet they're gone."

Finn saw he was flustered, "Have you been fishing at all?"

"Eh? Oh, too dry. Need a good rain for the fish to run. Now, I must have a chat with Hattie and work out what we are going to do with you."

Harry got to work applying to look after him. He cajoled his connections into flexing their muscles but it backfired and Social Services dug their heels in. One day there was a knock on the door—it was a Mrs Bateman. She was a big lady with curly hair and glasses and although she wasn't a bad sort she had a bad job to do. The three inseparables sat glum whilst she had a heated argument with Harry and Hattie then left in a huff. The next day a taxi arrived carrying her and a Miss Graddleson who clutched a green handbag and a fat brown envelope covered with official stamps. She was a skinny middle aged woman with wispy hair and a very thin mouth.

They had come to take Finn away.

Finn fought the big lady and the thin lady whilst Hattie and Harry clung onto Tom and Maggie. Eventually they got him into the taxi and sat either side of him in the back seat. Finn pressed his hands to the rear window and stared out with a grim expression. The taxi squirted gravel from under its wheels and headed up the track, over the brow of the hill and that was the last Finn saw of Tom and Maggie for a whole year.

He acquired Lucy and Scott as foster parents. They lived in an average sized house in an average sized cul-de-sac in an average sized town in Surrey. They were average sized themselves, average looking and had average views about everything.

Except their church.

When Finn told them about the ghost who stole his parents they developed an above average desire to save his soul. They had been forbidden by Social Services to take him to visit the Finkleys which suited them perfectly. Hattie and Harry had been warned by the authorities not to interfere, or else, which they hated.

Finn talked to Maggie and Tom from the telephone box near his school as often as he could, got a newspaper round and saved up. The first thing he bought was a small tent which he practised putting up in the dark, then he joined the scouts to learn outdoor stuff, particularly orienteering. He was too much of an outsider to make close friends but he forced himself to fit in and learned as much about camping as he could and filched some maps. One summer night he stole out of the house whilst his foster parents were asleep and headed for Hattie's cottage three counties distant.

For four nights he sneaked by torchlight through rustling woods and bramble strewn paths, avoiding the police by camping in hollows by day. Tom and Maggie knew exactly what was going on and followed the hunt on the news with Hattie and Harry, but they didn't tell. Finn arrived in the dead of night, went straight to the garden shed and found a chocolate bar, sandwiches and a thermos of soup, which Maggie had left for him. In the morning he gave himself up to Hattie. She listened attentively to his story and chose not to call the authorities immediately. Harry was unaware he was there because there'd been a big rain two days ago and he'd gone to Scotland after a salmon.

By the early afternoon Finn was sat with Tom and Maggie on the garden wall of Hattie's cottage. It was a glorious summer's day deep in tranquil English countryside, but, even so, Finn had a creepy premonition that something really bad was about to happen.

Falling Into Finkley Field

"Let's get off the wall." Tom said.

Finn checked out the twins. They were almost all he had left. Tom with his wild black hair, pale blue eyes and the best smirk ever, and Maggie, with her raucous laugh, mane of sandy hair and sparky green eyes that said everything and nothing. He frowned.

"What's up?" Maggie said.

Beneath his hands the wall felt rough and scaly, like a big dry fish. He sucked in a sweet summer gust, basked in the warmth of a perfect day and forced a grin.

"Nothing."

He faced forward again, blonde fringe flapping in the breeze. In front of him, juicy grass swayed in a cow-dotted field. His chestnut brown eyes traced a swallow homing in on frantic insects. A mile further out oak trees guarded the village. Unease slivered across his shoulder blades. He glanced behind. No one. Just Hattie's ancient white cottage overlooking her cherished garden. He faced forward, looked down and flinched.

Instead of grass below his feet there was a vast hole. Peering into it he saw, a long, long way down, a moat reflecting the bluest sky and the remotest clouds. The vision seemed so real that he felt he might fall into it. He shook his head and rubbed his eyes. When he looked again the apparition had disappeared. All he could see now was long green grass brushing against his feet and ahead, big green water-meadows stretching all the way to the oak trees. *I'm losing it*, he thought. Suddenly he felt the wall shift beneath him. He grabbed onto Tom and Maggie.

"Woah, steady!" Maggie said. "Are you ok?"

"The wall moved!"

She rolled her eyes, "Yeah, sure it did."

Weird, Finn thought, "Ok, let's jump."

However, before any of them could even move, the grass beneath their feet parted with a sigh then the ground ripped away from them with a tremendous crackling sound, as if the earth itself was yawning.

"It's an earthquake!" Maggie yelled.

But, as they gawped down into the massive rupture, they could see a moat, way, way below them. Then the wall tipped forward somewhat. Maggie gasped and clung onto Finn. Tom grabbed them both and strained to roll back, but, ever so slowly, the wall leaned farther and farther forwards until eventually, they lost their balance and toppled into the gaping rent in the meadow.

Finn's heart banged like it wanted to jump out of his chest. "Aaaaaaaaaahhh!" Down, down toward the moat they fell, accelerating like a lift in free-fall and the reflection of blue sky and clouds in the moat rushed up to meet them. Beside Finn, wind ripped at Maggie's luxurious hair. Even Tom screamed all the way down. But, instead of crashing into the moat, the reflection of the sky swallowed them up and now they were falling through a soft white cloud that fluffed against them like a vast cushion and somehow it broke their fall. When it vanished they were dumped onto the bare earth of a sizeable stone walled field. A big red sun hung low. Not a bird was in sight, nor was there any grass or crop or cows.

Finn had landed with a thud, face down in the dirt. It tasted of sulphur. He rolled onto his back, spat bits out and sniffed pungent air. Sitting up, he slapped dust off and gaped at Tom and Maggie, "We—we *fell through the sky!*"

"We're being watched!" Maggie hissed, nodding for him to look ahead.

He looked and saw a big man dressed in black with a full head of wild white hair sitting on the far wall and staring at them. He had a sallow face and there was something wrong about it. Something weird. Finn stared back. Then the big man raised his hand and pointed at them. Maggie flinched and edged back, but Tom just smirked. But then another man climbed up from behind the wall and sat beside him—then another—then another. All sallow faced, all dressed in black. Different hair. Weird looking, all of them. Younger. Tom lost his smirk. Maggie hugged herself. Others came, climbing over every wall of the field.

"We're being surrounded!" Finn said.

Then the white haired one got off the wall and walked fast toward them. Now Finn saw what was wrong with him. *Them*. Their skin was translucent. Weird yellowy flesh showed through it. Stringy. They reminded him of something. *Scarecrows!* He whirled around, scanning for an escape.

"Look!"

He pointed at the nearest corner of the field. Just there the wall was higher, but steps jutted out.

"Run!"

Tom and Maggie flew over the ground pelting for the steps. They feinted this way and that, dodging wide around five black garbed scarecrow-things that had got between them and the steps. Finn was slower. He pulled in a deep gulp of fetid air, scrambled out of the dust and charged after them.

Footfalls thudded behind him.

Finn beat across the loose soil and got around the first stringy-fleshed-scarecrow-thing. But the footfalls were closing. A chill slid down the back of his neck. He managed to accelerate but slipped as he dodged around the next one. Rolling in the dirt a sandal flew off, he stole a glance behind, the white haired one was coming fast. Finn threw himself off the ground and sped after Tom and Maggie who were in shadow now, almost at the wall. Those running after him sounded closer still but he didn't dare look back. He saw only what lay ahead—three of them garbed in black, woven strands of something or other for flesh. *Scarecrows?* They can't be—too spooky—got to be something else. He flashed past another one.

"Stop!" It yelled at him.

Yeah, sure, Finn thought. He saw Tom make it to the top of the wall, pull Maggie up alongside, wave encouragement to him—but then they jumped over and disappeared. Finn became frenzied to catch them up. He smashed out at the arms of the next scarecrow-thing—a small one with vermilion hair wearing a black skirt over black pants—got past easily. Hurtling at the last one he dived into its midriff and felt its stomach give way like a feather pillow. They went down in a bundle. Finn whirled, bit, scratched, snapped back onto his feet, kicked off his other sandal and charged for the wall. Adrenaline pumped into his veins, his legs spun, his feet pounded, stinking soil squeezed between his toes. Seconds later his hands gripped cool stone and he thrust himself up—first step—second step—third step—got his hands on top of the wall—got his stomach on top of it—the footfalls behind him stopped—something grabbed his leg.

Tight.

He twisted onto his back, now everything appeared to be moving in slow motion giving him time to study his aggressor. Beads of sweat dripped at snail speed across the furrows on its brow. Apart from translucent skin stretched over straw-like flesh it had all the features of a human. Blue-grey eyes squinted at him from under unruly and thick white eyebrows, and its mouth was drawn tight, as if it were imperative he be captured. Whatever the scarecrow-thing was, it was squeezing his calf harder and harder with its right hand, the long finger of which was missing.

"Wait!" It wheezed.

It's out of breath! Finn lifted his free leg, screamed out a lungful of air and rammed his filthy bare foot into its eye. It gasped, staggered back and brought its hands up to its face. Finn sat up then, and took a good long look at the big crowd of black garbed scarecrow things who had come to a halt on the blighted earth. All were staring at him. *They look like a hoard of lost mourners searching for a funeral.* He leaned back, flipped himself over the other side of the wall, and got a last glimpse of an angry red sunset before he shot through a hole in the air and landed in a heap on top of Tom and Maggie. Somehow they'd arrived back in bright sunshine at the foot of the garden wall that encircled Hattie's cottage. They untangled themselves. Maggie and Tom stared at him with bulging eyes. Finn sniffed sweet air and listened to insects buzzing and birds twittering. A cow stopped chewing grass and stared at them. Then a familiar voice called out from the other side of the wall.

"Tea's ready."

It was followed by Hattie's smiling face. However, her ruddy cheeks turned ashen and her smiley expression melted into a deep frown as she took in their contorted faces and dishevelled clothes.

"Finn, your feet are bleeding! And, Tom and Maggie Finkley! I've told you many, many times that this wall can sometimes be so much higher than it looks!" Contrary to her scolding there was an excited gleam in her eyes. Simultaneously, they burst out talking fast and loud, but their wild visions crashed into a jumble that made no sense at all. They shut up and stared at each other. "Come inside and wash." Hattie said, all businesslike. "I'll bandage your feet for you, Finn, and then, you three can tell me your story."

As soon as she'd gone Maggie insisted they tell their tale as an imaginary happening.

"Why?" Tom said.

"Because, *dearest brother*, I don't want Aunt Hattie to have a heart attack."

It was gone sundown before Hattie got any sense out of them. She smiled serenely and knitted continuously throughout their tales. Afterwards, they sat in the garden under a sickle moon, keeping an eye on Hattie through a window, and whispered excitedly about their adventure.

Later, in his cramped attic-room beneath the thatch, Finn thought about how he'd felt when Tom and Maggie jumped over the wall leaving him alone with the scarecrow-beings. He tensed up. Even though it had only taken thirty-seconds to catch up with them it had seemed endless. He knew it would be hours before he found sleep so he lit a candle before hitting the light switch. Slipping under the covers he stretched out, luxuriating in the feel of crisp cotton sheets, and for a while he watched dancing shadows cast off the candles' flame. Suddenly, the face of the scarecrow-thing loomed in his mind. To forget it he concentrated on the moon as it inched its way across the roof window above him. He thought about *the disappearance*. It was a year now since his parents had set out ghost hunting, never to come back. Tom and Maggie had got him through it. They were cool. They were his friends. His only true friends. *Life without them is unthinkable.* He wondered how long he would have with them before the police or social services came and took him away again. Eventually his candle spluttered out and exhaustion overtook him. His last thought was that something Hattie had said didn't make any sense, something about the height of the wall, but he was asleep before he could remember exactly what it was.

Next day, Maggie wandered into the garden. Tom was already there, sat on the grass. Cottage flowers were everywhere. Maggie smiled at a rickety basket swing made eons ago by her Uncle Harry and plonked herself down on it. Its chains jangled a welcome.

"Mind you don't break it." Tom said.

She pulled a face at him, lay her hands on the basket-weave and explored its intricate patterns with her fingertips. Dangling her head back she became lost in the sky, cloud watching. "It's different for him." She said, after a while, whilst peering at a cloud shaped like a strange head.

Tom was studying the garden wall. He puffed his cheeks out, "It changes to the right of the gate, I never noticed that before."

Maggie sat up and contemplated the shaggy black mop he called a haircut, "But he knew his parents, we didn't know ours."

"If you look at the wall here it definitely changes—"

"*Tom!*"

"Hmm?"

She sighed, examined her nails, and chewed on an errant one, "Our parents disappeared when we were only three years old."

Tom peered at his twin and frowned, "Finn's cool. He can look after himself."

"*But he knew his—we didn't know ours!*"

A white dove cooed from the top of a chimney pot that presided over the thatched roof of Hattie's cottage. Tom looked up, cupped his hands and cooed back, then turned and raised his left eyebrow at Maggie, "You've already said that, so what are you really trying to say?"

"*We shouldn't have abandoned him yesterday.*"

Finn was upstairs, squirming into a black T shirt emblazoned with a wicked white skull with tusks, the emblem of his favourite band. Then he sat on his bed and gently squeezed the dressings on his toes—no pain. He pulled on his denims, plodded down the stairs and headed to the kitchen with his mind set on a cup of tea.

"Hi, Finn," Hattie said, "you've had a proper good sleep, it's after midday already. Tom and Maggie are in the garden, can you call them for lunch?"

"Something smells well scrummy."

Hattie smiled. "Thank you." She said, and opened the oven to show him her creation.

He forgot about tea, walked down the hall and heard voices. *They're talking about me.* He sped up and breezed out into the garden, "Hi guys—lunch is ready." He made it sound as cheerful as he could.

Tom whirled his head. Maggie jerked to her feet and scrunched her sandy hair into a lion's main before turning and giving Finn the best smile in the world. He always went a bit wobbly when she did that.

"Great, I'm starving. Come on, Tom." They hurried inside.

Finn managed to resist the aroma of hot pastry wafting from the doorway and went to study the wall. The place where they were thrown off was formed from irregular stones different from those elsewhere. They seemed ancient somehow and blotched with unusual lichen. Hairy. He rubbed it and it reminded him of stroking the back of his dad's head. He didn't want to be reminded. He peered beyond the wall—nothing but grass and cows. Looking further out, a church spire poked above the oak trees. Everything was in its place. He leaned over the wall and checked where the grass had parted. Nothing. He breathed out slowly through pursed lips then trotted back into the cottage, he was starving too.

Plates clacked, knives jingled into place. Maggie poured lashings of gravy over their mash. It was an unusual lunch for summer but at the same time exactly what they craved. There was no conversation for a minute or two whilst Finn and the twins concentrated on filling their bellies. Hattie, however, scrutinised each of them in turn.

"Did you know that our family history goes all the way back to Baron Finkley and beyond?"

Tom and Maggie rolled their eyes and replied in a weary tone.

"Yes, Auntie."

"Ah, but did you know that this cottage is built on the original site of Baron Finkley's castle? Also, that part of the garden wall—the bit you jumped off yesterday—is believed to be all that is left of the top of the old castle wall. The ground level has been altered though—there used to be a fall of over a hundred feet at the other side, *and a moat.*" She stopped speaking and looked at them over her spectacles, her blue eyes sparkled and she wore an inscrutable smile.

Tom and Maggie's forks stopped midway towards their mouths and Finn choked on his chicken pie.

"When I was a teenager, like you three," she continued, "I used to jump off that part of the wall too—just playing games you know. The first time I did it, I felt like I would never reach the ground. It's silly when I look back, and when I tried to tell your Uncle Harry about it—he just laughed and said, 'What vivid imaginations young girls have'." With that she stood abruptly. "Must be off now—got to catch the baker before he closes and I want to walk to the village—it's such a lovely day. Don't forget to wash up before you go climbing garden walls again."

They didn't find their voices until after she had left.

"She knows." Finn ventured

"She does." Tom agreed.

"*She's been there,*" Maggie said, "she must have. And what's more it's ok to go back, because Aunt Hattie is nobody's fool and she would have warned us off if it wasn't." She scrunched her hair up whilst thinking it through. "I reckon she's gone to the village so we can talk freely and maybe get up the courage to do it again. There must either be something we need to do there or it's just a fun thing to do and, I think she was slightly envious of us too, so maybe adults can't go there."

Finn leaned back in his chair. A queasiness gripped his stomach, "Maybe we could . . . maybe we should . . . wait 'till she returns?"

"No, Maggie's right." Tom said. "She's cleared off so we can make up our own minds. And, we have to go *now* because Uncle Harry is back tomorrow from Scotland and you know what *that* means."

Finn grimaced, *he'll have to call the police about me,* "But—but what about those scarecrow-things?"

Maggie and Tom glanced at each other, an indiscernible something passed between them. Maggie squeezed Finn's hand, he felt a sensation like miniature electric sparks, "Maybe we read it wrong," she said, "they might have been welcoming us."

"But I told you about the big one—it grabbed my leg!"

"Ok," Tom said, "what do you want to do?"

Finn was caught. *There's no way I'm staying here if they're going back.* He sat straight and looked them in the eyes, lingering as long as he dare on Maggie's, "Ok, let's go."

Half an hour later they'd done the washing up and were stood by the old part of the wall. Finn had swopped his trainers for oxblood Doc's, Maggie wore dungarees and Tom a tracksuit.

"Right," Maggie said, "this time we stay put and see what those scarecrow people want—agreed?"

"Agreed."

They clambered onto the wall where the old stones were and waited. And waited. And waited. Nothing happened.

"What did we do yesterday?" Maggie said.

"I said 'let's get off the wall.'" Tom said.

"And I said, 'Let's jump.'" Finn said.

"Ok, well you've said it so let's try jumping." They launched themselves into space only to land with a bump at the foot of the garden wall. Tom frowned. Finn lay in the grass and smiled at the sky. "We must have done something wrong," Maggie said, "lets recap what we did yesterday."

They went over everything several times then Tom declared, "We're getting nowhere. Let's get back on the wall and wait for inspiration."

They didn't have to wait long because as soon as they stopped trying to will something to happen Finn got a vision of the moat a hundred feet below reflecting the most beautiful sky he had ever seen. He turned to the others, "Can you see what I see?"

"Grass?" Tom said.

"Nothing but long grass and cows." From Maggie.

Finn looked down again and, indeed, the apparition had disappeared. But, before he could say anything else the grass sighed away, the ground ripped open with the same tremendous crackling sound, and the wall lurched farther and farther forwards until it tipped them into a massive rent in the earth. Just like before they fell, accelerating ridiculously fast and screaming all the way down, but this time with grinning countenances like they were on a ride at an amusement park, rather than terror. Then, instead of plunging into the moat, they got swallowed into the reflection of the sky, flipped out of a fluffy cloud, and landed with a thump in the dust of the crop-less field. Finn brushed sulphurous bits out of his hair, pulled himself up and yanked Tom up beside him. Maggie was already stood. Her big green eyes were focussed intently on the spectacle before them.

Scarecrow-beings garbed in black.

Loads of them, a crowd of maybe two hundred or so, all watching them. This time though, they were huddled at one end of the field, apart from one, who stood a little way forward—the big one with wild white hair. It had an angry red smear around one eye. Suddenly, all the scarecrow-beings raised one hand in the air—like a greeting—like a salute—like a sign to attack.

"Let's get out of here!" Finn said. Right as he said it the big one stepped forwards and began to close the gap between them. *"Come on!"*

"Don't move." Maggie whispered. "It wants to speak to us."

Finn looked at her, then at Tom, then behind, searching for the corner where the steps would be. He located it—no steps, the other corner—no steps. He glared at the hoard of scarecrows, "They're blocking off the steps! But if we run now we can easily climb over the wall before that freak catches us."

"Relax mate," Tom said, "we're gonna wait and see what happens."

Finn looked at Tom with his unruly black hair and pale blue eyes. He had his smirk on. That smirk. The one that meant he was enjoying himself. Damn, he thought. He looked back at the scarecrow-thing. It was much closer now—big strides—big scarecrow-man or whatever the hell it was. It ruffled up puffs of dust as it advanced. Twenty paces away it stopped.

"Greetings, young people, and welcome to Finkley Field." It said in a voice that was both deep and dignified. If Tom and Maggie were surprised at hearing their surname they didn't let on. It studied Finn, "You've got quite a kick for a young warrior."

Warrior? Who's it kidding? Finn regarded his enemy. Again he peered at its translucent skin beneath which he could plainly see straw-like strands, ochre in colour and woven in ways that formed the contours of its face and hands. It wore all black like the others—a jacket, a shirt and trousers and a thick black belt with a chunky silver buckle. He admired the big bruise he'd caused on its face, "I was in a hurry to catch up with my friends." He replied.

"No matter. You're back now—you need to come with us."

Finn shrunk down and got ready to run. Maggie stepped forwards, "He's not going anywhere without us."

"I meant *all* of you."

Tom was still smirking. He slipped his hands into his tracksuit pockets, *"Try it."* The scarecrow man began walking forwards again. Tom extracted an aerosol can and a red Zippo.

Scarecrow man halted, "What's that you have?"

"A flame thrower."

"I see."

"You wont if you come any closer. You wont ever see again cos your head will be a ball of fire."

Woah, Finn thought, he'll do it, too.

Scarecrow man sat down in the dust, "Have it your way—we've got off to a bad start. I apologise for that. Just now I thought I had the advantage but clearly I don't—I might win—you might win."

"You'll lose." Tom said.

"Without me you're in big trouble."

"Oh yeah?"

"Oh yeah."

Maggie stared goggle eyed at Tom, "What were you thinking of? Why did you bring that? Oh—you—you—*barbarian!* Put that weapon away!"

"Just a little insurance, Sis."

Scarecrow man leaned back, splayed his legs out front and propped himself with his arms. His black boots were big, "So you're the twins."

Maggie glared at him, "And you—you—you—*great big arrogant excuse for a scarecrow!* Going around in gangs of hundreds just so you can play the big shot—*how did you know we're twins?"*

"The Book Of Writing That Cannot Be Unwritten told us to expect twins and another."

"What—?"

"You're not the only people to ever come here from your world. Princess Hattie was the last one."

"What—?"

"Baron Finkley before her—in fact this field is named after him."

"What—?"

"Do you want to hear what I have to say?"

Maggie didn't answer. She stood tapping her foot then folded her arms and turned her attention to the sky. Tom slipped his makeshift weapons back into his tracksuit and, as scarecrow-man made no attempt to get up and attack, he sat down and folded his arms.

Finn sat with him and looked squarely at the white haired being, "What do you want with us?"

Instead of answering the scarecrow-man glanced behind, "Grindlebrook! Prepare some refreshments—our visitors have managed to calm themselves." Tom bristled—scarecrow-man held up his hands. "They need to know we're not going to fight."

"Yet."

"Now I can see you're twins."

"How?"

"Easy."

Silence.

Maggie sighed and sat down between Tom and Finn, "Now, Mr. whatever your name is. We're used to people messing with us so you'd best be telling us your story, and then we'll be on our way."

"Goodhook the Elder is my title but people just call me Goodhook."

"Well, Mr Goodhook, we're all sitting comfortably . . ."

The faintest twitch of a smile disturbed the translucent skin at the edge of his pale lips, "Look, I'm not a scarecrow—"

"You don't say." Finn said.

Tom chortled, Maggie covered her mouth with her hand. Her shoulders shook. Goodhook cracked a smile which spread and spread. Just then, the hoard behind him began to advance. Their laughter died and Tom jumped to his feet. Goodhook glanced back.

"It's ok. They're just leaving Finkley Field, that's all." Sure enough, Goodhook's entourage all began filing through a narrow one-man stile they hadn't noticed before. Tom sat again and watched Goodhook whilst Finn kept his eyes on the far corner of the field, waiting for the steps to come into view. "Don't," Goodhook said to him, "you'll die if you do."

"What—?"

"There's a drop of hundreds of feet onto jagged rocks beyond where those steps are." Finn looked about wildly, scanning all the way around the wall. "Doesn't work." Goodhook said. "The only way back to your world is up those steps. Fact is you nearly died yesterday. You escaped only because you got over quick enough."

"You—you've trapped us!"

"No—we've saved your lives. You used up all your free time on your last visit. We stood there to block you off. If you'd jumped over just now you'd be dead."

Finn's shoulders slumped. The only sound he could hear was that of hundreds of feet pushing into dust as the scarecrow-beings, or whatever they were, formed a queue to leave the field. It was a gentle sound but seemed massive inside his head. He stared into the broken expressions of Tom and Maggie. Soon Finkley Field had emptied out. Goodhook left too.

With heavy hearts the three inseparables tramped across the blighted earth. They let Maggie climb up the steps first. When her eyes cleared the top of the wall her whole body stiffened then she trembled.

"*Guys, you'd better get up here and take a look at this.*"

The Black Diamond

※

Finn and Tom scrambled up the wall. The vista awaiting them was more aftermath than view. Gazing out, Finn saw land scorched to the horizon, teetering skeletons of black trees, lazy curls of smoke, and, when he looked directly below, a fall of hundreds of feet onto jagged rocks. Filtering up to him, and mingled with the dead smell of charred wood, came a noxious aroma of something he couldn't quite place and didn't want to guess at.

"How are we ever going to get back home?" Maggie said.

"That Goodhook character will know." Tom said.

"Be polite with him."

Tom didn't answer her, he just stared outward.

When they got down again Finn scratched his head, "Well, at least they didn't attack us."

Tom kicked at the dust of Finkley Field with his feet. "If they had—"

"*Keep that damn can in your pocket!*" Maggie said.

Then, with shoulders slumped they made their way silently across the stinking earth.

"Guys, I need a hug." Maggie said. The three of them stopped by the stile and clamped themselves together. "Ok, thanks, I guess we better go see what's waiting for us."

Tom and Maggie clambered through the stile but Finn paused for a few seconds, savouring the moment he had been closer to Maggie than ever before. Her sweet smell fought with the stink of Finkley Field and the warmth and feel of her breath on his neck lingered. Then, when he was about to squeeze through the stile, he chose to climb the wall instead, *just in case*. Once atop it, lush green grass peppered with wild flowers and new fragrances awaited him. The scarecrow people had crowded near a wooden signpost; its paint had faded to a mossy white but he could make out its large black letters. In one direction it read, 'Nowhere Land', in the other, 'The Nothing'. Goodhook was sat there with his back leant against it. In front of him ran a dirt track. Maggie and Tom were ploughing through long grass toward him. Finn looked to his right. That way the track ran off the edge of the escarpment. But when he looked to his left he nearly fell of the wall because, maybe only a half mile away, a vast herd of enormous and unfamiliar long necked beasts were grazing in water meadows.

"Hey, check out the zoo!" He shouted.

Tom and Maggie halted and turned to him, then followed his gaze. They froze with mouths agape. The beasts were too far away to make out clearly but they were definitely unknown to them. Finn leapt off the wall, crashed through the grass and caught them up, not even registering that he hadn't been catapulted back to England. Keeping close together, they made their way to the edge of the track then stopped.

"So what's with the animals?" Finn called to Goodhook, "Are you some sort of farmers?"

In their black garb they looked more like a religious cult than a gathering of land dwellers. His comment seemed to amuse them, all apart from a small one with short cropped vermillion hair. He was pretty sure she was the one whose arms he'd bashed away on their first visit. She wore a black skirt, had a bandage on one arm and was busy stirring the contents of a pan by a small fire.

"So what's going on—is this a kidnapping or a lunch party?"

The scarecrow girl scowled at him.

Goodhook spoke, "You three are unlike other visitors we've had from your world—suspicious, hostile."

"What did you expect?"

Goodhook looked around his throng before answering. Smiles were everywhere, "Like I said, The Book Of Writing That Cannot Be Unwritten told us to meet you at Finkley Field."

"Is that a weird law book or some dodgy bible?" Finn immediately felt a change of atmosphere. Everyone stopped smiling, a few shuffled about, a few coughed, the small one scowled again.

Goodhook narrowed his eyes. "Neither. It just gives messages."

"Here's a message," Tom said, "we don't take kindly to being crossed."

"You won't be happy here then," Goodhook said, "because there are plenty in this world who are going to cross you."

Tom's reply came out almost as a snarl, "Let them try!"

Goodhook snorted and made a dismissive shrug.

Maggie whispered in Tom's ear, "Please be careful."

"So what's going on?" Finn said.

"Our enemy is your enemy."

"What enemy? And don't say you read it in some weird book—give us some proof."

Goodhook sighed. "I have no proof, but if you don't accept our help you'll be dead by nightfall."

Finn swallowed, Tom smirked.

Maggie's eyebrows shot up, "I think we're going to need that statement explaining properly, Mr Goodhook." She glanced at the scarecrow girl. "My name is Maggie. Are you making the refreshments Goodhook offered?"

The small scarecrow smiled at Maggie then replaced it with a scowl at the boys. She returned her attention to cooking.

"Please, come and sit with us." Goodhook said.

Maggie whispered to her companions, "The way I see it we don't have many choices. Tom, I already know you're brave and loyal so you don't need to prove it by—"

"But we need to show we're gonna stick up for ourselves!" He hissed.

"Well, I'm going to go and sit with Mr Goodhook!" Maggie said in a raised voice. "You can wander down the hill and take on that field full of monsters with your little can and your plastic Zippo if you think you're up to it!" She folded her arms, crossed the track smartly then sat and stared at Tom.

"Come on," Finn whispered, "lets go check our options."

"If they lay a hand on you or Maggie—I swear I'm gonna lose it."

"I know you will, mate—but try not to—eh?" Finn crossed the track.

Tom paused a few seconds then stuck his chest out and followed. "Damn, that scarecrow thing is huge." He whispered to himself.

They settled onto the grass.

"Those animals down the slope," Maggie said, "are they dangerous?"

"They're called mucklebacks—you'll be riding them soon."

"We'll be what?" Maggie stared at Goodhook as if he'd just declared he was going to chop her head off. She glanced at the monstrous beasts. "Tell me you just made that up!"

"Never been more serious."

"Oh my—is that why you said we'd be dead without your help?"

"No."

Silence.

"Look, just what is going on?" Finn said, "Me and—"

"We came to give you a message—two actually."

"Who from?"

Goodhook sighed. "The Book Of Writing That Cannot Be Unwritten."

"Ok, show it to us."

"I can't, it's disappeared, it—"

"Oh, how very convenient." Tom said.

Maggie frowned at Tom.

"Ok, just tell us." Finn said.

"The ones you've lost are in this world."

A shiver flushed through Finn. "What!"

Silence.

"That's what 'The Book' said to tell you."

Maggie grabbed Finn's arm, "Be careful. It's vague."

"But—but—it must mean our parents!"

"Steady mate." Tom said.

"So, it means something to you?" Goodhook said.

Finn's hands shook so much he folded his arms. He frowned at Goodhook. "Well—it could mean something to anyone—but our—"

"Krukill wants you dead." Goodhook said.

"What?"

"That was the other message."

The young people stared between each other.

"Who—who's Krukill?" Maggie said.

Goodhook stroked his cheek, "See this," he said, pointing to his translucent skin and stringy straw-like flesh, "Krukill did that to us. She placed an unbreakable curse on us that can only end if she dies. We used to be ordinary humans like yourselves. She is High Empress of this world. She's also an extremely powerful sorceress. She sent fire breathers and drunes to hunt you down. It was they who torched the land beyond the escarpment, burning up every living creature in a vast ancient forest. She'll come after you again."

"Oh, I get it," Tom said, "we've arrived in the land of the faeries having been summoned here to rescue the scarecrow nation."

"*I—am not a scarecrow!*"

A hubbub broke out amongst the gathering.

Tom smirked.

Goodhook glared at him. "I—we—are . . ." He beat the ground with a fist. "*Attuks!* That is who we are! Attuks."

Maggie glared at Tom whilst shaking her head slowly.

"We're English." Finn said.

"I already know that! People have been here from England before you. Be thankful for your country. We have no nation anymore. We are the dispossessed of the Atta Desert—no longer capable of living there because of our curse. Krukill slaughtered most of our race, hundreds of thousands of us—men, women, and young people like yourselves. She cursed the last of us. We're dying now. Her curse can only reverse if she dies."

Finn felt a tiny kindling of warmth for Goodhook and the Attuks. Tom stared blankly. Maggie tried to take his hand in hers. He pulled it away. She shrugged.

"Mr. Goodhook, can you understand that this is very difficult for us. We've been yanked out of our world and maybe it was a big mistake coming back. Now, why would this Krukill woman—sorceress, empress or whatever she is—want to hurt us?"

"Because one of you may be a Ring Bearer."

"What's a—"

"Food's ready." The small cook announced and scowled at Finn. He stared right back into her shining hazel eyes. Her piercing glare didn't budge.

"This is my granddaughter," Goodhook said, "her name is Grindlebrook. Let's eat whilst we talk."

Grindlebrook fired another black look at Finn then returned to her pot. The twins and Finn watched the prickly cook ladle soup into five earthenware bowls. Elsewhere, the crowd separated into smaller groups, took food parcels out and chatted amongst themselves. Goodhook passed a large rustic loaf of bread to Maggie. She broke a chunk off and offered it to Tom, but he got up and walked off.

"Tom! Show some respect!"

Tom just kept on walking.

"Damn." Maggie said and passed the bread to Finn but, as soon as Finn had the loaf in his hands, Grindlebrook sprang at him, jerked his head back and scraped a silver dagger against his neck.

"If you ever hurt my grandfather again I'll slit your throat!"

Maggie gasped, she stared, helpless.

"Grindlebrook!" Goodhook shouted, "Release him! Now!"

Finn heard a click and a whoosh. Tom came charging back with a ferocious flame surging out of his aerosol. Maggie jumped up and got between him and Grindlebrook.

"Tom!—Tom!—Stop!"

All the Attuks let out a huge gasp but fell silent when Tom closed off the flame. He glowered at Grindlebrook. "Drop it—or burn —*Grindly!*" He fairly spat out.

"*What did you call me!*" The small Attuk shrieked. She let go Finn and turned her dagger toward Tom.

"You heard—*Grindly!* Back off or I swear I'll burn you up."

Finn seized his chance. He grabbed Grindlebrook's arm and twisted her weapon free. Maggie snatched it up and held the silver dagger at the ready looking slowly around the Attuk crowd. There was something quite regal about her bearing in that moment.

"Now let's get something straight!" She stated, in her loudest proudest voice, "I don't know what your little game is but here's how this meeting is going to progress. Goodhook, you are going to come back into Finkley Field with us and explain the whole situation properly, and the rest of you—especially you, *Grindlybok* or whatever your damn name is—are going to stay here. Got it!"

Grindlebrook took a step forward but Tom held up his aerosol, "Just try it—*Grindly*."

The little Attuk stood still glaring at him.

Goodhook got to his feet, "I do like your style, Maggie Finkley." He peered down at his granddaughter, "*You,* are staying here!" Grindlebrook put her hands on her hips. She gave her Grandfather the blackest look but he stared her down. "Good." He said when she finally lowered her eyes. Then he faced his Attuks, "Now everybody listen up. I am going into Finkley Field with our guests. We are not to be disturbed. *Androver,* pick some help and settle the mucklebacks. They're grouping up and probably saw the flames."

A thickset Attuk with lush black hair and a straight nose stood up and checked the herd of huge creatures, "Ok." He said. His face was scratched. Finn recognised him as the one whose stomach he'd head butted.

Goodhook led off and they followed his large frame.

Tom smirked at his sister.

She looked at his aerosol, "Oh, put it away . . . please, dearest brother."

Still smirking Tom put his makeshift weapon away. The sulphurous smell of Finkley Field greeted them at the other side of the stile.

"Where would you like to sit?" Goodhook said. Maggie pointed to the middle of the field. They sat there on warm barren soil, invisible from the other Attuks. "First let me apologise for my—"

Suddenly, Maggie stabbed Grindlebrook's silver dagger into the earth up to its hilt, "Unwritten books," She snapped, "Finkley Field, Krukill, Ring Bearers—get on with it!"

"We're supposed to be allies, friends maybe."

"Really?"

"There's been misunderstandings."

Maggie waited for more, but he was not forthcoming. She sighed, "This field smells bad."

"It used to be full of wild flowers and was one of the sweetest smelling fields in the whole of this world. In summer swarms of butterflies would gather here before beginning their final journey into the sky, then more and more would arrive and follow them. Soon afterward Baron Finkley would come from your world, store his harvest here, and join our ancestors for a while."

"What are you blabbering about?" Tom said.

Goodhook ignored him and carried on, "The Baron was a friend of Albinonus, who was the greatest sorcerer who ever lived. Baron Finkley helped Albinonus secure The Black Diamond—an instrument of great evil—and they hid it well. As a result all wars ended. Albinonus rewarded the Baron by creating Finkley Field for him to travel freely between your world and ours. The Baron used it to store his harvest so that there was always plenty of food for his subjects. Otherwise it would have been taken away in taxes. One year the butterflies didn't turn up, and Baron Finkley never came back."

Maggie settled herself and rested her chin on her palms, "What happened next?"

"When Albinonus died, the Black Diamond was buried with him. Guardian magicians kept watch over his tomb but that evil jewel was stolen by Krukill, the ungrateful daughter of one of the guardians. She one day broke into his tomb and made away with it. However, she became corrupted by its enormous power and began the dark wars. We Attuks fought against her alongside many other races but none can resist the power of the Black Diamond. Krukill upended the natural order of this world and made Queens and Kings subservient—they are mere vassals to her now, clinging to their territories in name only, ruling only by her whim. At the end of the wars she cursed we Attuks and slaughtered all our children. I managed to hide my Grindlebrook —but she was the only child who survived. Krukill attempted to destroy Finkley Field too, but it seems the magic of Albinonus prevailed somewhat, and she failed to entirely close the gap between our worlds. It has opened just long enough for you to get through."

"The book?" Finn said.

"The Book Of Writing That Cannot Be Unwritten was created by Albinonus to guide people in times of adversity. It appears only when it is most needed."

"Appears?" Tom said.

"Yes, it only exists for moments in order to pass important messages."

Tom snorted, "Surely you guys don't believe any of this rubbish?"

Maggie glowered at her brother, "Haven't you noticed yet we're in a different world? We're sat with a talking scarecrow who says that soon we're going to be riding those great big monsters that are grazing just the other side of that wall! And that, dearest brother, is why his story has more credence than your scepticism! Humph! Please carry on, Mr Goodhook."

"I am not a scarecrow!"

"Sorry, Attuk."

"Thank you."

"Ok," Maggie continued, "so you can't show us the book. Now, what's this Ring Bearer thingy?"

"There is a ring that gives the wearer the power to see inside the Black Diamond. The Ultimate Spell lies there. Incanting that spell is the only way to break open the Black Diamond and kill its dark magic."

"So how come *you* haven't used it?" Tom said.

Goodhook held up his right hand. His big finger was missing, "I tried. That particular ring is a tad fussy about who wears it."

Maggie swallowed, "You said earlier your curse will end if she dies?"

"That's right."

"And that this book thingy told you that one of us is a Ring Bearer?"

"That's right."

Her hands flew to her mouth. When she lowered them they were shaking, *"You want us to kill her for you!"*

"Exactly right."

"Bloody Hell!"

"Yes," Goodhook said, almost in a whisper, "it will be."

The Attack

Tom snorted, "So where is it—this Black Diamond?"
Goodhook pushed his chunky hands through his rebellious white hair, failing to bring any order to it, "Hanging on a chain around Krukill's neck."

"Sis—we need to talk."

Maggie bit her lip and made patterns in the soil with her fingertips, "No, Tom—we need to listen."

Finn's mind whirled between possibilities and threats, "What options do we have?"

"Options?" Goodhook said.

"Yeah, options."

Goodhook's eyes were steady as a rock, "Krukill will already know you're here because you've disturbed her curse on Finkley Field. She will come after you with creatures beyond your imagination. You need to run. You don't have options."

Tom shook his head. He cupped Finn's upper arm, "How about we have a talk?"

Finn squirmed out of his grip, "No, let's listen."

"Ok, well I need a think—you two can carry on the parley."

"Tom—" Maggie said.

But he was off, eyes glued to the dusty earth. He stomped across the field, all the way to the steps, then settled down and propped his back hard against the wall. Scooping up a handful of soil it felt as dry to him as sand from a hot beach. He sniffed at it, jerked his head back and pulled a face, then slung it and closed his eyes to think.

Something huge shot up in the air behind him.

Maggie screamed.

Tom's eyes flashed open. He rolled forwards and leapt into a sprint but all he could see was Maggie standing quite still with her hands clasped to her head, screaming like a banshee. Goodhook though, was hurtling toward him and he was brandishing a half-sword in his right hand. Tom skidded to a dead stop and groped for his aerosol and lighter.

Goodhook roared out, *"Drune! Everybody into Finkley Field! Now!"*

Finn howled, *"Tom! It's behind you!"*

Tom twisted his head but saw only the wall, then he looked up and froze. A demonic rust coloured flying beast with triangular wings as big as bedsheets was hovering not far above him. At the same moment Tom looked into its huge red eyes it folded its wings and dived straight for him. He pelted off to his right.

Goodhook, coming even faster now, had his arm held wide and was spinning his sword. Tom feared what he was up to and repeatedly flicked the thumbwheel on his lighter, but it couldn't ignite whilst he ran. Then, the nefarious flying demon uttered an ungodly shriek and Tom, chancing a glance, saw that it was already almost upon him, splaying out viciously hooked claws and snapping swept-back rows of spiked teeth. When he tried to change direction again his legs tangled up and he crashed to the dirt. His red Zippo got jarred from his grasp. Rolling madly off to one side he caught a glimpse of Goodhook letting fly his sword. Gracefully, it sliced through the air, shimmering with every revolution and, just as the great beast got at him, Goodhook's sword pierced it between its shoulder and neck. Tom heard bone crack and saw hot purple blood spurt. Then the infernal thing was all over him, claws slicing and cutting across his backbone and shoulder blades. *"Aaaarrgh!"* Just then hoards of Attuks, uttering a tremendous roar, streamed over the wall. Seeing them, the vile creature faltered in its murderous task and took flight. But, its maddened wing beats churned Goodhook's sword around and around and it coughed out big splashes of purple blood. Then the Attuks hurled a barrage of half-swords. Many pieced it. The creatures' wings gave in and it plummeted to the ground, helpless now, it lay there flopping about. The Attuks swarmed and hacked its head off. Its body juddered madly for a few moments, then it lay still.

Tom panted, filthy with dust and bloodied. Maggie and Finn rushed to him but Goodhook got there first and offered his hand. Tom grimaced and squirmed away, but then relented. He raised his hand, accepting Goodhook's, and the big Attuk pulled him up.

"What the hell was that?" Tom groaned.

"A drune."

Tom winced, "I'm hurt." Gingerly, he pulled off his tracksuit top.

Goodhook appraised his cuts, "We have a special balm that will heal your wounds."

Tom stared at him, "I thought you were attacking me."

"I know."

Then Tom did something totally out of character. He attempted to get his arms around Goodhook, failing by over a foot, "Thank you." He said in a hoarse whisper. He wasn't even half the bulk of Goodhook, who patted him gently on the back of his head. Tom released his grip and gave Goodhook's hand his strongest squeeze.

Goodhook raised his eyebrows, "Follow me." He led Tom through milling Attuks, pulled his sword from out of the defunct drune and scraped it through the dust to get most of the purple blood off it. He finished it off with a rag then sheathed it. Grindlebrook, who had waited off to one side and scowled throughout their exchange, retrieved her dagger then scurried to her grandfather, standing the other side of him to Tom.

Meanwhile, Maggie was dabbing tears away with a sleeve. "Thank heavens he's ok." She said to Finn. They hugged tight. She was trembling, "Oh, Finn—I'm so scared. I—I—*they've got swords!*"

Finn drew in a deep breath, then puffed out his cheeks. He stepped back leaving his hands on Maggie's shoulders, "Look, I reckon we're with the good guys."

"But—"

"Come on, let's go take a look at that drune thing."

The Attuks had slit it from throat to abdomen. Finn and Maggie held their noses.

"Whew—that's disgusting." She said.

Goodhook pointed to its head, "See that tube on the back of its skull? It whistles when it dives from a great height but only animals and young people can hear it. Its claws—"

"Can I have its amulet?" Grindlebrook said.

Finn watched her kneel and examine a hefty but intricate metal band adorning its ankle. Turning to her grandfather she caught sight of him and her face made a kaleidoscope of expressions. Suddenly, scraping sounds from just beyond the wall grabbed the attention of everyone. Finn watched mesmerised as a drune poked its pointed head above it. It had bat-like ears, loose flaps of skin like a turkey's wattle swung below its jaws and it breathed with a suckling sound.

Swords whispered against leather.

"Steady now," Goodhook called out, "there may be many more of them."

A hush fell. Maggie swallowed and grasped Finn's hand. Tom glowered at the drune.

Leaning forwards the drune saw its decapitated comrade and hissed. Its big red eyes narrowed then it flashed its gaze over everyone, finally coming to rest on the young people. It vented a gurgle. In response another three drunes poked their heads up from behind the wall.

"Back up slowly," Goodhook commanded in his deep and dignified voice, "and no sword throwing—there'll be no retrieving them from over the escarpment." Everyone obeyed. When they'd retreated maybe half way along the field the drunes clambered up from where they had been clinging behind the wall and stood to their full height. Sentinel-like, they left their wings folded. They were thin, elongated creatures and their rust-hued skin hung loose in wrinkled folds. One of them flicked a claw indicating everyone should keep moving back. "Let's do its bidding." Goodhook said, "We don't know the extent of what we're dealing with here."

Everyone backed up until they were bunched near the far end of the field. Satisfied, the drune that had flicked its claw jumped off the wall onto the dead earth. With a waddling gait it approached the carcass of its fallen comrade all the while making suckling noises, then it dropped to its knees and removed its amulet. It turned it this way and that, appraising it, then clasped it around its own ankle. Glaring at those responsible for the kill, it spat then it raised its head to the sky and shrieked the most hideous shriek imaginable.

Finn expected a deluge of drunes to come pouring over the wall or drop out of the sky but nothing happened.

The drune then made a gesture to its companions. They glanced between themselves. Then it issued a noise that seemed like a command and they jumped off the wall and waddled to it. The one wearing the amulet then ripped the heart out of the corpse, bit off a chunk and passed it around.

Maggie's eyes were drawn to their devilish feast but she felt a frothing in her belly. She battled to contain it, failed, bent forward and vomited. When she arose hot breath breezed on the back of her head strong enough to part her hair

Animal breath.

Not wanting to embarrass the Attuks by showing distaste, particularly as she'd just vomited, she raised her hands to smooth her hair and got hold of something warm and sticky. She screamed, spun round to look, screamed again, lost her balance and fell, narrowly missing her splatters of vomit. The thing that had breathed on her followed her down. It had a three horned head atop a long neck and again attempted to lick her. She saw that one of its horns had the tip missing but most of its body remained hidden from her by the wall. Grindlebrook burst into fits of laughter as Maggie squirmed away as fast as she could go.

"It's just a muckleback." She said.

"Just a muckleback!" Maggie exclaimed, then pointed over the back of her head. "I suppose they're '*just*' drunes then!"

The muckleback looked to where Maggie was pointing, caught sight of the drunes and its big green eyes clouded up. It jerked its head high into the air and howled like a hundred dogs. A thunderous racket erupted from beyond the wall and the ground began to shake.

"Run!" Goodhook yelled.

Everyone bolted for the edges of the field. Seconds later masses of the most powerful creatures the young people had ever seen launched themselves into Finkley Field and charged the drunes, who fled, flying low over the far wall.

Maggie wheezed and puffed madly. Grindlebrook, who had dragged her up and run with her hugged her, "Welcome to the world of the Attuks, Maggie."

Maggie gawped at Grindlebrook who again erupted into raucous laughter. Tom and Finn stared at them, then at the mucklebacks. Goodhook's attention though, was fixed firmly on the sky and the four drunes flapping away. He followed their flight until he could no longer see them. Androver wandered over to him.

"Those drunes played a good bluff."

Goodhook let go a deep sigh, "They certainly did. I called it wrong there. But, at least everyone's safe. We'd better be on our way."

"What about them?" Androver thumbed over his shoulder at Finn, Tom and Maggie.

"I don't think they'll be giving us any more trouble. Would you be good enough to get everyone mobilised?"

Androver surveyed the scene with hands on hips, then drew a deep breath, "Attuks!" He bellowed. "Get these mucklebacks out of Finkley Field. We go to The Great Oak."

Goodhook approached the young people. Finn saw behind him mighty multi-horned camel shaped beasts being shooed out of Finkley Field. However, the resemblance to camels ended there as the mucklebacks exuded power. Massive power. "We are leaving." Goodhook said, "You either ride on mucklebacks with us or die when those drunes return."

Maggie stared open mouthed, "What—you'd just leave us?" Goodhook didn't answer. He made for the stile, and Grindlebrook bounded after him. Maggie bit her lip, "Looks like we've got no choice."

Tom cocked his head at Grindlebrook, "There's something about that little scarecrow . . ."

They set off after them, Finn fell in behind. Damn—Tom's smirking. I'm scared out of my wits and he's enjoying himself. Once back by the track Finn regarded the wooden signpost.

"What's 'The Nothing'?"

Goodhook followed his gaze, "Exactly what it says."

Finn scratched his head, "But that means nothing—I mean, where we come from nothing means . . . actually I've never needed to describe nothing before, I'm not sure if I can."

"It's the same for us. The Nothing is like walking into a fog except there's no fog. Everything becomes indistinct and disappears in the space of an arms length. There's just *nothing*. It's deadly. In the past people have walked into it attached by ropes. After a while the rope jitters then becomes slack. Nobody returns. People stopped trying it but every few centuries some curious fool has to have a go, but they never come back. Does that explain it to you?"

"Perfectly. Can we go the other way?"

"Ha, ha, that is exactly what we're going to do. Nowhere Land is our destination. We will camp tonight by the Great Oak, a sacred tree that grows where Nowhere Land begins. Wait here with Grindlebrook, I will ask Androver to choose some quiet mucklebacks for you."

"Granddad's lying to you." Grindlebrook said, as soon as he was out of earshot.

Maggie spun on her, "What? You mean there isn't a Nothing? Or a Black Diamond? Or you're not going to take us with you? Or—or—"

Grindlebrook beamed at Maggie and her nose did a couple of twitches, "No, he's lying about the mucklebacks—there aren't any quiet ones."

Maggie clamped her hands on her hips, "Grindly, you're an imp!"

The young scarecrow pulled a face, "My name is *Grindlebrook!*" Then her face softened, "What's an imp?"

"It's a mischievous, vexing, elfin being that plays tricks on you."

"Oh—hmm—yes, I'm all of that." She addressed Tom. "And what do *you* think of me—fire boy?"

"Huh?"

Grindlebrook and Maggie grinned.

"What's going on, Sis?"

"Oh, Tom, you're so—"

Tom grabbed her arm, "We're going to have a little chat."

"Tom that hurts—"

"No, it doesn't." He pulled his sister away. Finn made to follow, "No —not you—this is between Maggie and me."

Finn felt like he'd been slapped. His brow furrowed up as he watched them swish away through the grass. Then he shrugged —*there's bigger things to worry about now*. He took a deep breath of refreshingly sweet air and became aware of insects clicking and fussing in the grass. But then he heard a noise that sent a chill to his core—an almost imperceptible rustling of clothing.

Grindly's behind me!

The Dark Tower

Thousands and thousands of miles away, around the far side of that world, the fist of a long winter had the Southlands in its grip. There, an icy fortress reared up atop a precipice. It dominated a desolate snow-blown valley, deep within the mountains of the province of Trag. From its highest tower, Verko, Krukill's daughter, gazed out over a snow splattered landscape. She had coloured her lips blood red to set off her white skin to the effect she desired. Her black hair draped either side of her strong nose. From beneath sparse eyebrows and even sparser eyelashes, she peered out at her world.

A lone drune caught her attention as it beat its wings hard through thin air to gain the final two thousand feet needed to clear the rock face. Its difficulties were compounded by the weight of two firebreathers it carried. When the drune was close enough for her to make out its less than precious cargo Verko hissed and slumped into a heavy wooden chair inlaid with exquisite carvings of every depravity known. Her mother had told her that several drunes would come bringing two boys and a girl. A single drune with a pair of firebreathers was way beyond disappointing. She kicked out with her feet and the chair revolved, giving the illusion of the walls spinning. Once upon a time that simple act would have been enough to please her, but, now she was almost a woman, her tastes for diversions had become more complex.

The drune was relentless. Back and forth across the precipice it flew, inexorably gaining height. Finally it alighted on the huge ledge that accommodated the fortress. Breathing out a huge gasp it released the two small creatures it carried. A light snowfall peppered them as they chattered about their journey and admired leering gargoyles. When the drune had recovered somewhat, they satisfied the guards of their right of entry—they had important news to deliver and a reward to collect.

Sometime later Verko heard footsteps. Recognising the stealthy movements of her mother, she slid off the chair and peered down a dark spiral stairwell. She tapped her foot whilst watching the progress of a candlelit shadow twirling far below. Eventually, her mother, an older image of herself, completed her assent. Black eyes met black eyes.

"Verko darling, I've been searching for you."

"Where are the girl and boys you promised!"

"Darling, sometimes there are delays."

"Give me the drune!"

Krukill put her hands on her hips and glared at her daughter, "I've already had the dracs take it to the dungeon for you, dear."

"Can I kill it?"

"Of course you can. It brought me bad news. Bringers of bad news should always be discreetly punished or given a task they probably won't survive. Do whatever you like with it. Have the dracs open the stretching room if it pleases you."

"And the firebreathers?"

"I thought we might have them for supper."

"But they're gristly!"

Krukill pondered her daughter. She's more upset than I thought, she loves roasted firebreather, "Darling, I *will* capture the boys and girl for you because I must."

"Why?"

"Like I said, because I must. I'll have the firebreathers taken to the dungeon too. Be satisfied with that."

"Promise you'll make it up to me!"

"I promise!"

Krukill descended the stairwell more than somewhat faster than she had climbed it. The drune and the firebreathers had followed her instructions but hadn't found anyone when they torched the ancient forest and searched the area. Expecting a reward when returning empty handed was naive and it was far more important to keep her daughter happy. Verko was becoming impatient, she hadn't had any girls or boys to amuse her for a while. Unknown to her, Krukill had eaten a girl quite recently without sharing. At least she hoped she didn't know.

I love her and I fear her.

She suspected Verko would try to vanquish her one day, because that's what magicians did if they were born lusting power, and, Verko had lusts aplenty. However, the pressing need was to find and kill those who had dared enter Finkley Field.

Family issues could wait.

The Great Oak

Finn whipped around. Grindlebrook had her silver dagger out but she was simply picking her nails with it. She cocked her head to one side, "Aw—did your friends leave you all alone?"

He took a pace forward, "Have another try with that blade, *Grindly!*"

She edged back and hissed, "Touch me and you're dead."

He took another step, "You're not so brave without your granddad."

She blinked, then backed up further.

"*Grindlebrook!*" Goodhook yelled. She stuffed her weapon into her jacket and ran to him.

Problem child, thought Finn. He took a look at his surroundings. Everything was refreshingly green. The track led a zigzag route through water meadows, beyond were gentle slopes as far as he could see. Maggie and Tom returned just as Androver turned up, both their faces were flushed.

"I'm Androver. Time for your riding lesson." He handed Tom his tracksuit top.

"Thanks. Did you find my lighter?"

"If you mean your little red fire box, Goodhook has it."

"Why am I not surprised?"

Maggie sighed, "Tom—"

"*Just joking*—he saved my life."

Androver prised a cork out from an earthenware pot. "Before you put that back on let Maggie smear some balm over your gashes."

She sniffed it and wrinkled her nose, "Smells spiky."

She pushed a couple of fingers into the mustard coloured ointment then gently began anointing Tom's wounds. Whilst they were intent on that Finn perused the scratches on Androver's face. Around them the straw-like strands beneath his translucent skin had acquired a bluish tinge. Finn kicked a pebble with his foot then decided to fess up, "Was it me who scratched you?"

The Attuk stroked the dark lines on his cheek and nodded, "You proper winded me too."

"I've upset Grindlebrook again."

Androver let out a snort, "Everybody upsets her."

Maggie frowned, "Finn—what have you done? We were only away a—"

"We need to get going." Androver said. "Just walk towards those mucklebacks."

Maggie saw three alarming looking beasts, lined up, watching them, "I—I've been dreading this."

Tom took her arm, but gently this time, "Our first bit of real fun." Finn held her other arm and they guided her toward the mucklebacks.

"Guys!" Then her attention was caught by a distinguishing mark—a horn with a broken point. "That's the one that tried to lick me! There's no way I'm getting on that!"

Their mucklebacks were triple horned four legged beasts. Finn studied the horns of one of them. They were curved, thick and black at the base but came to a stiletto-like red point. And long. He judged they could gore straight through him and stick out of his back a long way. The horns were arranged a in similar pattern to those he'd seen on a triceratops that had impressed him at the Natural History Museum. But there the resemblance ended because the muckleback's necks grew as long as a giraffes, nowhere near as graceful though and much thicker. He guessed they stood about as high as an elephant. Each had a pronounced hump adorning their backs and they were whippet-slim for their size with deep chests, giving the impression they would be fast. Then, while making various grunts and snorts, their three mucklebacks settled themselves to the ground. The scene beyond them was a veritable army of golden brown mucklebacks, some on the ground, some chomping vegetation and others cavorting around. Attuks wandered amongst them, splashing through the water meadow like black shadows.

"Ok, it's safe to approach now." Androver said, "Just remember that they are our friends and you'll be fine."

"Where we come from," Finn said, "we say tame rather than friends."

Androver drew his pale lips into a tight circle and ran his eyes over their mucklebacks, *"Tame?* The last thing they are is tame—the only reason they let us ride them is because we have mutual enemies."

Maggie squinted at him, "Androver! Before you say anything else and I get even more scared can we just get on with it?"

"I already said it was safe to approach."

"Oh, yes—yes, you did. Well, here goes—guys—I'm not having that one with the broken horn!"

They sidled steadily toward the mucklebacks aware of Attuks everywhere turning to watch. Suddenly the three mucklebacks rose up and turned their behinds to them. The trio flinched and backed up. All the Attuks burst out laughing. What particularly galled Finn was seeing Grindlebrook in hysterics.

"She's going to make a mistake sooner or later." He said under his breath.

"I heard that." Androver said, still chortling. "Ok, the first lesson is—you don't choose your muckleback—your muckleback chooses you. Now spread out a little and wait. And, when they turn around don't make any sudden movements." Soon the mucklebacks clumped around to face them again. Maggie relaxed a bit when the one with a broken horn ambled toward Finn and picked him out by lowering its head which alone was almost as big as him. It puffed hot animal breath onto him and its big green eyes stared into his intently.

"It's bowing to you." Androver said, "You need to do the same."

Finn was quivering a little. He looked from one eye to the other then bowed to it. Soon the other two mucklebacks ambled forwards and bowed to Tom and Maggie who returned their bows. Satisfied with their greetings, the mucklebacks wheezed loudly, nodded to each other, then lowered themselves to the ground. Finn felt his body relax a bit.

"Well done." Said Androver, "Ok, walk around the side of your steed and scramble onto its back. You'll find a natural seat on their humps."

Finn got on with it. The flank of his muckleback was smooth and rock hard but there were notches here and there. Using them, he climbed up onto its back and sat in a hairy depression in its hump. It was surprisingly comfortable. He checked Maggie out.

"That was nothing like as scary as I was expecting." She called to him, but then screamed and held her heart when her muckleback suddenly stood up, "Whew! I hope they don't go fast."

"Well done, Maggie!" Grindlebrook yelled from atop a muckleback, then she scowled at Finn.

Tom mounted up without incident. A few Attuks clapped then one whistled. Within seconds all joined in, some cheered.

"What's that all about?" Finn shouted.

"They're impressed." Androver called back, "Mucklebacks can be cantankerous when novices first mount up—sometimes they get killed—now listen up, Goodhook always leads but I'm going to stay with you."

Finn wondered if he was kidding about novices dying. He searched out Goodhook and saw him rummaging in his jacket. He took out a curved horn, then blew a long strident note on it and pointed forwards. All the mucklebacks set off as one, following the direction of the track.

Maggie bounced up and down and had trouble balancing, "There's nothing to hang on to!"

Finn though, swayed easy with the movements of his steed, "Stop fighting and relax!"

Never before had Finn told Maggie what to do. She stared at him, "Pardon?" But the distraction had caused her to stop bouncing. She relaxed and gazed at her muckleback's long muscular neck and the back of its triple horned head. "Hello muckleback." She said. Its ears immediately shot up, sticking out more than a foot. Then it turned its head and gazed at her with big dreamy green eyes encircled by thick black lashes. Suddenly, it stuck its tongue out and winked then its head shot back around. "No! That's not possible!"

"What's up?" Tom shouted.

"I think my muckleback understands me."

"Glad something does."

"Very funny, dearest brother."

Ahead, the track marked a route across rolling grassland. A warm breeze ruffled Finn's hair. He took a last glance behind at Finkley Field then wondered about the possibility his parents were somewhere in this world. Wouldn't the Attuks have heard about it? He closed his eyes and tried to feel if they were here like he could feel they were gone back in England. But the thought suffocated him. He gave up and opened his eyes again.

Androver guided his muckleback to Maggie's, "About two-thirds up its neck there's a wide slit at either side." He said.

"Oh yes. Has it been hurt?"

"No, they all have those. We use them to ride faster."

"Androver, please tell me I don't have to go fast—I've only just properly relaxed and I'm enjoying this bit."

"Once you're up there in the high perch—"

"Woah—if you think I'm going to climb its neck—"

"Getting up there is easy—"

"What!" Her voice had altered to a squeak. "You mean we really do have to get up there? Please don't tease me, I'm not sure I can take any more big surprises today."

"Just watch everybody else. It's easy. When your muckleback lowers its neck, slide your legs into those slits, then wrap your arms around its neck and you'll find some bony handholds."

"What—?"

"They're like small horns, you just—"

"No! Tell me you're kidding!" But out of the corner of her eye she saw a muckleback roll its neck back just like a swan would. She turned to watch. The Attuk riding it performed exactly the movements that Androver had described, got lifted high into the air and waved to her. Maggie's hands shot to her mouth. It was Grindlebrook. She waved to Maggie. Maggie bit her lip and gave a hesitant wave back.

Meanwhile, Finn rode perfectly in tune with the gait of his muckleback. He leaned back into its seat, stretched his arms out and gazed up at a cloudless sky. *I'm going to remember this moment forever.* Beneath him his muckleback swished and thudded its way forwards grunting and snorting as it went.

"Hey Finn, something's happening." Tom called.

"Damn—what now?" Then he saw Attuks all around him being

hoisted up high in the air, "Wow!" Androver pulled up alongside. "How do we get them to lower their necks?"

"Glad to hear you're ready for it—Maggie isn't—we'll stop soon and the three of you can learn the moves together." He got their muckle-backs to halt at the brow of the next hill. The rest of the herd pressed onward.

"Androver has this crazy idea that I'm going to get up the neck of my muckleback!"

Tom scratched his head, "You've got to do it, Sis—it's gonna be amazing."

"But I'm scared! And we've only been riding for like five minutes and a bit and now I've got to be a damned acrobat!"

Finn pointed to the others getting further away, "We're being left behind."

"It's not safe to be left on our own," Androver said, "if the drunes return . . ."

Maggie wiped her eyes with her sleeve and drew a sniffle up her nose, "Are they not going to wait?"

"No." Androver said.

Her muckleback turned its head and twinkled at her with its deep green eyes. "Don't you start!" She said, but managed a tentative smile. Her muckleback nodded to her then returned to facing forwards. Ever so slowly, it lowered its neck backwards and down. It was so slow and gentle that Maggie wasn't spooked and soon she was able to stroke the back of its head and scratch between its ears. Its skin just there had a comforting feel. A few thick hairs grew straight upward. Gently she pulled them through her fingers. "What's your name?" She said in a quiet voice.

"Its up to you to make one up." Androver said. "It's a he."

"Oh, ok, well—everything that's happened here today has been loopy—and I've always loved that word so you're going to be—Loopy." Her muckleback waggled its ears forwards and back-wards. "I guess that's ok then." She found the slits either side of Loopy's neck, which were like a pair of deep leathery sheaths, and slid her legs in. Feeling around his neck she located two bony handholds and gripped them as tightly as she could, then, laying her cheek against his neck, she closed her eyes. A deep pulse throbbed through his tough hide. "Ok Loopy," she whispered, "I'm ready." She shook as Loopy raised her up to his full height.

"Well done! Androver exclaimed. "You're a brave girl."

Her eyes were squeezed tight shut, "No I'm not! I'm a bloody wimp."

"You were petrified," Finn said, "but you still did it—that makes you fierce."

Tom clapped as hard as he could, "Come on, take the compliments, that was dead impressive."

"Really? That's so kind of you to say that." Tears meandered down her cheeks. She tasted salt as she licked them away. "Please can you get up high on yours now guys so I can look around at you not down. I think I'll be ok then."

As soon as their mucklebacks lowered their necks the boys slid their legs into the sheaths grabbed the bony handholds and were hoisted up as high as Maggie.

"Ok we're up." Tom said.

She opened her eyes and smiled at her brother, "You can be truly kind sometimes. Thank you. Androver, please, please will you speed up gently and stay with us?"

Androver patted the side of his muckleback's neck.

"You'll feel safer going fast in the high perch than traveling slow on Loopy's hump but we'll take it steady before we let them rip up the trail, ok, Loopy?"

Loopy looked at Androver and nodded.

"They *can* understand!"

"Course they can—ready?"

"No—I'll never be ready. But I'll do the best I can—I promise." Androver led off and true to what he said it did feel safer in the high perches than riding on their backs. As they sped up a breeze blew harder on their cheeks and their hearts lifted. They accelerated faster and faster and even when their hair blew back and the ground was whizzing past it felt completely safe. Maggie stole a glance at Finn and Tom. They wore the biggest grins she'd ever seen. "Are we galloping yet?" She yelled.

"Not quite." Androver hollered.

"Let it rip then!" She fairly screamed out.

A sudden punch of power surged through them as their mucklebacks accelerated to full pelt. Maggie and Tom's rapturous expressions became tattooed into Finn's memory. He felt supremely alive in that moment atop an unknown beast in an unknown world with an unknown Attuk alongside Maggie and her wild twin brother.

Androver let the beasts have their heads until, silhouetted by the red orb of the setting sun, a huge tree rose up on the horizon. He got their mucklebacks to slow, then stop, and the three of them took in the vista. The tree dwarfed mucklebacks and Attuks milling around it to ant size.

"Wow!"

"The Great Oak." Androver said. They sat silent for a long moment, just drinking in the sunset. "Now listen up," Androver said, "there's something I need to tell you, and, you may not like it—you must learn to trust Grindlebrook."

"But—" Finn started to say.

"All she wants is to protect her grandfather, which is ridiculous because he's ten times more powerful than she is. But, the truth is she's fiercely loyal and that's a good thing."

"But she attacked—"

"Give her a chance—that's all I'm going to say."

He couldn't be drawn further and they pressed on. When they arrived at the colossal tree Androver made a throaty sound. Instantly, their mucklebacks lowered themselves to the ground and rolled their necks back. They extricated themselves from the high perches and slid down their flanks onto thick grass.

Then they stared up at the tree.

Its trunk was as wide as Hattie's cottage and stood higher than a church even before the first branches appeared. Two hundred Attuks plus mucklebacks could comfortably shelter beneath its branches. Scuttling up and down the trunk were huge squirrels with yellow chests and blue backs the size of young bears. They were just as cheerful as ordinary squirrels. More fascinating to Finn though were the birds. They perched in long lines, had green backs, red chests and black heads with orange eyes. They squawked through beaks shaped like a hawks. But, what really caught his attention was their rainbow coloured necks. Just like real rainbows, there was a part that his eyes couldn't see, making their heads look like they weren't joined to their bodies.

"Spooky." Finn said.

"Rainbow chasers." Androver said. He grabbed blankets then led them to a raised area with springy grass a little way beyond the tree. "Best bed around here."

Finn pointed to a substantial block of white marble, "What's that?"

"Albinonus's tomb," Androver replied in a reverent tone, "the greatest magician who ever lived. Several thousand years ago, at his funeral, a young oak was planted. It never died, nobody knows why, and became known as The Great Oak. I'll call you when supper's ready—Grindlebrook's cooking."

Androver wandered off and Maggie held out her arms, "Never mind about that old tomb or the size of that tree—I need a gigantic hug."

They all did and embraced fiercely.

"Sis, I'm gonna get us out of this, I promise."

"Don't make promises you can't keep. Thank you though."

"I have a little idea." Finn said.

"What's that?"

"How about we give Grindly a chance, like Androver said? I mean, if these guys are actually helping us, it might be a dangerous thing for them to do. We could be in their debt big time." Tom frowned and drew a breath to speak. "We can always go back to fighting if we need to," Finn added before he could say anything, "and I'm not saying that we should trust them completely."

Tom exhaled slowly, "You know what? You're absolutely right—and I'm starving. I was dying to try that soup Grindly made this afternoon—it smelt well good—but you understand why I walked away—yeah guys?"

Maggie gave him an extra tight squeeze, "Course we do. Come on, let's not wait for Androver to come back—let's check out what's happening."

"Definitely." The boys agreed.

"Race you to the tree!" She bounded off the grassy knoll and they charged after her.

Grindlebrook was sat by a cooking fire fussing over a steaming pot. They had decided to wait until Goodhook was with her and open up with her full name. When the moment seemed right they approached and dropped to their haunches, so that they weren't looking down at her. She didn't notice them at first being intent on stirring a big stew.

"Hello, *Grindlebrook*, that smells good." Tom said.

She looked up from the pan and almost fell backwards but Goodhook got a hand behind her and steadied her.

"What . . . ?" She managed.

"Smells great." Tom said and smiled.

Then their eyes met and something ignited, but not anger, not fear, not anything previously known to either of them.

"It's stew." Grindlebrook said, almost in a whisper.

"Can I taste it?" Tom whispered back.

Like an automation Grindlebrook lifted a big steaming spoon to his lips. Goodhook made a polite cough. Grindlebrook blinked and pulled the spoon away sharply,

"No! Don't—you'll burn yourself!" The moment was broken and Grindlebrook lowered her gaze. When she looked back up her eyes were flashing. "Why are you being nice to me!"

Tom pulled back and looked to Maggie for support.

"We're sorry we were rude to you earlier," she said, "and we mean no harm to your grandfather."

Grindlebrook looked at her and smiled, "I like you, Maggie—but —*these boys!*" She looked down again.

Maggie checked out Tom and Finn. They nodded and gestured for her to continue. Goodhook was smiling now.

"*Grindlebrook*, Tom is my twin brother and Finn is my—my—" she glanced at him, "—best friend!" She finished with a flourish.

Grindlebrook peered at her, then at Finn, "Promise me you wont hurt granddad ever—ever—*ever again!*"

"I Promise." Finn said.

She returned her attention to the pan stirring it a few times then said quietly, "I guess that will be all right then."

"I can't wait to try your stew," Maggie said, "it smells delicious."

"It's ready! Pass me a bowl—there's some bread over there too." Grindlebrook caught Finn's little twitch when she mentioned bread. Her eyes flashed again. "I would have done it you know—with my dagger I mean!"

"I know you would—you really scared me."

A smile spread over her face. She stirred her stew once more and made sure they got plenty of chunky bits. Then they tore off hunks of bread and withdrew beyond the tree to eat.

By then it was quite dark, Tom gazed at the sky, "Those stars are so beautiful, and Grindly's turned out ok after all. In fact I think that went quite well. Actually I think she's quite sweet."

Finn and Maggie burst out laughing.

"What?" Tom said.

"Nothing, Tom." Maggie said. She held it together for all of five-seconds then burst out laughing again.

"Did you see—?" Finn said.

"Yep!"

They laughed even harder.

"What's going on with you two!"

Finn was in fits.

"He's fallen for—"

"A bloody Attuk!" Maggie exclaimed and they howled.

Tom's protests did him no good. They just laughed more.

Meanwhile, most Attuks were preparing places for themselves to sleep and the mucklebacks had wandered off into the dark a while ago. Goodhook though, was sat with Androver and a few others having some sort of conference. Above them the dark shadow of the Great Oak blocked out a sizeable portion of the stars.

Presently the young people snuggled beneath their blankets and gazed into the firmament, picking out patterns that might be constellations.

"Anybody know what the southern sky back home looks like?" Tom said.

"I do." Maggie said. "It's nothing like this."

"I wonder where our parents are?" Finn said.

Maggie and Tom fidgeted.

"Maybe—maybe that message meant something else." Maggie ventured.

"I know you think I'm a bit nuts but—"

"Your not nuts, but getting your hopes up—"

"Well, *I* reckon we've got nothing to worry about." Tom said.

"How so?" Maggie said.

"Well, Aunt Hattie was here—in fact, she's probably slept right here on this grassy knoll and she managed to get home safely, so we must be able to. All we've got to do is persuade Goodhook to tell us how to do it."

Finn considered it, "I want to find out if our parents are here somewhere before we go back, I mean someone must know if they are, and —hey—there's a moon coming up!" As they watched it climb they realised its craters were unfamiliar to them. After it had cleared the horizon, Finn spoke again, "I think the Attuks are on our side."

"Hate to say it," Tom said, "but I reckon you're right. You know, when that *drune* thing ripped my back I thought I was dead—"

"Oh my God, Tom," Maggie exclaimed, *"that was so scary!"*

And they were off. They began dissecting their thoughts and emotions and recapping their wild and hairy experiences. But they stopped abruptly a couple of hours later when Finn declared, "I guess that settles it then."

"Sorry?" Maggie said, turning to him. "Oh wow!"

Wondering what was happening, Tom turned over too. "Wow!" He propped himself up to get a better view.

A second moon was climbing the horizon. But this one was huge, way bigger than the moon back home. So big they could see its craters as clearly as if they were using binoculars.

"Where are we?" Maggie whispered.

Nobody answered, Finn and Tom being too awed by the beauty of the second moon unveiling itself. Eventually though, their eyes grew tired from staring and, overcome by weariness, they dozed of.

During the night Finn stirred. By his side, his best friends in the world breathed peacefully. *But which world can we possibly be in?* He wondered. Looking up he saw the second moon was directly overhead. It's either half way to full or the opposite, he thought. Its light was bright enough for him to see around and about and he picked out the black snake of a river some way off. In the other direction the white marble tomb of Albinonus sparkled in the moonlight as if it had a frost. His gaze wandered back to the moon and he was lost in the wonder of it until he heard a grating sound. He searched around for its source and at first perceived nothing.

Then his blood chilled.

The white marble slab covering Albinonus's tomb was opening. He drew in a sharp breath and watched it slowly raise up until the tombs' lid was pointing skywards. A dim light flickered from within the grave and Finn heard footsteps scraping on stone, as if someone was ascending a staircase.

Suddenly, a luminous white head appeared out of the tomb and looked about. Finn let out a gasp but so far, he didn't think he'd been seen. Trembling now, he turned over and shook Maggie and Tom but they were in a deep, deep sleep. Then he heard more scraping and looking again, he saw, climbing carefully out of the sparkling white marble tomb, the full apparition of a man.

A ghost! He thought. It must be Albinonus's ghost!

It was tall, had very long hair and a beard and its luminescent white cloak reached all the way to the ground. Right at that moment it looked his way. Finn flinched back. He tried to get up but his limbs had gone to jelly. Then the ghost began moving slowly forwards, bent over, as if stalking him. Nearer and nearer it came and with each step Finn's heart beat louder and louder. He struggled madly to move but his body had locked solid as if petrified. When it was almost upon him, the ghost curled its fingers open and raised its hands. Finn was petrified, thinking it had come to strangle him. But, just when he thought it was going to make its final lunge, its hands performed some creepy gesticulations and he heard it murmur a string of unintelligible words.

Instantly, he lost consciousness.

The Morning Of The Ceremony

A while later a second figure climbed out of the tomb, a big man with wild white hair, this time clothed in black. It was Goodhook. He went to join the man whose pale cloak was lit up magnificently by the huge moon, and stood by his side.

"Are these they?" The man in white said.

"Yes."

The man's nostrils twitched, "I suppose they'll have to do then."

"They are all we have."

Without replying the white cloaked man went and sat by the camp fire. Goodhook followed.

"I don't think much of the one who saw me."

Goodhook rubbed his cheek, "See this bruise? *He* did that."

"It'll take a lot more than that to convince me. You might as well get some sleep. I'll close the tomb."

Goodhook offered his hand, "Good to see you, old friend."

Instead of taking it the man stood and embraced him, "And you too, forgive my manners, I'm preoccupied." After Goodhook left, the man pulled a long stemmed smoking pipe out of his cloak, primed it and sparked it up. Then he stared into the fire, smoking absently until his pipe fizzled out.

Next morning Grindlebrook and her grandfather were sat with their backs against the Great Oak.
"I've been bad haven't I?"
"Bad? You've been the most courageous and loyal granddaughter I could wish for."
"Really?"
"Really. Now go wake our guests up. And be polite."
Grindlebrook hadn't taken her eyes off them since waking. Goodhook watched her scoot away then, rummaging through his jacket, he plucked out a small burnished metal tool, about as long as a cigar with complicated prongs at one end. It had been entrusted to him years ago and he always carried it on his person. Countless times he had wondered at its purpose. He stroked its exquisite lines, before slipping it back into an inner pocket of his jacket.
"I saw a ghost!" Finn told Grindlebrook.
Goodhook overheard and burst out laughing. He went to the young people.
"What's funny about seeing a ghost?" Finn said.
"All sorts of spirits visit this tree but that was no ghost—that was Philadini. He's a magician!"
"But—"
"Look over there." A white robed man with long hair and a beard was sat on Albinonus's tomb filling his pipe. Finn felt his face go hot. "Grindlebrook," Goodhook said, "we need to prepare breakfast for our guests."
Grindlebrook sneaked a glance at Tom before they left. Tom watched her all the way to some stores stashed under The Great Oak.
Maggie nudged Finn and winked, "Weirdo." She said.
"Yep." Finn replied.
"What—"
Maggie smiled sweetly at Tom, "Nothing."
Finn peered at the magician, "Do you think we should go talk to him?"
"You can." Maggie said, "I don't like the look of him."
Tom had his smirk on.
"What are you up to?" Finn said.
"Nothing." Tom said, echoing his twin. "I'm wondering what

Grindly's knocking up for breakfast, that's all." He wandered off, Maggie shrugged at Finn then followed her brother.

Finn was in two minds but his strongest urge was to meet the magician. He wandered toward him but with each step he felt more and more doubtful. The magician didn't make it any easier for him by just puffing away on his pipe and offering no sign of welcome. By the time he had reached him Finn felt as skittish as a mountain goat.

"You scared the wits out of me." He said.

The magician's deep-set eyes were almost black giving the impression of huge pupils. But they didn't even acknowledge Finn's presence.

"Why?" Finn demanded.

No answer.

"Goodhook says you're a magician."

Still no answer.

"Well, you'd better be good cos we don't impress easy."

Again no answer but Finn did perceive the slightest twitch at the corner of his mouth. Ha! He's going to speak. He waited. And waited. And waited. Finally the magician sighed and gazed up at the sky. When he looked down again Finn felt a dark shadow pass right through him.

"Run away, boy whilst you can."

When Finn still didn't leave, the magician mumbled something and made a small gesture with his hand. Instantly, Finn was knocked flat onto his back. No one saw it except Goodhook who, standing some way off and unseen by either of them, shook his head slowly. Then the magician closed his hand into a fist. Finn felt something cold slip right inside his chest and take a hold of his heart. He scrambled to his feet and ran away as fast as he was able, and didn't feel the chill hand relax until he had caught up with Tom and Maggie.

Maggie was biting into a big wrap folded like a burrito, "Mmmm—delicious! Whatever is the matter?" She added, on seeing Finn's expression.

Absently, Finn took a wrap offered to him by Grindlebrook. "Thanks—that big guy in the cloak really is a magician."

Tom smirked between munching, "He'd better be good."

"He is, and damn scary too." He took a bite of the wrap, "Mmm—wow, Grindly! This is well good!"

Grindlebrook picked up a pan and pretended she was going to bash him with it.

"What's my name?"

"Sorry—*Grindlebrook*."

"You will be. Maggie, would you like another?"

"Hey, what about me?" Tom said, pushing forwards. "I was here first." Grindlebrook put a firm hand on his chest, Tom frowned, surprised by how strong she was.

"Maggie first." Grindlebrook commanded.

A little way off, Androver and Goodhook were watching them.

"Looks like your granddaughter actually likes them."

"Yes, it's a delight to witness Grindlebrook melting. It is so sad there have been no young Attuks for her."

Androver grimaced, "We're doomed unless our guests from Finkley Field can triumph against Krukill."

Goodhook ran his big hands through his uncontrollable hair, "Better not to think about that—lets get on with preparations—it is going to be interesting how the ceremony turns out."

"What was it like in the tomb?"

Goodhook's eyes widened, "Spooky! But serene too, in an odd way. There were strange instruments and pots of powder and liquids and animal parts—books too, and steps leading further down but Philadini said no one who'd descended them had ever come back. He didn't know what lurks down there but he was scared of it. Shook like a bush in a storm, he did and, once he'd retrieved the ring, he wanted to get out fast."

"Philadini was telling me earlier that he's researched for more spells to help us and our women." Androver said.

"Anything?"

"Nothing. He said that it remains true we will remain unable to sire or our women to bear children until Krukill dies and the curse ends."

Goodhook sighed from the deepest part of his being, "It is as I expected."

Meanwhile, Finn was telling Tom what Philadini had done to him.

"Woah—nobody can do that."

"Exactly! But he damn well did."

Tom put his hand in his pocket and gripped his aerosol of fuel, "I've gotta get my lighter back."

"What are you guys blabbering on about?" Maggie said.

Tom ignored his sister, he was looking wide-eyed at Grindlebrook, "Can you and me have a little chat on our own?"

Grindlebrook took a step back but then smiled, "Er . . . yes."

"Tom—" Maggie said.

"What?"

"Just be nice. Ok?"

Tom rolled his eyes at his sister then took Grindlebrook's arm and led her out of earshot.

"It's gonna end in tears." Finn said.

"Always does." Maggie said.

"Will you do something for me?" Tom said to Grindlebrook once they were out of earshot.

Grindlebrook raised her eyebrows, "That depends . . . *Tom*." It was the first time she'd ever said his name. Her voice quivered ever so slightly.

"Well, do you remember yesterday when I lit my flaming gas can and came charging at you?"

Grindlebrook looked down and scraped her foot around, "I do," she said, almost in a whisper, "it was terrible."

"I'm sorry I called you *'Grindly'*."

"Oh that's all right!" She perked her head up, "I quite like it really. But I was madder than a pot of hoppers! You can call me Grindly if you like." She was wide-eyed and smiling now.

"What are hoppers?"

"Big jumping insects—they're scrummy baked."

"Hmm, ok, well—I need my lighter back from Goodhook, you know, my little red fire box."

"But . . . but . . . I thought you asked me to walk with you because . . . because . . ." Her eyes became watery, "You're a horrible boy!" She dashed away.

"Tom!" Maggie shouted.

"Damn!" Tom said as he watched Grindlebrook running away.

"What did you say to her!" Maggie demanded.

"I just asked her to get my lighter back and she—"

"Tell me you didn't." Finn said. "Haven't you noticed how careful she is around fires?"

"What—"

"I bet that stringy flesh burns real easy."

"No—I—uh oh." He raised his hand to his mouth and stroked it. "I'm off to apologise." He said, and turned on his heels and ran after her. Shaking their heads, Maggie and Finn watched him go. A while later though, Tom was back, he gave them a quick flash of his lighter. "I've smoothed things over with Grindly—it's ok to call her that now by the way—and I had a little chat with Goodhook too. He gave me my lighter back before I even asked for it—but, he also gave me some bad news—we're definitely not going home anytime soon."

Maggie's eyes narrowed, "How do you mean! What's happened!"

"Don't get suspicious on me, it's all about that Krukill."

"Just tell us." Finn said.

"Well, I asked Goodhook how we can get home and mentioned Aunt Hattie to him. It *was* her that came—perfect description and all that, and she's been right here too, right under this huge oak tree and she got back home by jumping off the wall in Finkley Field, just like we did."

"So we must be able to." Maggie said.

"No, she went back *before* Krukill destroyed the magic passage. He hasn't got a clue how we're gonna get home."

"Damn."

"Apparently Aunt Hattie had a lovely time—went muckleback riding, hunting and fishing and met some crazy sounding creatures called merfyns who we're gonna meet. Last he saw of her, he said she was going back to fetch someone called Harry but never returned."

Finn grinned, "I can just see your Uncle Harry here."

Tom laughed, "That would be priceless."

"How can you be so blasé?" Maggie said. "You've just told us we're totally screwed!"

Tom's shrugged, "Look Sis, it's simple—we're in the middle of our own fairy tale—no school, no homework, just adventures. The way I see it we're either gonna get back or we're not, but I'm damned if I'm not going to have a great time while we're here."

"But we're hanging out with the losers!" Maggie said. We could die in the next five minutes if a bunch of those drune things turn up!"

"No way. We were caught off guard that's all. And, Goodhook says we'll get help. I trust him. He gave me back my lighter didn't he?" With that Tom wandered off to chat with Grindlebrook.

He carries himself so easily, Finn thought, but trusting someone just because they return a fake plastic Zippo to you? Got to be mad. Glad he's on my side though.

"*Vultures ho!*" Yelled a voice from high above Finn. He gazed up and saw an Attuk sat on a branch way up high in The Great Oak. He was waving franticly and pointing toward the river. Finn looked to the river and, seeing random flashes in the sky just above it, wondered at first what was happening, then, after a few moments, he realised they were birds and made out nine of the extraordinary creatures flying toward him in V formation. Soon they descended on the camp in a wide sweeping arc and alighted. Their plumage shone a mixture of silver, gold and platinum, giving them the appearance of burnished metal. Bright red flight feathers set off their metallic sheen perfectly. Tinsel-like strands, flushing upwards from the top of their heads, formed glittering halos that swayed when they strutted. Red, banana shaped beaks completed their striking appearance. They stood as tall and proud as Goodhook.

No bird tugged at the heartstrings of an Attuk as strongly as a desert vulture. Because they lived and hunted in the Atta Desert, the vultures represented an old freedom the Attuks might never again enjoy. Once it had been their homeland, but since Krukill's curse none had ever visited that scorching place and survived. Some Attuks wiped away tears, but all saluted the desert vultures with a bow and applause.

The birds strutted to Philadini who had remained sat on Albinonus's tomb, and gathered around him. He greeted them like old friends, chatting with them and laughing at their squawky replies.

A short while later a lone black eagle turned up. It was huge. Bigger even than the desert vultures. A hush descended when it landed and even the magician stood to get a better view of it. When he held a hand up in greeting the black eagle bobbed its head once in response. All the desert vultures bowed, deferring to it. Then the black eagle stood to one side, composed, watching.

The Great Oak meanwhile, was heaving with squirrels and a mob of rainbow chasers had flown out of it to greet the desert vultures. They steered clear of the black eagle though.

The coming of the birds galvanised the mucklebacks. They had been enjoying a watering hole at the river, now they left it to join the gathering. They swished and thudded sedately across grassland, becoming larger and grander the nearer they got.

Tom came rushing up to Finn and Maggie, "Goodhook says they're going to choose who gets the ring!"

Maggie looked worried.

"The ring?" Finn said.

"The magic ring! You know—Goodhook told us about Ring Bearers!"

Maggie bit her lip. Soon the mucklebacks arrived in a thunder of hooves and she tried to pick out Loopy but there were so many of them that she couldn't recognise him. Then Goodhook separated himself from the Attuk throng and addressed the whole gathering.

"Friends, today is a special day!"

His voice projected well. It was deep and mellow and more dignified than dignified usually gets.

"It is a day that we meet again as friends and comrades. It is a day of thanks and an opportunity to be grateful for what we have. And—more importantly—it is a day that may change the history of our world!"

He paused and took a long slow look at all around him making sure that every Attuk, human and creature knew they were included then raised his hands in the air.

"Friends—it is time—to attempt—a ceremony of the ring!"

There was tumult. Everyone cheered, clapped, squawked or howled.

Finn hissed into Maggie's ear, *"They believe we're going to liberate them!"* His expression was grim.

"I've got this terrible sense of foreboding." Maggie said.

Tom though, was smirking, "You guys," he said, "it'd be amazing to have a magic ring!"

"Have it, dearest brother. I'd prefer to be on my basket swing cloud watching, or sipping a nice cup of tea with Aunt Hattie."

"Oh come on it's—"

"But I haven't seen a single cloud since we got here!"

"Clouds?" Tom exclaimed. "Who wants clouds? We've got seven-foot sparkling vultures and—"

"I do!" Maggie said, so loudly that some Attuks turned to see.

"Well I'm off!" Tom declared.

"Where to?"

"To check out the birds."

"Tom!"

He stalked off. Maggie folded her arms and bit her lip. Goodhook meanwhile, was barking out orders with a huge rainbow chaser perched on his shoulder.

"Goodhook looks just like a mad pirate." Finn said.

Maggie followed his gaze and couldn't suppress a grin, "Oh, come on, Finn, let's just get on with it."

Verko

Verko caught a whiff of wet fur whilst making her way to the dungeons—drac fur. She snorted. The allegiance of dracs lay with her mother.

Half human, half bear, way bigger than both and highly intelligent, dracs were possessed with no desire to vanquish but would defend themselves to the death. When Krukill declared herself empress of everything she elevated their status, from being hunted to the death as a royal privilege, to her own personal bodyguards. It proved to be a wise move as, besides demoting royalty, the dracs became ferociously loyal to her.

Verko prowled deeper and deeper into the fortress innards, halting only when she smelt fear. Animal fear.

She licked her lips.

Stepping into a dark and dank chamber she heard water drip, rustling chains and stilted breathing. Something large was struggling by the far wall. She lit a fire torch. Its flames illuminated an enormous drune, manacled there—crammed in like a body in a barrel. Two firebreathers scuttled within a robust metal cage. No dracs. A shallow grin crossed Verko's face. She paced the chamber, plotting. She liked it to be fun, ritualistic, like a murder. Three pairs of terrified eyes darted after her every move

Firebreathers were similar in shape to a monkey and had an ability to emit a spray that burst into flames. They hunted in packs, lit fires to flush out their prey then pounced, ripping their flesh like piranhas.

Verko ignored them and slunk up to the drune.

"Hello."

The drune attempted to make itself smaller. Verko gazed up and shook her head.

"No mercy for you, big drune, the firebreathers are going to get hungry."

She turned her back on it, went to the firebreathers' cage and muttered an incantation. The firebreathers first perceived a slight gnawing sensation in their bellies but it rapidly grew into a hunger they'd never known. The hunger of a thousand rats. A hunger so strong they hurled themselves at the bars of their cage, eyes transfixed on the drune.

Verko hauled the heavy metal door of the dungeon shut and turned the old key in the lock. The rattling of its tumblers signalled a finality. The drune thrashed and squirmed against its chains.

"Soon, dear creature, soon—be patient."

She stood still and stared at the drune until it became so unnerved it screeched. Then she probed into its mind, wallowing in its fear. *Exquisite*. Fear was the best bit. Without the fear there was no fun. She went to the firebreathers, maddened now, and stoked their hunger up to a fresh intensity.

"We're going to play a game. The prize is . . . you get to eat your friend!"

The firebreathers shook deliriously and sprayed saliva at the trembling drune.

"But—there are rules. First you have to cook it with your fire. When you've cooked a bit, then you can eat a bit."

The firebreathers became frenzied.

Verko leered at the drune, "However if you fail, and take a bite before it's cooked, the drune gets to eat you two instead."

Both firebreathers stilled themselves and stared at Verko. She was demanding the impossible. Their tails stopped wagging.

The drune spat at her.

"Naughty drune! Now I have to punish you!" She slipped a bunch of keys off a hook and paraded them in front of it, drinking in its terror. "That's better, much more entertaining. Change in the rules, *drune*.

Because you've misbehaved I'm going to leave the dungeon door open. When the firebreathers have eaten all they can of you, they can play at evading the dracs."

She waited until she felt the drune's fear reach its fullest fever of foreboding then unlocked the firebreather's cage.

"Eat, little creatures, *then run!*"

The firebreathers went berserk on the drune. Purple blood and bits of drune fountained everywhere. True to her word Verko left the dungeon door open and headed off to the kitchens.

The drune's screeches reached all the way up through the fortress to Krukill's chambers who paused for a moment and smiled at the thought that Verko might be having fun, then she went back to planning her own murders.

Meanwhile, munching in the kitchens, Verko was thinking about her mother. She hoped the firebreathers would make good their escape —that would definitely upset her—but it wouldn't make them even—it had been mean of her mother to keep that girl all to herself.

The Ceremony Of The Ring

A purple cushion, embroidered with silver tassels, was placed reverently by an Attuk onto the long flat top of Albinonus's white marble tomb. Everyone jostled for places around it.

"Steady now!" Goodhook said.

He instructed Androver to get the mucklebacks to sit at the rear and many Attuks climbed into their high perches to get a better view. The birds and squirrels sorted out one representative each. Finn and Maggie were ushered forwards and crammed themselves in around the tomb. Tom was already there. He winked at Grindlebrook who clung to her grandfather. She grinned and lowered her eyes. Alongside them were a desert vulture, the lone black eagle, a rainbow chaser and a squirrel who attempted to sit on the tomb but got shooed off and had to peep over the edge. Finally Philadini the magician made his entrance. He jumped from muckleback to muckleback, slapping shoulders of Attuks he recognised and shaking hands with those he knew better until he got to the front. He rummaged in his robes, took out a small wooden box and passed it to Goodhook who opened it and extracted a simple gold band, held it high, then placed it on the centre of the cushion. A sigh spread through the assembly. He closed the box with a snap and put it to one-side. Next he fished inside his jacket, flourished a pair of silver pincers, clinked them onto the marble next to the cushion and held up his right hand—the one with the missing finger.

"Just in case." He said to Philadini.

Their eyes met. The magician gave a slight nod.

Tom reached out to pick the pincers up but the magician grabbed his wrist.

"Don't touch without being invited!"

Tom struggled but a mysterious force flew up his arm paralysing it, "Ow!" He exclaimed.

Maggie glared at the magician, Finn scrunched his hands into knots.

Goodhook cleared his throat, "Friends," he began, in his dignified beyond dignified voice, "first, we should acknowledge the three brave young people who were called upon to enter our world. Although they have their doubts as to our integrity they've already shown us inner strengths and the beginnings of comradeship."

He clapped and the whole entourage joined in. A few cheered. Maggie and Finn passed a worried glance, Tom rubbed his arm and did a half smirk.

Then Goodhook held up his hands for silence, "Maggie, would you like to try the ring on first?"

She bit her lip, then shrugged and put her hand out to pick it up but, just before she touched it, she drew in a sharp breath and pulled her hand back.

"Do I have to?"

"Philadini?" Goodhook said. The magician indicated that Goodhook should do the talking. The big Attuk spoke in a gentle voice, "We all believe that the three of you will have a better chance against Krukill with the ring than without it."

"But do we have a choice! I mean, what will happen if we refuse?"

Goodhook's expression became soft. He said, almost in a whisper, "Whatever you do in this world, the one thing that is sure is that Krukill will come after you." Unable to hear, the crowd leaned forward.

"But we only have your word for that." Maggie said.

"If you wont try it on, I will!" Tom said.

Maggie took a deep breath, *"Dearest brother—*this is an opportunity to have things declared—important things."

Tom pursed his lips, "Ok."

"Now, Mr Goodhook, do you declare that what you are asking us to do is right? By that I mean, are you doing this because you stand to gain something, or because you truly believe that you can help us?"

Goodhook was about to answer then paused and considered, "My dear Maggie, your question is profound. You must already know I stand to gain. How can I deny that and be honest in my reply? Even though I believe I am doing this to help you three and all the good people and creatures in this world, I cannot deny that I stand to gain great things if you are successful."

He lowered his head like a guilty man.

Maggie seemed to grow a little, "That is exactly why I asked you. The only way you can answer truthfully is by admitting that you personally stand to gain a lot. That is the answer I was looking for and now I trust you. Maybe I shouldn't because you might just be being clever, but I do."

She looked at all the faces crammed in tight and made sure she included the birds and the squirrel too. To help her remember the moment she took a deep sniff and picked out the scents of warm feathers, sweat and oak leaves. Her hand shook a little as she picked up the ring.

"Long finger, right hand." Goodhook said.

"Ok."

She slipped the ring on and it fit perfectly. She cringed inside, stole a glance at Finn then held up her hand to get a better look at it.

"Take it off!" Philadini said in a commanding tone.

"What—?"

"Take it off," Goodhook echoed in a more sympathetic tone, "it's not yours."

She eased the ring off. It felt warm in her hand, hotter than it should have been. She frowned at it then replaced it on the cushion. Tom picked it up without being asked. He was about to put it on then offered it to Finn who shook his head.

"You first."

Tom twisted it onto the second finger of his right hand and again it fit perfectly. He held it up to his eyes and smirked.

"Take it off." Said Philadini.

Tom zipped his hand behind his back, "It's mine! It fits perfectly!"

"Take it off or it will hurt you!"

"What—?"

Goodhook held up his right hand with the missing finger, "If you don't want to lose your finger like me I suggest you take it off—now!"

Tom felt the ring growing hot. He took his hand from behind his back and gawped at it. Suddenly it turned red.

"Aaaaagh!

"Grab him!" Goodhook shouted—but Philadini was already on to it and forced Tom's hand onto the marble. Tom screamed again, but not from the magician's magic—his finger was smoking.

Maggie's hands shot to her mouth, *"Do something!"*

Goodhook snatched up the silver pincers, gripped the ring in its jaws and wrenched it off Tom's finger. Tom screamed once more then the searing pain subsided and his finger stopped smoking.

"Owwww!"

Finn clutched him and held him steady,

"Tom, Tom—are you ok!" Maggie said.

"He'll be ok if he listens to the advice offered." Philadini said.

Maggie glared at him, *"Why didn't you warn us!"* Philadini sighed and looked to the sky. "How dare you sigh! You—you—ridiculous impresario!"

"By the honour of Albinonus!" Philadini exclaimed loudly. "None of us knows exactly what this ring is going to do!"

Silence.

Goodhook opened the pincers, dropping the ring onto the tomb. It tinkled and rolled in a circle before falling onto its side. The crowd strained to see what was going on, "Friends, please be calm." Goodhook announced. "Unfortunately, the ring has rejected both Maggie and Tom." A hubbub of mutterings erupted. All the while Finn watched the ring. *It can't be me, what would Tom think?* He regarded Goodhook who raised his eyebrows and pointed at the ring. Finn felt a powerful urge to run—to run and run and keep on running and never look back, "Are you ready?" Goodhook said.

Tom grabbed his shoulder, Finn turned to face him. "It'll be good if it's you." Tom said and gave Finn one of his best ever smirks. It cheered Finn to his core and he relaxed a little.

"Thanks mate."

Goodhook picked up the ring and replaced it on the purple cushion, "It won't hurt you if you do what we say."

Finn stared at it. Gingerly he reached out and touched it. It was quite cool. He plucked it up and laid it on his palm. Everyone bunched in closer. *All this fuss for a little gold band.*

Maggie placed her hand over the ring and squeezed his hand, "Don't do it! Let's go back to Finkley Field—we can jump off every bit of the wall! We'll find the way home!"

If I don't at least try it, Finn thought, I'll never find the courage to take a big risk ever again. "I have to find out if my parents are trapped here someplace—yours too." He lifted Maggie's hand away and slipped the ring on. It hung loose. His body sagged as a wonderful sweep of relief spread through him.

"It doesn't fit."

"Wait." Philadini said.

"But—"

"Watch it." Goodhook said.

Finn looked at the ring. Then he stared at it. Then he brought it close to his eyes. Five small bumps had appeared on it. Within seconds they transmuted into three sparkling jewels and two opaque ones. The metal blistered but remained cool and morphed from a single band of gold into many intricately woven threads which passed straight through the gems and the opaque stones. Then the ring took hold of his finger.

"*Oh!*"

Goodhook leaned forwards, "What's happening?"

"*It grabbed me!*"

"That's good. Now watch the jewels."

He did as he was told. Cut with many facets were two midnight blue gems and, between them, cut into a spike, was a crimson jewel. The opaque stones lay either side. For a while nothing happened. Then in one swift moment the three gemstones flared brilliantly, the spike retracted and all three gems settled to a light amber hue flecked with dark blue. Flames suddenly burst out within them, licking at the insides of the jewels.

"Woah." Tom said.

"It's going to burn you!" Maggie exclaimed.

Finn shook his head, "No, it's not hot—but how can that be?"

Philadini shrugged.

"No one knows—*but one thing is absolutely certain.*" He jumped up onto the tomb, raised his hands to the sky and bellowed out, "*We've found ourselves a Ring Bearer!*"

"Lucky boy." Tom whispered to himself.

Tumult erupted. Clapping, laughing, cheering, hugging, backslapping and hurrahs—every Attuk was either saying, "Told you so!" or "No! I told you first!" The mucklebacks roared and snorted and the birds shrieked and cawed.

Goodhook bellowed into the cacophony, "It is time . . . " and again —this time as loud as he could, "*It is time!*" The hubbub subsided and in a more steadied and grand voice he declared, "It is time—*to test the ring!*" The mucklebacks couldn't contain themselves any longer and they shooed the Attuks off their backs like a swan would eject her signets. Goodhook regarded Philadini atop the tomb, "You look like you are about to dance on a grave and that is not just any old grave."

Philadini sat on the purple cushion, "You're right, my old friend. That wouldn't do."

Maggie grabbed Finn's hand and gawped at the flames flickering merrily within the jewels in the ring, "Are you sure it doesn't hurt?"

Tom leaned in to see, "We're going to have some proper fun with that."

Philadini and Goodhook rolled their eyes to the heavens. Grindlebrook pushed in between Tom and Maggie, "Let me see! Let me see!"

The magician and the big Attuk left them to it, "What's next?" Goodhook said.

Philadini stroked his long grey beard, "Next, I'll attempt to get some magic out of him. Have three small logs collected. I'll start with something simple and best we stay away from The Great Oak, we don't want him damaging it."

Once he had the logs sorted Goodhook fetched Finn, "Philadini wants to give you a magic lesson."

He led him to the edge of the crowd. Philadini was standing a little way apart. Goodhook gave Finn a gentle push forwards. Like before, the magician didn't move or raise a smile as he approached but his lip curled up, "I didn't expect it to be you!" He hissed. A hush dropped over the assemblage. The magician's pointed grey beard quivered as he glared at Finn. A sinking feeling infiltrated Finn's stomach. *What's going on,* he thought, and glanced to Goodhook for support, "You wont find any help there!" The magician stated emphatically.

THE BOY WHO FELL THROUGH THE SKY

Maggie scrunched her hair up, "He's a beast!" She hissed to Tom.

"Now, now, Philadini," Goodhook called, "there's no need for that. Today's events will be talked about for hundreds of years. You wouldn't want to be viewed from the future in a bad light, would you?"

Philadini snorted, "The future is already set and you know it! It can only change if this boy is capable of learning and I doubt he has capacity." He spun on his heels and strode away, white robes billowing.

Goodhook rushed to Finn and whispered, "Follow him quickly—don't be scared—he's testing you."

The encouragement set Finn tiptoeing fast after him. When Philadini spun around, mouth wide open ready to shout, he found Finn standing right in front of him. He curled his lip again and glowered. Finn stared along the magicians hooked nose straight into his pinched and almost black eyes. The magician snapped his fingers at the crowd, "Bring three of those logs!" Grindlebrook grabbed them, brought them over then retreated. No please or thank you was offered. Finn ground his teeth.

"Boy," Philadini said, "I, am going to set fire to one of these logs with a simple spell that even an Attuk could achieve." The crowd mumbled at this and shuffled about a bit. He ignored them and continued. "If you are any good at it you'll be able to use it as a weapon. *But I doubt you are any good at it!*" He pointed to one of the logs and incanted.

"*Leivitus-Ignito!*"

The log immediately obeyed by jumping off the ground and exploding into flames. Sparks shot around wildly and some Attuks needed to jump away to avoid flying embers.

Woah, Finn thought, that was amazing. But what came out of his mouth was a whimper. The gathering cheered Philadini then looked to Finn to follow suit. Tom gave him the thumbs up. Maggie crossed her fingers.

"Well, *boy*—what are you waiting for? *Impress us with your talent!*"

Finn wanted to be back home in bed with a good book, a cup of hot milk and some biscuits. His taste for adventure had spilled out of him faster than a fish could swallow a fly. Hundreds of eyes were trained on him expecting an impressive piece of magic but he felt powerless. Then, the ring squeezed his finger. Hard.

"Ouch!"

Some Attuks laughed. But being squeezed by the ring brought Finn back to his senses. He took his time, looked Philadini in the eye, and in the most ingratiating voice he could summon up said, "Please could you repeat that little spell . . . ever so nice and slowly . . . so that I may incant it correctly?"

Philadini's face flushed, "L-e-i-v-i-t-u-s I-g-n-i-t-o!" He fairly spat out.

Finn paused a few seconds then said, "Would you mind repeating that once more, *please?*" He smirked in a manner that would have done credit to Tom. Some Attuks sniggered, others hooted and whistled.

"*Rub it in deep!*" Tom shouted.

His comment galvanised Philadini who pointed at another log with a flourish and incanted, "*Leivitus-Ignito!*" This time the log flew over the crowd and exploded with a loud bang. Attuks ran this way and that. Philadini scowled menacingly at Finn, "Do it!" He hissed.

The ring squeezed Finn hard again. *This thing's got an attitude!* He thought. Suddenly, Finn felt anger stream purposefully out of it and instinctively he knew how to use it.

"*Leivitus-Ignito!*" He shouted out, pointing straight at the last log.

An electric buzz ran along Finn's arm right up to his shoulder blade and to his amazement the log shot into the air higher than a house and exploded into a fireball larger than Philadini had achieved. Sparks, embers and lumps of blazing wood shot out in majestic arcs. Philadini strode up to him with eyes flashing and raised his arm high above him. Finn froze. *He's going to blast me into oblivion!* But the magician merely slapped him on the back and roared with laughter.

"Well done, Finn!" He shouted. "It takes a lot of anger to do your first piece of magic!" Then he whooped and pointed at the cloud of smoke, "I knew you were up to it the minute you challenged me!" With that he dashed into the cheering crowd, slapping hands and hugging Attuks as he went. "We've got a live one!" He exclaimed, over and over.

Maggie and Tom ran to Finn and hugged him tight, jabbering compliments after compliments but he didn't hear them. His mind was elsewhere, spinning in a whirl of flying robes and sparks and weird incantations. He was brought back to the present by Maggie pinching him.

"Hello! Maggie calling Finn, is anybody in there?"

THE BOY WHO FELL THROUGH THE SKY

He blinked and became aware of masses of Attuks and animals all clamouring to get a look at his ring.

"Stay with me, guys, please." As soon as they were able they wandered off in the direction of the river. When they were far enough from the crowd to feel comfortable Finn lay on the grass with his hands behind his head and tried to relax. Maggie and Tom sat either side of him. "What have we got ourselves into?" Finn said.

Maggie sighed, she propped herself with her arms and gazed upwards, "Oh for a cloud! *I want to get out of this damn place.*"

"I don't get you two," Tom said, "it just keeps getting better and better."

Finn stared at him, "I wish it had been you, Tom. The ring I mean."

Tom grabbed his wrist, "Lets have a proper gander at it." He got his eyes close enough to see the flames inside the gems and smirked. "Hah! You're a magician!" Then he thumped Finn playfully. "Take that, *magician!*"

The boys grinned at each other then launched into a mock fight. Suddenly, Maggie felt a heavy weight placed in her lap and looked down, "Guys!" She squealed but they took no notice. "Guys! Stop fighting! Pleeeeease!" Still they carried on. "Guys! Stop! *Something's happened!*" She fairly screamed.

That sent a chill down their spines and even Tom forgot their scrap and stared at his sister. Maggie was sat cross-legged with a huge metal-bound book on her lap.

"Woah—where'd you get that from, Sis?"

"I swear it just appeared out of nowhere!" She said in a trembling voice.

Tom and Finn scrambled across the grass and gawped at it. Its big gold cover reflected the sun back into their faces. Exquisite script stood proud of its surface proclaiming its title.

"The Book Of Writing That Cannot Be Unwritten!" Finn exclaimed.

"So it really does exist." Tom whispered.

"Where's Goodhook when you need him?" Maggie said.

Finn and Tom grabbed the book and heaved it up high.

"*GOODHOOK!*" The three of them shouted at the tops of their voices.

Hearing their hollers both Goodhook and Philadini stopped dead in their tracks. Instantly they recognised the golden book. They stole a troubled glance at each other.

"We might not get there before it disappears." Philadini said.

Goodhook raised his hands to his mouth, *"Don't open it!"* He bawled. "We're coming!"

The Book Of Writing That Cannot Be Unwritten

❦

Finn and Tom lowered the heavy tome to the ground and waited. Philadini and Goodhook sprinted to the trio. Masses of Attuks scrambled after them. Philadini was fast for a three hundred year old magician, he arrived puffing though. Goodhook dropped to his haunches next to Maggie and panted. Everyone gathered around.

"You can open it now." Goodhook wheezed. "Anywhere will do."

Maggie opened it and read aloud. Her voice got slower and slower and almost trailed off by the end.

'Finn must release the three cousins from beneath the Atta Desert and take them to Itako.'

Maggie looked up, her expression a mixture of incredulity and wonder.

"Turn the page!" Philadini demanded.

'The trail of the lost ones began there.'

"Again!"

But The Book Of Writing That Cannot Be Unwritten simply disappeared.

"Oh!" Tom and Finn leaned in, Maggie stroked the flattened grass where it had lain, "It's definitely gone."

Finn blinked a few times then whispered, *"But, how can it know my name?"*

"It's a very, very, very clever book," Philadini said.

The Attuks all looked glum. They pulled away into groups and, muttering amongst themselves, headed back to The Great Oak. The lines on Goodhook's face seemed to get deeper.

"That was well spooky!" Tom said. "How does it disappear?"

"We have no idea." Goodhook said quietly. He looked sad, disturbed almost.

"There's something bad about that message, isn't there?" Maggie said.

Goodhook's shoulders slumped, "I'm afraid I've let you down."

"How do you mean?" Her voice had an edge to it. "What have you done?"

"The Attuks can't go with you and I can't help you anymore."

He made to get up, Maggie grabbed his sleeve, "But you promised! You said the ring was good! I trusted you!"

Tom and Finn stared at Goodhook.

"It's not his fault." Philadini said. "Attuks can't go to the Atta Desert."

"Why-ever not?" Maggie demanded.

"Because we burn." Goodhook said.

"Everybody gets sunburn!"

"I meant—we set on fire."

"Told you." Finn whispered to Tom.

Maggie looked like she'd been slapped, "Well, who are these cousins!"

"Magicians," Philadini said, "Krukill incarcerated them within Uderzandu prison, which lies beneath the Atta Desert. There's three of them, Juslusan, Zabbax and Chankalghar."

"What? We get to break into a prison?" Tom said wearing a fine smirk.

Maggie frowned at him, "So, who, actually, *can* come with us?" Maggie said.

Philadini stroked his beard, "Well, I suppose I could."

"Who else?"

Silence.

"I'd better go tell Grindlebrook." Goodhook said, and looked pleadingly at Maggie. "She thinks you three are the best thing that's ever happened to her—she's helping prepare a banquet to celebrate your—such a good granddaughter she is—I couldn't wish for better." He wiped his eyes, "I'm sorry."

He set off back to camp leaving them with Philadini. Whilst Maggie glowered and Tom and Finn were lost in their thoughts, the magician filled his pipe then snapped his fingers over the bowl to ignite it. He took several long puffs until it smouldered to his satisfaction.

"It's not all bad—"

"For who exactly!" Maggie said. "You're more concerned with attracting attention than watching out for us." Finn took her hand but she pushed it away. "No, I'm going to say what I think. Now look here, Mr. Magician, you best get yourself a proper plan together and some recruits or were not going anywhere!" She jumped to her feet. "Come on guys—I've had enough of him." She strode away fast. Tom and Finn got up to go.

"Now just a moment you young men—"

They ignored him and followed Maggie. He watched them scurry away then shrugged and went back to smoking his pipe.

Grindlebrook came flying across the grass, "Granddad's just told me! You can't leave me here—I have to go with you!" She fell into Maggie's arms and sobbed and sobbed. "Please!"

Maggie looked wide-eyed at the boys. Tom spoke up first, "We could demand Philadini makes it safe for Grindly to come. He's a magician, he must be able to fix it."

Maggie looked aghast, "But—it will be horrible going with him without the Attuks. He's a nasty sort! And—and Grindlebrook will set on fire and die!"

Grindlebrook's eyes flashed, she pulled away from Maggie, "But you have to take me—it's going to be dangerous wherever I am and I'd rather die in the desert with you three, fighting for something worthwhile than just get killed here for helping you."

"You can't mean that." Maggie said.

Grindlebrook squeezed Maggie so tight she could hardly catch a breath, "Krukill will come after us. If we're caught she'll give us to her depraved daughter to torture. But we knew that before we came to help you in Finkley field. We all talked about it for hours and days before we came. Everybody voted—everybody said yes—*everybody came to help you.* But we couldn't tell you—we knew it would be too much of a burden—I—I shouldn't tell you now . . . oh I'm so . . . weak!" She broke down and became wracked with sobs. Maggie slowly helped her to the grass and let her head lay on her lap, then looked helplessly at the boys.

"Damn—if I'd known that," Tom said, "I mean, if I'd known that I wouldn't have . . . damn, I've been such a jerk."

"No Tom, no." Grindlebrook said, wiping her tears away. "You been just the best person, the best . . . you all have. You've all been brilliant . . . so brave and it's not your fight—why should you even bother to help us?"

"Actually I do want you to come," Maggie said, "but only if you're safe."

"That's a kind thing to say, but it can't be like that. It can't be safe—for anybody. I'd have to trick granddad somehow, and I don't want to. I don't want to hurt him."

The cooks working beneath the Great Oak looked wretched. They abandoned their pots and pans, kicked dirt over cooking fires and the succulent aromas of a planned banquet in honour of the Ring Bearer faded. Groups of Attucks muttered amongst themselves. Goodhook strayed alone to the Great Oak, spread his arms out and leaned against the ancient trunk. He'd done it innumerable times when troubled but always alone. Now he didn't care who saw. He bit his lip and sniffed the gnarly bark. The desert had already taken his wife, his daughter and son in law away. Grindlebrook was all the family he had. Whilst he whispered a prayer for wisdom he became aware of a presence. Small arms gripped him with familiar warmth. He peered down.

"*Grindlebrook!*"

Her eyes misted up and her young heart tugged, "Tell me about the desert, granddad." She whispered.

Finn, Maggie and Tom sought out Androver. He led them to a big rock. From atop it they got a fuller view of the landscape through which the twisting silver band of the river flowed. The watering hole the mucklebacks enjoyed gleamed at them like a blob of mercury. The terrain was gentle and particularly verdant by the water. Beyond it rolling hills provided a fitting backdrop.

"That message from The Book," Androver said, "no one expected that."

Maggie pressed her lips to a thin line, "Do you like Philadini?"

Androver grinned, "Well, he's a proper boxful of personalities but he *is* on our side. I've seen him kill for us, save us all really."

Maggie swallowed and said in a quiet voice, "Ok. I'll try and give him the benefit of the doubt."

"Does the 'lost ones' mean anything to you?" Finn said.

"Nothing."

Finn lowered his eyes, *"It does to me."* He said quietly.

Hearing Finn's words Tom and Maggie frowned at each other, "Where's the Atta Desert?" Maggie asked.

"It was my homeland—we're nomads now. It's a tough journey, you'll never make it without help."

Meanwhile, Grindlebrook and Goodhook sat with their backs against the Great Oak. He draped his arm around her and she had her arms wrapped tight around him as far as they would go.

"I love sitting against this old tree with you." She said.

"It's the safest place in the whole world. None would dare attack us here."

Grindlebrook peered up at him, "So why cant we just stay here forever?"

He patted her head, "You know we cant do that."

They sat on in silence watching their clan bumble about having mini squabbles about what the future held. It had gone midday when the three inseparables met again with Philadini to parley. They had asked Goodhook to be with them. The magician and Maggie glared at each other.

"You either come with me willingly," Philadini said, "or I leave you here. You'd last at most two days."

"We'll never go with just you!" Maggie said. "We'll stay with the Attuks."

"The Attuks will all leave you soon. Forget them. They will obey me. It's over. Stay here and die or come with me."

Goodhook wore a dark expression but nodded his agreement. Maggie looked like she was going to slap Philadini.

"Finn?" Tom said.

"Yeah?"

"Let's just go with him."

Finn gazed at the sky for a few seconds then seemed to make his mind up, *"The lost ones,"* he said to Philadini, "do you know who they are?"

"No, I have never heard of them." The magician replied.

It has to mean our parents, Finn thought. He steadied his eyes on Philadini, "Can you get us safely to Itako?"

"I will do everything in my power to make that happen."

Finn glanced at Tom, "Yeah," he said, "let's go with him."

"Finn!" Maggie exclaimed.

Philadini and Goodhook left them to argue. The whole Attuk clan were staring at them, looking troubled. "We need to tell everyone what we're up to," Philadini said, "then you and I must take Finn into the tomb. I need to show him where the ring is kept in case I don't make it back."

Goodhook pursed his lips, "You always return."

"Somehow, old friend, I think not this time. Have you still got that clever tool I trusted you to look after?"

They had been friends and comrades forever. Goodhook watched Philadini with sad eyes as he fished the exquisite tool out of an inner pocket. He gave its complicated prongs a last look. "You never told me what it does." He said quietly, as he handed it over.

"Now's not the time, but I thank you deeply you for looking after it for me."

Philadini put it in his cloak, patting it to make sure it was secure. Then, when they had got the Attuks gathered it was Philadini who spoke out.

> "Finn has received a tremendous challenge from the Book Of Writing That Cannot Be Unwritten and now we all face new difficulties but, we mustn't forget this—" he paused then until the silence became uncomfortable, *"today, Finn became our Ring Bearer!"*

His statement sank home. None denied its meaning. There were no complaints.

> "I must go now with the Ring Bearer and his friends. We will follow the River Rhand to the Unfillable Lake and I will be honoured if you

would accompany us. Beyond there our trail leads to the Atta Desert and we must part."

The Attuks regained their sense of purpose. They disassembled and broke camp. Then Philadini took Tom to one side. They sat by the campfire. The magician poked it with a stick, "The one thing I enjoy more than poking fires is starting them." He said, and got his pipe out and primed it. "I don't need any distractions right now and we have no space for prisoners. Your sister *will* come with us willingly. Are you ok with that or do I have to put a spell on her?"

"She loved riding a muckleback so I reckon that might help cool her off."

"Good. I need Finn to come with me into Albinonus's tomb and you must stay here and watch her."

"But—"

"If you try to follow us you will fall a hundred feet and break your neck. There's old magic in there. Magic I am scared of myself. Understand?"

Tom lowered his head and nodded.

Finn was arguing with Maggie when Philadini approached and tapped him on the shoulder, "Come with me, Finn, we are going into Albinonus's Tomb. I need to show you where the ring is kept."

"Why?"

"So you know where to return it." Finn shrugged. When they moved off Maggie looked like she was going to follow. "Not you." Philadini said. "Tom will explain." Maggie looked apoplectic. She stormed off to talk to Tom. Next Philadini asked Androver to prevent anyone following them into the tomb. Then they were ready. He went to the bulky white marble resting place, uttered some incantations and made a few complex hand movements. The lid of Albinonus's Tomb opened with a sigh of rushing air then angled up slowly until it pointed to the sky. Finn placed his hands on its thick edge, peering inside he saw white marble steps leading down into darkness.

To Finn Philadini said, "Wait until I reach the bottom. I'll call you when I'm down. *That is very important.* If two people touch the steps at the same time they disappear. It's a challenge to get back out with broken limbs and no stairs—clever magician, that Albinonus." He clambered up and stood on the top step, steadied himself, then slowly and carefully he began working his way down. Presently, they heard him incant, "*Ignito!*" and a dim light swelled from far below. A faint echoey voice called out, "Ok, Finn, you can make your way down."

Finn swallowed then blew out a steady puff of air. Taking his time, he climbed up onto the lip of the tomb and steadied himself on the top step. *What's he talking about breaking limbs? I'll break my neck if I slip.* He took a step down, then another and another until his head was level with the edge of the tomb. He took a last glance at daylight then concentrated as hard as he could and continued down into the gloom. When he was only halfway down tremors in his legs threatened his balance. He quickly sat and anchored himself as best he could.

"Take your time." Philadini called out.

When he was ready, Finn gingerly stood and climbed the rest of the way down.

"That was hairy!"

"Good work. Now take your foot off the bottom step and move away."

Finn looked down, "Damn." He quickly moved away.

"Finn's clear!"

Whilst Goodhook descended Finn gawped about by the light of several fire torches Philadini had lit. The air smelt ancient and stale—he picked out musty stone, decayed cloth, old leather and something complicated and sweet. Curiosity caused him to search for the source. He found it amongst a multitude of strange artefacts and preserved specimens of creatures the like of which didn't exist in any museum he'd ever visited. The aroma was coming from an elegant urn, set atop a dais in a recess. He couldn't quite place the ingredients. Honey, he thought, that's the sweet part, but it's mixed with something like the whiff of—a wet dog?—or—blood—strong blood—*rusty iron,* maybe. Muffled voices told him Goodhook had made it down.

"Finn?"

"Over here."

Goodhook found him. "Eerie isn't it? What are you doing?"

"Sniff that."

Goodhook leaned in and sniffed, "Ugh." He pinched his nose and stepped out of the recess.

Finn got in close for a better look at the urn. Exquisite script ornamented its lip and he picked out the name Albinonus. The urn had crescent moons for handles and the scene of a large chamber lined with statues guarding a sarcophagus, was hand painted on it. Goodhook made his way back to Philadini who was rummaging about collecting things. Philadini saw the big Attuk was alone. He peered around him but couldn't see Finn because he was hidden in the recess.

"What are you up to, Finn?" He called out.

"Just checking something out."

"*Don't touch anything!*"

But Finn already had the urn in his hands. With a whoosh and a bang a huge stone slab dropped behind him trapping him in the recess and plunging him into darkness. Philadini and Goodhook rushed to where Finn had stood. Goodhook whipped out his half sword and scraped it over the slab. Wherever he scraped a violet aura sparkled.

"I shouldn't have let him wander." Philadini said, almost in a whisper. "Put your sword away, there is no hidden trigger."

Goodhook pointed to the instruments and jars assembled around the chamber, "There must be something here you can use to break this rock."

Philadini shook his head, "Not even a magician can help him now. That rock will rebound anything I throw at it. A violet aura means *old magic*. I'm helpless against it."

The big Attuk grabbed his arm, "What's on the other side?"

Philadini averted his eyes. Goodhook squeezed him harder. The magician seemed unsure how to answer, "Finn only knows—only has —a simple fire spell—"

"*What are you saying!*"

"I'm afraid there is little hope for him."

Krukill

Krukill became aware that the drune had ceased screaming and guessed Verko had finished playing with it. She was confident that her daughter would be unharmed but curious as to what she had done to it. After descending many stairways she arrived in the bowels of her fortress and found, in a rank cell, what was left of the drune. No firebreathers. No Verko.

Wrinkling her nose at the stink coming off a pool of congealing drune blood, she stepped out of the cell and caressed a chunky black stone, about the size of a ravens' egg, hanging from a hefty silver chain around her neck. The Black Diamond felt cold to her touch. Sometimes it felt warm, sometimes hot, sometimes sharp. It had its moods. She let her mind empty. Often a message would come.

But, not this time.

She needed to choose her next step. Relying on the Book Of Writing That Cannot Be Unwritten to turn up with more information about the Ring Bearer would be a mistake. That very clever book only told what was needed, never what you wanted, and she wanted to know plenty. The Black Diamond would be a more reliable source.

But perhaps not today.

Today, was council day. There was the small matter of her empire to attend to. However, the meeting, due to commence, she would postpone.

She searched for Verko and found her asleep in front of a fire in a day room, snuggled up to her pet lizard, a carnivorous chameleon as big as a crocodile. The reptile raised its head and hissed and flicked its tongue at Krukill, unaware she could murder it by a flick of her hand. The fire crackled out orange ambiance and warmth. Krukill settled herself onto a chaise-longue and gazed into it.

It had been a mistake to give the chameleon to Verko because it had developed an appetite for servants. It would be an even worse mistake to kill it now. She sighed, lowered her head back and, once relaxed, let her thoughts be absorbed deeper into the flames. Reaching up she fondled the Black Diamond again. This time she got something, a cryptic response, just a feeling rather than a clear vision. Something is burning, she interpreted. A cold burn. Small. A long way away. Anger crossed with anguish arose in her breast. The ring, someone is wearing the ring! Time to prepare. Lightly, she kicked her daughter's ankle. The chameleon hissed harder.

"Verko, wake up." No response. Verko could sleep for the empire. She rang for a servant. An elderly woman entered. "When Verko wakes tell her to come to me." The servant bowed and took a step backwards. "Watch out for the lizard."

But it was too late—the chameleon had her by the leg. Krukill sighed and drummed her fingers on her elegant seat. The lizards' thrashings woke her daughter.

"Hello darling," Krukill called over the screams, "did you have fun with the drune?"

Verko yawned and stretched. She watched the chameleon wrestling the servant into its mouth, "I wondered when Zilla was going to eat, it's been weeks. What were you saying?"

"The drune—"

"Oh, that. Boring. The firebreathers were more fun. Why didn't you share the girl with me?"

Krukill flinched, "Sometimes your mother needs . . . needs things for herself. I know you like to share but—"

"You're mean!"

"I'm an empress darling. One day you'll understand. How did you kill the firebreathers?"

"I fed them and let them go."

"What! But they had sensitive information!" Krukill saw the look in her daughter's eyes. It was pleasure. "Well, that makes us even—"

"Two firebreathers for a girl makes us even?"

"Darling, I promise I'll make it up to you. We'll be going on a trip shortly and there'll be girls to capture. Dragons to fly too."

Verko patted the chameleon. It was having difficulty swallowing. A pair of shoed feet stuck out of its jaws.

"Can Zilla come?"

"No darling, he can't fly a dragon. We'll have an army though. I'll let you give out some orders."

"I think I'll stay at home."

"All right, have it your own way."

Krukill knew Verko would come around. She never missed the chance to fly a dragon. Or the spoils. There were always spoils. She left to summon the dracs, there might still be a chance of recapturing the firebreathers. It would be awkward if they spread news about a drune being tortured. Trouble with the drunes she could do without. There was a war coming.

The Tomb

Although Finn was enveloped by the deepest black he had ever known, he could still make out a tiny glow seeping from his ring. To better look at it, he fumbled the urn back onto the dais. Immediately he did so the floor beneath his feet began to revolve, unbalancing him. He flailed his arms about in the dark and managed to grasp the dais. He steadied himself. When the floor ceased turning he felt behind. His hands found emptiness. He shuffled around to face the other way and stood quite still. His breath wheezed in and out. Thud, thud, thud thumped his heart. He took a deep sniff, the air here smelled different, even more ancient somehow.

"Damn, damn, and triple damn!" He hissed.

His words echoed back and their timbre told him that he was in a large space. *I wonder,* he thought, and pointed his ring hand into the dark.

"*Ignito!*"

A stream of sparks flew out of his ring and careered about like drunken fireflies. Some found homes and soon half a dozen fire torches spluttered then burst into life, their flames casting warm light around a huge stone chamber, as big as a church.

The first thing he saw, not twenty paces away, made him flinch. He didn't want to dwell on *that* so he scooted his eyes around the chamber, checking out the other stuff. I'm alone—good—I'm safe—no—bad —there's no doors and there's that thing in front of me.

He saw walls and ceilings fashioned from pale stone, and a marble floor patterned with blood red flecks and swirls. Against the opposite wall stood statues of men and women, a long line of them—he counted—twenty. The men were posed as if in battle, brandishing swords and spears. The women stood in more gentle poses as if amused by them. He smiled at the expression of one that resembled his mother watching his father screwing up. To his right, resting on four stone blocks, lay a dark and substantial stone slab, bigger than the biggest gravestone. Heavy manacles sprouted at its corners. A little way away from the slab hung four huge bronze barrels, suspended by heavy chains. He wondered at their purpose, then decided he didn't want to know. Painted on the walls at either end of this great chamber were identical images of a lunging demon with a black head. Part reptile and part hell dog, it had hooked claws and spiked teeth. The fire torches caused spooky shadows to be thrown off the statues and dance with the demons and Finn allowed himself to be distracted by them, putting off looking at the thing that was really bothering him for a few moments longer. Finally, he surrendered and studied it.

A big black sarcophagus.

Surrounding its base, the floor was inlaid with an intricate mosaic depicting torn bodies and emerging from it was a sculpture of a five headed snake, enamelled in green and gold, which coiled itself around the sarcophagus. Its diamond pupils sparkled and seemed to be watching him. It took him right back to a memory of sitting between his parents, watching an old horror movie that didn't end well for an archeologist who entered a sacred tomb.

Finn knew exactly where he was, it was the scene depicted on the urn. If I step out of this recess, he thought, I may set off another trap. He squatted and gently stroked the marble floor. Nothing happened.

At first.

But then he thought he saw a movement to his right. His eyes darted to it. There was nothing there though, just the far wall and upon it the painting of a demon. With his heart bumping he got back to his feet, looked at the sarcophagus again and worried what evil thing might rest within. Then, out of the corner of his left eye he thought he saw another movement. Again his eyes darted to it, and again he saw nothing but the painting on the other wall. His breathing became faster and shallower. Then he sensed movement from both sides at once and his head shot to and fro until it dawned on him what was actually happening. The paintings of the demons were becoming more vivid. He peered at one of them intently, saw dashes of colour change, and got a sensation like icicles were slipping down his spine.

Then, scratches, something like a match scraping along the gritty side of a matchbox, caught his attention. Listening harder, he realised it came from behind him. *Goodhook and Philadini!* He felt a glimmer of hope. It was short lived. Looking back at the demon pictured to his right he saw that its eyes had become a vivid yellow with piercing black pupils. In itself, that was no big deal, but the fact that they were blinking, was. His neck muscles jammed up and his teeth clenched.

A soggy slap sounded to his left. The hairs on the back of his neck prickled up. He jerked around. A long and steaming pink tongue was poking out from the jaws of the demon in the painting. It licked the air then slapped back against the wall. He heard sniffling, shot a glance at the other picture, and saw a wet nosed snout probing out of it with fangs bared. It growled. Now Finn's whole body quivered.

When he saw the arm of a female statue creak upwards Finn staggered backwards and bumped against the dais. Through widestretched eyes he watched it scrape its forehead, then yawn, before letting go the groan of something dark and vile. Then the lid of the sarcophagus slammed open and Finn's legs gave up, he wobbled down, banging his knees hard onto the floor.

The statue took a faltering step off her plinth, then another, and another, her feet bashing down, scouring the marble, each step more confident than the last. A second female statue followed it. Both held their hands out and smiled invitations for him to approach. When he shook his head their benign expressions grated into snarls. His eyes whizzed between them, the painted demons, and the sarcophagus. He made a decision and dashed out of his alcove to the nearest fire torch, grabbed it, and sprinted for another. With his flaming weapons he got ready to take on the hard faced statues, but their vapid grins told him fire would be useless.

He switched his attention to the demons, picked out the one most fully formed and hastened to it. A long hairy arm, freed now from the painting, struck out at him with razor sharp claws. The malevolence of its swipe overpowered Finn's giddy bravado. He sprang back panting, clutching his torches, forcing his will not to buckle.

Glancing behind he saw the statues were almost upon him. He felt part of himself crumbling into helpless panic but, banishing those thoughts, he plummeted deeper inside his mind and discovered a locked vault of seething rage. Ripping his defences away, he let his own demons flood out and, after dodging a particularly vicious slanting swipe from his adversary, he screamed fury from every part of his being and rushed at the demon, thrusting out his torches to blind it. But he was too late. The statues grabbed his arms with cold stone hands of immeasurable strength, and ripped his torches away. Finn howled out his years of pent up rage and kicked out at the statues for all he was worth but they dragged him with ease to the big stone slab, tossed him onto it, then shackled his wrists and ankles with the manacles. For all his twisting and writhing he succeeded only in bruising and grazing himself. Their function complete, the statues retired to either end of the slab and folded their arms. Meanwhile, more statues had awoken, males too this time. Zombie like, they shuffled to him, peering down or stroking their chins as if puzzled.

He was tethered almost within striking distance of the demon he'd enraged by his flaming attack. Its upper torso, blue skinned with clumps of long straggly red hair, strained at the wall, grunting and thrashing, impatient to free its legs. Hungry saliva flew from its gnashing jaws. It paused, leering at him whilst catching its breath then resumed its efforts.

Finn glowered at his captors, the veins in his neck pumping like swollen rivers. *I'm going to die and it's going to be horrific.* He too, squirmed, twisted and yanked at his own manacles. His clothes, wet now with sweat, stuck to him, and his wrists and ankles bled. He wished his heart would burst and it be over. He attempted to visualise Maggie and Tom for his last thought but the terror of the present ripped their images away because the demon from the painting on the far wall had broken free. With an ecstatic howl it bounded past the sarcophagus, fangs glistening and claws flexed, speeding to tear and intrude his flesh. Its trajectory was true but just before it could indulge its lusts two statues grabbed a stout leash embedded into its back. The demon raved and howled and struck out with the madness of a thousand year hunger, but the statues had it held fast. Then the second demon broke free, but again the statues were ready for it and seized its leash. The demons snapped their jaws on empty air, roaring dark displeasures, however the statues kept them gripped at heel.

Two male statues stepped up either side of him, drew their swords and raised them, tips downward. Finn knew no one was coming to rescue him, a hissed profanity escaped him then faintly he whispered an unheard goodbye to Maggie and Tom. However, before either of the male statues could impale him, the female statues grasped their arms, shaking their heads and pointed to the four huge bronze barrels suspended on chains. The males at first frowned then nodded their heads sagely and sheathed their swords. Marching to the barrels, they pulled on levers set into them. Sand began to course out of them in thin streams. The statues returned to their posts either side of Finn, inclined their heads respectfully to their stone women, then resumed peering contemptuously at him.

He gawped at the barrels and escaping sand wondering what hell would happen next. Then the barrels jerked upward a notch and he heard muffled squeaks of pulley wheels. Looking straight up he saw, nestling between the pale stone blocks of the ceiling, a big dark slab the exact shape and size of the one he was tethered to. Ever so slowly it scraped out of its home and began to descend. Finn quaked. The barrels were counterbalancing the dark slab above him, and, as sand trickled out, they lost weight. Pulleys beyond the ceiling were creaking the slab down.

He was to be crushed.

At that very moment, a demon made a ferocious lunge and managed to wrench those tethering it off balance. The statues crashed to the floor, one smashed to pieces and its stone head bounced up, narrowly missing Finn's skull. The demon snatched it up, yanked it high and brought it down hard to finish him off. Finn wriggled like a worm pierced by a hook to avoid it. At the last instant the stone head was knocked away by a statue and the demon got overpowered by several others.

Above him, continuing its leisurely descent, the big dark slab had reached a quarter way down.

Suddenly Finn's ring throbbed, gripping him with incessant pulsations and then became hot. *The damn thing's going to burn my finger off and abandon me!* Then he laughed. He laughed the laughter of one who wallows in the ironies of life. *What the hell does it matter now?* He closed his eyes calmly and at last he managed to conjure up a clear picture of Maggie. She was scrunching her hair up, smiling the best smile in the whole world, and, from the depths of his imagination, she spoke to him.

"Finn, look to your ring."

He lifted his head and peered at it. Immediately, his eyes widened and a faint trickle of hope percolated into his mind. Red, green and purple smoke was pouring out of it, puffing over the side of his slab, then it advanced snake-like, all the way to the open sarcophagus and up its side, gushing into it until it filled up and overflowed.

Above him, the dark slab was half way down and gaining speed.

From within the smoke filled sarcophagus Finn first heard coughing then manic chattering. He strained against his shackles to see. The statues and demons followed his gaze. For the first time their expressions looked unsure, worried even.

A moment later a white monkey's head appeared above the tricoloured smoke. It took one glance at the events unfolding in the chamber then shrieked and shot back into the smoke. Squabbling and bangs emitted from within the sarcophagus followed by deep yawning, finally a wizened hand frantically wafted smoke away revealing a bleary eyed man with ridiculously long white hair and an even longer beard.

"Hmm." He mused, in a slightly annoyed way.

He climbed out of the sarcophagus and all the statues bowed to him. Even the demons became hushed. The man was clothed in a mildewed sleeping smock. Swaying a little he ambled forwards lifting his beard as he went rather than tripping on it. He stopped once to yawn and stretch, then came right up to Finn. By now the dark slab had descended so low it was hanging at waist height on the sleepy man. Finn grinned his biggest ever grin. However, the man simply scowled at him, then, placing a hand on the slab to steady himself, he bent low and studied Finn's face.

"Who are you!" He yelled. "What's the meaning of this!" He wheezed to catch his breath. "And how dare you wake me up! Have you any idea how many months it took me to get back to sleep after the previous greedy grave robber broke into here?"

"What!" Finn exclaimed. "Get—Me—Out—Of—Here!"

The old man blinked a couple of times, "Vagabond! How dare you order me around! I've a mind to stick you into that black box for monkey fodder and go walk the world again." Then, completely ignoring Finn's plea, he bent down, snatched his wrist and twiddled his ring around.

"Hah! A Ring Bearer! Might have known. He stood and waved his arms about. "Statues, get back to your stations, demons, get back into the wall. No fun for you lot today."

He turned and walked back to his sarcophagus, pushing a couple of statues out of the way as he went. Finn couldn't see much more of him than his ankles, the slab now being just a foot above his head.

"Wait!" He squealed, "Who are you? Why are you going to let me be crushed?"

The old man paused and clamped his hands on his hips, "What? Oh, stop playing games with me—you're a Ring Bearer—do it yourself!"

He climbed back into the sarcophagus.

"But I only got the damn thing today! The only spell I know is how to light a fire!"

The old man paused and stroked the upper part of his long beard, "So why didn't you torch the demons?"

"What? But—but—I—*but I didn't know I could do that!*"

"If you are making fun of me, you irritating little individual, I'll blast you into the gap between the moons!"

"Please—please—I only came into your world yesterday. It was just an accident—I jumped into Finkley Field with my friends and the scarecrows brought us here—"

"*Scarecrows?*"

"Attuks, I mean."

The old man glared, "*I made Finkley Field solely for Baron Finkley!*" He paused then and became even more engrossed with his beard, stretching it out seeming to be gauging how long it had grown.

"Heeeelp!"

Finally, the old man looked up and paid attention to Finn again, "Oh well, even the best magic sometimes slips over the centuries."

Wearily he got back out of his sarcophagus, walked beneath each barrel and waved his arms about muttering incantations. The sand ceased flowing and the slab halted its descent. By now it was pressing into Finn's chest.

"I can't move." He managed to squeeze out.

The old man sat on the floor and peered into the gap between the slabs.

"I can see that. You really are a novice, aren't you?"

Finn swallowed and thought hard. *Hold it together! Don't make demands,* "Yes. Yes, I am a novice."

"What are you doing here?"

"I already told you, I got stuck in your world by accident. A day later I got told to stick this damn ring on my finger and now I'm stuck under this slab in your bedroom."

Their eyes met and the old man's twinkled.

"I've never followed anybody's orders myself but I suppose you not being a real magician allows you for that. You are a lucky young man. I'm beginning to like you. This pesky magic stuff used to get me into all sorts of scrapes too."

He walked about incanting at the piles of sand accumulated on the floor. Obediently the sand arose in streams and began refilling the metal barrels. Creaks and snaps from beyond the ceiling signalled pulleys reversing and the slab commenced to ascend. The old magician released Finn's shackles and he squirmed out from underneath it. His ankles and wrists bled, his body ached everywhere and he was bruised all over but he didn't care. He got to his feet unsteadily.

"Thank you, I died twenty deaths in my thoughts before you rescued me."

The old man peered at him.

"Why is it that captives always thank you when you release them? I'll never understand it. You were free before you were caught so I haven't given you anything."

"But—you saved my life—"

"No, I didn't. I simply chose not to take it. It was *I* who set the traps"

Finn tried to make sense of it but gave up. He still felt massively grateful.

The old man yawned, "I must get back to sleep, you have woken me too early. But first, because you've shown me some misplaced gratitude I'm going to lend you a little something. However, you must promise me you will return it."

Finn balked, "You mean come back and get attacked by these demons and statues?"

The old man smiled, "I'm sure by then you'll have learned enough to be able to subdue a couple of demons and a few stone effigies."

Finn regarded him steadily. All he could perceive was kindness. I'm not going to risk upsetting him by refusing. If the demons and statues are scared of him . . .

"Ok, I promise, and thank you."

The old man went to the sarcophagus, bent over and reached inside. Finn heard an animal scurrying about. The white monkey poked its head out and gawped at him. The man returned with a rectangle of gold metal in the shape of a small diary complete with gold pencil and offered it to Finn.

"This is my book of spells. Take it and guard it well. *Don't let it fall into the wrong hands!*"

Finn accepted it. It fit snug into the palm of his hand. It was thin and quite light, as if hollow. He tried to open it but failed. When he looked closer he saw it didn't have any pages, being a single piece of metal, and the pencil was moulded into its case and wouldn't come off.

"No, it doesn't work like that. It only opens when you really need it."

"But—"

"No buts. It's a clever little tool. Far too complicated to explain. Don't forget to replace the urn on your way out." With that he returned to his sarcophagus and climbed in. "Just lift it up and it'll return you to the first chamber—and don't mess around—there are plenty more traps waiting for you. Now I must get some sleep."

Finn stared dumbly at the urn, "Could I have just picked it up and left?"

"No, it only resets when the demons return into the walls, which reminds me . . ."

He glared sternly at the demons who were hanging around whilst wagging their tails slowly. Heeding him now they began to dissolve back into the walls. Each gave out a low growl before becoming petrified once more. Then the statues grated and scraped themselves more firmly onto their plinths. They assumed their favourite poses, let go a few last rasping wheezes and became still.

"What if I kill a demon when I return?" Finn said, trying to keep the conversation going.

"Then you will be trapped in here forever." The old man said sternly.

Finn swallowed before asking his next question, "Are you who I think you are?"

"Oh, I was forgetting—you asked me who I was—Albinonus is my name, you may have heard of me, I'm one of the good magicians—at least I like to think I am. Some days I wasn't so sure about that. Have a great life, farewell."

"I've heard of you. You are spoken of with great respect."

"Is that so? Well—*goodbye then*."

Finn pushed for more, "Is it true, that Krukill is bad and Philadini is good?"

"Never heard of either of them." The old man said.

"But you must have—you created the Book Of Writing That Cannot Be Unwritten—so you must know everything!"

"Oh that." He chuckled. "Well, I lied to everybody about that. I didn't make it—I found it hidden deep within the Tombs Of The Ancients. Told everybody it was my creation and they were stupid enough to believe me. But as soon as I said it the damn thing disappeared and I never saw it again. It kept appearing for other people and ignored me for the rest of that particular life. Confounded thing. *Goodbye!*"

He lowered himself, grumbled at the monkey then slammed down the lid of his sarcophagus and Finn was alone again apart from the statues, but they didn't move. He looked to the demons. All that was left of them were faded images on the walls at either end of the tomb. He approached the sarcophagus and stroked an engraving on its lid. It was a good likeness of Albinonus. Faintly, he heard the white monkey chattering.

"Go away." Came a muffled voice from within.

Finn grinned, "Bye, Albinonus!"

He returned to the recess, lifted the urn and without a backward glance spun into the outer chamber.

Philadini and Goodhook rushed to grab him but he calmly replaced the urn then stood firm. He grinned the biggest grin ever and shone the little golden book of spells at them.

"You'll never guess who I just met." He said in the most casual voice he could muster. Then he thought back to the demons and felt his legs wobble. "I think I need to sit for a bit."

They guided him to the bottom of the stairs and he perched on the second step.

Goodhook noticed his wounds, "Finn, your feet are bleeding."

Finn stared up at the Attuk. "That's the second time somebody said that." He smirked a Tom-like smirk unsure how to begin, "I just met Albinonus—"

Philadini frowned, "Be careful, it's not a good idea to make irreverent comments in his tomb."

Finn stiffened. "But I did!" He offered the golden book to Philadini. "Look! He gave me this. It's his book of spells."

Philadini's brow knotted as he examined it then his expression became troubled, "Don't be ridiculous. Albinonus would never give *you* his book of spells. The fact is, there are many rooms hidden within this tomb, each guarded by spirits and demons and all containing a sarcophagus with a sleeping guard. If you are very lucky the guard lets you out. You didn't meet Albinonus. He's long dead."

Finn's heart sank, *"I thought I did something special."* He said quietly.

Goodhook sat next to him and put his arm around his shoulders. Immediately, the stairs disappeared and they bumped to the ground.

"Ouch!"

"Damn!"

Philadini's eyes grew huge and he gripped the golden book so hard his hands shook. He didn't say a word. Finn and Goodhook leaned back and gazed up. The opening to the tomb was way above. A few tiny heads were peering into it.

"Sorry." Goodhook whispered.

Philadini lifted his shoulders and let out a huge sigh, "I hate climbing out of here." He said, "Wait here you two, I need to collect the things we actually came down here for. Don't move and—*don't touch anything.*" He tossed the little gold book to Finn who fumbled it. It fell to the floor and he left it there.

"Are you ok?" Goodhook said.

Finn's brow knotted, "No," he said, quietly, "no, I'm not ok. I nearly died just a few minutes ago. And he doesn't care. I wish I was back in England with Maggie and Tom."

"Tell me what happened."

"You wont believe me! There's no point."

"I've seen some things. Things that maybe you wouldn't believe."

Finn struggled really hard to quell his temper, "It was very, very dark . . . blacker than black ever gets . . ."

By the time he had finished telling his tale Goodhook was mesmerised.

"*That* is one scary story. I'm staggered. You did so well."

Philadini returned with a couple of sacks and plonked them down. One rustled, the other clanked. "Ok, I've collected what we need. Let's get out of here." He gazed up and shouted at those peering down from above. "*Get ready. I'm sending up a magic rope.*"

Under his breath Philadini incanted a few strange words and a glowing yellow cord flowed out of his palm. Circling his hand around and around it grew and grew until he had a coil plenty long enough to escape the tomb. Holding it in one hand, he pointed with the other and the yellow cord obediently rose higher and higher until the onlookers could grasp it.

"Make it fast!"

Then he incanted again to thicken the rope and create four loops at the end of it for their hands and legs. "Ok Finn, put your legs through the big loops and hang on to the smaller ones." He did as he was bade. Philadini stooped to pick up the little golden book and stuffed it into Finn's back pocket. "Don't forget your little trinket."

Finn scowled at him.

Philadini scowled back, then, after checking the line was secure, he whirled his arm twice. The glowing rope quickly became shorter and Finn shot into the air. Seconds later he was helped out of the tomb by Androver. He said his thanks then rushed to Tom, Maggie and Grindlebrook. He was furious as he recounted his tale, showing them the cuts on his wrists and ankles then pulled the golden book out of his pocket and shared with them his opinion of Philadini's attitude.

"Let me see." Grindlebrook said. Finn tossed it to her. Feeling how light it was she pursed her lips, frowned and passed it to Tom. Tom didn't say anything but didn't smirk either. He passed it to his sister. She tried to open it.

They don't believe me, "Albinonus said it would only open if I really needed it."

THE BOY WHO FELL THROUGH THE SKY

Back in the tomb Philadini first sent the sacks up, then Goodhook, before following himself. After he had resealed the tomb he asked Androver and Goodhook to join him by the campfire. They waited in silence whilst he primed his pipe and drew on it until it glowed strongly. He poked the fire with a stick before settling back and blowing a smoke ring which transformed into the perfect shape of a book, then Philadini twinkled his eyes at the Attuks.

"I lied to Finn." He said.

Vrix

❧

Krukill went to the drac's quarters to glean information about the firebreathers. However, no drac was yet aware of their escape because, the firebreathers being merely playthings for Verko, Krukill herself had ordered they place no guards.

She glanced at the head drac, acknowledging him with a tiny flick of her head, "Vrix, walk with me."

Vrix ordered his clan to hunt out the firebreathers and followed her. He was a cantankerous creature but Krukill had a soft spot for him. During her campaigns for supremacy Vrix had carried her lover's body for two days without rest, evaded her enemies and laid him out respectfully. She hadn't asked it of him but he undertook it anyway, risking himself and so preventing his body being defiled. Many more years had passed. Many more years he had remained loyal. She had offered him land and wealth. He refused, choosing only to serve.

Krukill led him to the kitchens. The cooks, when not summoned to stay, pulled cooking pots off fires, levered oven flues closed and left.

Being well over ten feet tall Vrix needed to stoop to enter. His half bear, half human head was furred black with brown flecks. Big sea blue eyes below his thrusting animal forehead startled whoever he met. The bench by the table he chose creaked beneath his formidable frame. His familiar but not unpleasant animal scent dominated the kitchens.

"Vrix," Krukill began, "there may be trouble with the council. They are expecting concessions today and may see my absence as a sign of weakness. Inform me if you observe anything . . . interesting."

The drac nodded and waited for more. The woman who had saved his race from extinction wouldn't have required privacy to order him to listen out for traitors. It was a given.

Krukill, watching him from across the table, rested her chin on her fists. He fascinated her. Every person and animal she had ever come into contact with wanted something from her.

Except Vrix.

Vrix never asked, never coveted, never needed anything. He just was. Clever too. He knew he got leeway with her simply because he had nothing to lose. She smiled at him and he grunted back. Reaching out, she tapped the back of his hairy paw-hand.

"Sharpen your claws, Vrix. There's a war coming. I can feel it."

His eyes flashed and he leaned back checking they were completely alone.

"What do you wish from me?" His voice was a deep rumble, but articulate.

Krukill's brow furrowed, "It is not clear yet. The danger is small today but may run deep. Do you know what a Ring Bearer is?"

The dracs ears pricked up then pushed forwards, "I do. Go on."

Krukill smiled at his presumptuousness. No one but he would dare give her an instruction.

"A Ring Bearer is definitely afoot. A young person. They are always weak at first."

The drac formed a half smile. His killing teeth showed, "Do you want me to hunt him down?"

Krukill shook her head, "It may be a she. Three young people have entered our world through Finkley Field, two male, one female—you may remember the place—it's where I cursed the Attuks." Vrix stiffened. Krukill spread her hands. "I should have waited for you. You were away on a hunt. I entrusted the drunes to kill them."

The drac lifted a paw-hand and examined it, "Were firebreathers involved?"

Krukill laughed, "Vrix, you are the quickest creature beneath the winter sun."

"Perhaps I could go after this Ring Bearer in haste . . . *your majesty?*"

She smiled at the way his growl curled around her title, "No," she said and stood, "haste today will not help. Come, let us accompany your clan. Others are seeking out the Ring Bearer for me, I will have news soon enough."

Vrix got up and banged his head. He sat and rubbed it. "*Kitchens.* Give me the woods, any day."

Krukill grinned, Vrix was unstoppable in the wild but forever clumsy indoors.

"Fetch my cape and join me outside."

She strolled across a cobbled courtyard toward the dragon stables. Someone opening a window on the first floor distracted her. It was one of her council. He poked his head out looking to address her about the meeting. She paused and waited. The man caught her expression, and, although a well known figure of royalty, thought better of it and retracted his head. She smiled to herself and walked on knowing the council meeting would adjourn itself and not bother her today.

She had always enjoyed saddling her own dragon, and was in the stables when Vrix arrived carrying an elegant black cape edged with sparkling jewels. He steamed in the frosty air, towering over his mistress as he draped it around her.

Originally displayed in a glass case within a dressing chamber, Krukill had adored the cape on sight and requested Lord Transinden, the fortress owner, give it her. Unfortunately, Lady Transinden resisted, suggesting its ancestry gave her some sort of right to keep it. She wasn't given the chance to make another suggestion. That evening Krukill invited her husband to dine alone with her and tricked him into eating a steak sliced from his wife's buttocks. After he complemented Krukill on her hospitality she whispered to him its pedigree and had him cast over the ramparts. The cape became her favourite.

She always wore it on a hunt.

The Falls Of Rhandoror

Goodhook and Androver glared at Philadini.

"You lied to Finn!" Goodhook exclaimed.

"Old magicians need not die," Philadini said, "they can sleep for a few thousand years and eventually regenerate."

"What—?"

"In theory we're immortal—however, no magician has achieved the long sleep since the time of the ancients.

"But—"

"How many old magicians have you met?"

"Well, you have over three hundred years behind you."

"That's not old—I mean thousands of years."

"Well—"

"Exactly. We tend to either get killed fighting other magicians, or, sometimes, our over-ambitious magical experiments backfire on us. Anyways, we magicians have always suspected that Albinonus fashioned his tomb and its tricks to attempt the long sleep. Now, I have no idea if he will complete it and someday regenerate, but I do know Finn met him. *Definitely.*"

"What makes you so certain?"

"Apart from having absolutely no chance of escaping it's what he saw."

"Albinonus?"

"No, the white monkey. It was his favourite. Albinonus created it himself. Finn couldn't have made that up."

"But why lie to him?"

"Krukill! She has the greatest mind reading powers of all magicians. I don't want her sensing we have acquired such a powerful weapon."

"So that little golden book of spells is actually real?"

"For sure, it must be real, and, I think I'd better go take it off him."

"But Albinonus gave that book to him not you! He might do a better job with it!"

Silence.

Suddenly, Philadini stormed off towards the river. After he had gone about thirty paces he stopped and shouted back. "Get moving —and bring those sacks—we leave now!" He set off again at a fast lick.

"*Magicians!*" Goodhook said to Androver. "If he doesn't admit to Finn he lied I'm going to tell him."

Androver picked up the sacks and tossed one to him, "Oh?"

"It might not be wise, but that little man needs all the help he can get. It's not his fight—he didn't choose to come here and do battle for us."

"Agreed. It does look bad."

"Look, half of his battles could be against Philadini if we don't rein him in."

Androver stared after the magician, "But they'll be on their own with him after tomorrow."

Meanwhile, Grindlebrook saw Philadini stalk off, "I'm off to see Granddad."

Tom's eyes followed her. Finn punched him lightly on the shoulder.

"You really like that little Attuk, don't you mate?"

For the first time Tom didn't argue. He watched her all the way to the campfire, "Yeah, I guess I do."

Maggie grinned, "Knew it!"

Tom shrugged, "I wish she were a real girl."

Finn cocked his head to one side, "Well then, we'd better pull this caper off so that she can become one again."

Maggie saw that Goodhook and Grindlebrook were heading their way, almost within earshot, "Look out."

"Time to go." Goodhook said, when they arrived. He was holding a pot of the mustard coloured balm. "Let me dress those cuts." He said to Finn.

Once he'd applied the balm to Finn's abrasions they headed down the grassy slope toward the river. It was mid afternoon and another gloriously sunny day. The squirrels scampered around The Great Oak, jostling for places to watch them depart, some climbed the big rock. Meanwhile, the Attuks packed up their camp, swiftly loading a troop of sandy coloured four legged animals, which were waist high, had outsize ears, and were called pacuns.

The mucklebacks, who had spent their time wallowing in their watering hole, were now alert and watching the entourage troop toward them. When Loopy recognised Maggie he bounded out of the water.

"Loopy!" Maggie yelled and broke into a run.

Finn and Tom's mucklebacks splashed out of the river behind Loopy and thudded their way to them. Soon the three of them were seated on their humps. A commotion in the water caught their attention and it looked like two mucklebacks were about to fight then one of them, a huge albino, ploughed out of the river and bulled it's way toward Philadini. Loopy made way for it snorting all the while.

"That's Sulan," Grindlebrook said, "Philadini's muckleback. Trust him to pick a big angry white one."

"I heard that." Philadini called.

Grindlebrook pulled a face at him and Philadini grinned, then Grindlebrook's muckleback arrived and nuzzled her.

"Her name is Loola," Grindlebrook said to Maggie, "how strange, we've chosen similar sounding names for them."

Once everyone had mounted they set off downstream keeping the River Rhand to their left. The pacuns trotted behind the mucklebacks making up the rear. Finn checked over his shoulder frequently until Abinonus's tomb became too small to make out but he could still see the big rock and, of course, the Great Oak.

"Did you see the squirrels watching us?" He called to Maggie.

"Yes, and I'm sad in a way I didn't expect. I desperately want to get back home but now I'm unhappy leaving The Great Oak. Why do I always want to be where I'm not?"

Tom burst out laughing, "You two."

"What?" Maggie said.

"Crazy sentimentalists."

The mucklebacks ate up the terrain and the Great Oak disappeared from view. A while later, a grey blot appeared on the horizon.

"A cloud!" Maggie exclaimed.

"No," Grindlebrook said, "that's spray from the Falls of Rhandoror."

"Oh."

"You won't be disappointed when you get near and see it properly."

"But I miss clouds, Grindly."

Grindlebrook took no notice and guided her muckleback away so that she could ride next to her grandfather. Soon The River Rhand curved left and an open plain lay ahead. The mucklebacks halted and lowered their necks backwards, en masse. Everyone slid their legs eagerly into the high perches, grabbed the bony hand holds and the magnificent beasts sped off. Maggie's heart bumped powerfully, her luxuriant mane of sandy hair flew back horizontal and around her a thousand muckleback hoofs pounded the ground generating a deafening roar. Every face wore a glorious smile. Too soon, the end of the plain approached and the mucklebacks had to slow to a thudding trot. When the way became rocky and hazardous they halted once more.

"If you look as far as you can see," Goodhook called to the young people, "you should be able to pick out a line of blue—that's The Unfillable Lake." To Philadini he said, "We have enough time to show them The Falls Of Rhandoror–what do you think?"

Philadini sighed but didn't object so Goodhook guided everyone to the left and they picked their way forward until they were again plodding adjacent to the River Rhand. Here it ran moody and black until it poured fast into a gorge. From there, Finn could make out faint reverberations coming from the falls ahead. The mucklebacks pressed on, following the edge of the gorge until they encountered a thick wood.

"Ok, it's a walk from here," Goodhook said, "the mucklebacks can skirt the wood and meet us at The Unfillable Lake."

They dismounted and everyone took it in turns to pass through a slim gap between boulders that, once through, led them to a path alongside the gorge. High above them, spray from the falls caused the sunlight to sparkle. As they drew nearer and nearer to the falls the noise became more raucous and the ground actually shook. Spray drifted down. In no time Finn and everyone else were soaked but pleasantly so. A little further on, still stronger reverberations juddered into them and the River Rhand, now a mass of swirls and gushing waves, flashed onward at considerable speed. Finn's heart pounded. Goodhook motioned everyone should get down onto their hands and knees. Soon the path widened out somewhat enabling the English trio to crawl alongside Grindlebrook. Then they squeezed through a final slim gap between boulders and there, right ahead of them, and shooting skywards, Finn saw a massive wall of spray hundreds of yards across. Everyone stretched out prone and squirmed forwards until they got to the lip of the falls and gazed down.

Finn lay on hard and cool rock with Maggie to his right. To his left, the roaring River Rhand surged like an airplane about to take off then flung itself in a giant leap over the brink, forming a massive peat-brown tongue. Gyrating madly and splotched through with creamy foam, it licked the void below. Then, plunging down, down into the depths of an abyss, the stupendous waterfall finally exploded into a churning mass that roared like a thousand giants before flying back up to the sky, transmuted into the great wall of spray. Finn gawped, awed by the power of it. Suddenly, he felt the ground tipping. He flung himself back and rolled away fast, however, the ground had remained flat. The Attuks laughed at him. Although he couldn't hear them above the din, he could tell it was good natured; watching the river making its arc and descent had created the illusion to him of the ground slipping forwards, and Maggie and Tom's panicked expressions told him they had just gone through the same heart stopping experience.

He squirmed back to the rim and gawped, mesmerised by the tumbling water, until Goodhook crawled alongside and signalled him back. They rolled a good distance from the edge before standing up. Unable to talk above the din they made wild gesticulations to each other to share the marvel.

Then Goodhook motioned him to walk to where the din quieted somewhat and called everyone to follow him into the wood. A peaceful hush soon enveloped them. As they followed a leafy trail inquisitive birds about half the size of a sparrow fluttered around their heads. Maggie became enchanted by them. Pointing out a particularly persistent one, she held out her hand and it flew there. Cautiously, she raised it to eye level. It cheeped a little song.

"It's a zook." Grindlebrook said. "My favourite bird."

"I can see why. Is it saying anything?"

"No, it's just a sweet tune."

Maggie flipped her hand upwards and the teeny zook fluttered off into the undergrowth, "Walk with me Grindly, I want to learn more about zooks."

Further on, sunshine broke through the canopy of the trees. The sound of the falls returned louder and louder and the ground vibrated strongly again.

Goodhook, still leading, shouted back, "Go steady now, everyone, we're getting near to the edge, pushing from the back will be dangerous."

They slowed, making their way towards the brightness of a clearing then one by one walked out of the wood and onto an extensive rock platform. Here they had reached the far side of the massive wall of spray. Mist particles drifted down from hundreds of feet and sunlight was diffusing them into a myriad of small rainbows that appeared and disappeared within seconds. At any one time there were twenty or so of them, plus one huge rainbow which bridged right across a half-mile wide gorge. Zipping in and out of the shimmering rainbows were swarms of rainbow chasers—dive-bombing, looping and swooping majestically. After watching them for a while the young people sat down and, gazing to the right, took in their first clear and unimpeded view of the Unfillable Lake. There was nothing but deep blue water and more deep blue water stretching all the way to the horizon and beyond. Maggie was enraptured and grasped Tom and Finn's hands and squeezed them tight.

"Guys, I want us to remember this moment forever."

Finn however, sensed that the lake and everything around him had acquired an undercurrent of menace. And his ring felt tighter, like it was suspicious of something.

His pained expression troubled Maggie, "*Whatever* is the matter?" She said, looking hurt.

"I don't know yet but something's wrong."

He turned away from the Unfillable Lake and gawped at the rainbow chasers but instead of looking happy he looked terrified. They followed his gaze. Maggie contemplated them and the sparkling spray. Frowning, she turned to him, "Finn, it's the most beautiful scene I've ever—"

"*Drunes!*" Finn yelled and shot to his feet. He grabbed Maggie and Tom and ran, pulling them through clusters of bewildered Attuks toward the woods. Grindlebrook ran after them.

Suddenly, out of the spray shot four drunes and with claws extended and red eyes flashing, they swooped fast, each toppling an Attuk over the lip of the gorge. The Attuks fell screaming for hundreds of feet and smashed on jagged rocks at the waters edge. Speeding in a tight arc, the drunes sped back into the spray and were gone. Every Attuk whipped out their half-swords and faced the spray but it was too late. Stunned by the audacity of the attack. Goodhook and Philadini went and peered over the edge at those splattered below.

"Who were they?"

"I'm not sure," Goodhook said, his voice cracking, "It happened so quick—I never should have—"

"It's not your fault, the drunes killed them, not you."

"But I brought them here."

Finn and the others clung to the edges of the wood. Suddenly, Grindlebrook stood stock still and sniffed deeply. Her eyes widened.

"I can smell smoke—*fire!*" She shrieked, waiving her arms madly. "*Granddad! There's a fire somewhere close!*"

The Escape

❧❦❧

Krukill mounted her dragon—a snakla. Small for a dragon and nimble, snaklas were two winged and fast, ideal for a hunt. The snakla pranced in a circle awaiting Krukill's command. She pricked it delicately with her silver spurs and they shot into the air. Over the battlements they sped, then she willed it into a nose-dive. The frosty valley lay several thousand feet below. Her jewelled cape blew out and she revelled in their speed, flashing down, hugging close to the icy rock of the precipice.

Free falling was an early love.

When she was just a child she could stop the hearts of her parents by doing it—hurtling toward any old jagged death and leaving her dragon to pull out at the very last moment. Instinctively,' she had known never to attempt to steer a snakla at the end of a free fall—it was certain death, but she always chose a dragon that could time a free fall perfectly. Today her snakla did just that, scattering loose snow as it pulled out of their hair raising dive.

Vrix rode a larger steed, a dragla, there was no way that a twitchy snakla would be capable of manoeuvring fast under his weight, and he needed instant responses when tracking Krukill on a dragon. The dragla dropped at full tilt chasing her snakla, but Vrix guided it at a slightly less severe angle, sparkling at lightening speed toward the valley floor. He kept his sharp eyes on Krukill's dragon knowing he would have to keep up. He knew it would be a challenge. His empress had enemies everywhere and he wanted to keep her safe. It was his purpose, it was his life. He chose it. She permitted it. Krukill might be all powerful but if she had one weakness it was recklessness. He knew it. She knew it. The wind whistled through his fur, ice grew on his face.

He kept up.

Ahead were his dracs, methodically scouring over frost and snow for firebreather tracks. Krukill and Vrix scattered them as they flared past.

Meanwhile, back at the fortress, Dulgo, a worried guard, stood shivering by the gates knowing already that their hunt would be unsuccessful. The firebreathers were his friends, and he'd lent them his eagles as was his custom. He'd known them forever and they always looked him up when they were in the Southlands, always brought him something tasty when they returned from hunting, but this time he feared they wouldn't be coming back. The dracs had questioned him, had wanted to know if he'd seen the firebreathers, he'd lied, now he feared for himself and he feared for his wife also. Deeper inside though, he was sick with the boredom of guarding the gates. It gnawed at him, year in year out. Once, he had been of higher station, a loyal employee of Lord Transinden and Lady Transinden and head of all the other servants but, after Krukill murdered his masters, he took the gatekeepers job in preference to execution. He was bitter about it, angry at Krukill's ownership of his life, her daughter's tricks and taunts, and for his years of wretched drudgery. However, today he was not bored, today he was somewhat more alive, because today, he was cringing about the probability he would be discovered.

Verko prodded him in the ribs. Dulgo spun around, dagger instinctively drawn but blanched at the sight of the young woman perusing him. She'd been creeping up on him like that since she was a child, always dressed in black, like some tenacious sleuth-shadow. Instead of greeting her with his perennial humility, he drew in a sharp breath, though it was his eyes that really gave him away.

"What are you up to, *Dulgo?*" Verko said, with a grin that slowly distorted her lips.

Dulgo could never think fast and his mind, even more scrambled now by her presence, failed him, "I—I let them go." He stammered.

"*Oh?* And who, *exactly*, was it that you let go?"

"The—the firebreathers—I didn't know they were *bad* firebreathers

—I—I'd known them for a long time." The change in Verko's expression chilled his gut. He saw it was his time. He fell to his knees and clasped his hands. "Please don't hurt my wife."

Verko's chill laughter echoed around the cobbles and walls. A big black bird, preening itself on the battlements, squawked and flew off. Verko's black eyes followed it then she leaned into Dulgo's face, "Don't worry yourself, silly man. It will be our little secret."

She stepped back and watched him shuffle gratefully to his feet.

"Thank you, thank you, thank you—your majesty."

She gave him one of the scariest smiles on the planet. Dulgo's mind churned slow. But even he could see there would come a day when Verko would expect payment for this favour. He wiped his brow as she strutted away, clicking her elegant black heels onto cold cobbles.

Verko savoured the moments, reading his mind, feeling his fear leak away. Soon she would feel the sweetness of vandalising his hope before the final ecstasy of murder. At the far side of the courtyard she paused then spun to face her victim. She pursed her lips, tapped her chin with her finger, then the distorted grin was back. When she half closed her eyes Dulgo's knees twitched. He wobbled to the heavy wooden gates and clung on. Slowly, she sashayed her way back to him, relishing the twisting of his relief into terror. When she got close his eyes were stretched wide and he was drawing faster and faster and shallower and shallower breaths. Oh what joy. Sparing him, watching him relax . . . and then . . . she whispered just loud enough for him to hear.

"Thought you'd got away with it—didn't you, *Dulgo!*" Her last word she hissed then spat into his face.

He screamed all the way to the valley floor. Verko grinned at his slaps and scrapes against rock as he plummeted. The final minuscule thud when he collided with death was pure bliss. The moment particularly satisfied her, because, had she never freed the firebreathers, she would never have had an excuse to kill him. She congratulated herself. Not having excuses to kill people was so tiresome. Her mother always wanted an explanation.

∼

HALF A DAY AWAY, SECURE ON A REMOTE MOUNTAIN, THE FIREBREATHERS were long gone, ensconced in a cave known only to their clan and confident they would be safe. They had chosen to hunker down until spring and the eagles could never give their position away because they'd just eaten them. A pity—just like using Dulgo was a pity. But firebreathers weren't an overly pitiful race. They prepared to hibernate —each eying the others muscles—the hunger with which Verko had cursed them earlier hadn't entirely dissipated, not to mention the fact that firebreathers had been known to eat their own kind, especially if they woke up ravenous in the middle of winter.

~

THE FIRST THING THAT VRIX NOTICED WHEN HE AND KRUKILL ALIGHTED their dragons was that Dulgo wasn't on duty at the gates. He paused momentarily but said nothing. The hunt with Krukill had been exhilarating even if not fruitful and he and the dragons steamed. He passed their reins to a stable handler, saw Krukill into the fortress, returned her cape into its display case, then went to investigate. The news he got was awkward, he couldn't confront Verko directly, his standing with Krukill didn't stretch quite that far, and, if he caused a problem for Verko she might just kill him too, not straight away, she would pick her moment, find justification. He chose to leave it, some self seeking fool would turn up and offer up information to Krukill for a reward, Verko could kill that one instead. He sat down in the shadows to wait. Later, Dulgo's wife turned up at the fortress gate with a plate of hot food for her husband. Vrix watched her collapse mid conversation with the replacement guard. The dish shattered, echoing around the empty courtyard. Vrix felt a great sadness for her and fury that Dulgo's life was over, wasted on Verko's whim. He didn't show it though, showing feelings got you killed. He headed back to the drac's quarters and got drunk. Dulgo might have been slow witted, but he had been his friend.

Vrix didn't have another friend.

The Fire

※❦※

Grindlebrook's cry punctured the Attuk's already wretched spirits, some gasped, but others, mindful of drunes, kept watch. Goodhook and Philadini rushed to her, they too smelt smoke.

Philadini sent Androver to reconnoiter and asked Goodhook to lead the others and make haste for the Unfillable Lake. Finn, Tom and Maggie held back whilst Grindlebrook shinned up a tree to check the extent of the danger.

Soon Androver reported back,"There are many fires—it could only be firebreathers. There's been no rain—it'll be bad."

As if in answer, the Attuks Goodhook had been leading, poured out of the woods. "*It's an inferno up ahead!*" One called out.

Meanwhile, Grindlebrook, in her perch above the canopy, saw smoke pouring out of the woods in many places. She shuffled back down the tree trunk and went straight to Philadini, "I saw two routes between the fires," she reported, "one leads to a fall of hundreds of feet off the escarpment, the other to a ravine that comes out at the Unfillable Lake—Granddad and I used it on a hunt a while back."

Philadini frowned, "Neither way will be any good if its firebreather's work, the ravine is sure to be a trap."

Soon Goodhook arrived back, "The main track is hopeless."

Most of the Attuks gathered around their leaders, some however, stayed just within the wood, clinging to trees as if they were somehow giving them reassurance.

"Well, Mr. Magician," Maggie said, "in all the good books it's you who gets us out of this mess!"

Hearing the word 'book' Finn slipped his hand into his pocket and pulled out Albinonus's little book of spells. Philadini caught its golden flash.

"Kindly pass that to me."

Finn frowned, "Why?"

"We haven't much time!"

Finn looked squarely at him and repeated, louder this time, "Why?"

The magician didn't answer but his face flushed. A few Attuks let go their trees and moved closer. Goodhook spoke up.

"Finn, it really is Albinonus's book of spells."

The magician's eyes flashed and his eyebrows shot up. He took a pace toward Goodhook.

"You shouldn't have lied!" Goodhook said.

Finn smiled inside, *I did meet Albinonus,* "Goodhook's right! You should trust me—*us,* I mean."

However, he handed the book to the scowling magician who grumbled something. After scrutinising it all over, Philadini uttered incantation after incantation but failed to get it open and gave up. "We're going to have to risk the ravine." He said, and slipped the golden book of spells into his cloak.

"*Give it back!*" Finn said.

Philadini ignored him, "Lead the way, Goodhook."

But Goodhook didn't move, neither did anyone else.

Finn felt the hackles fly up on his neck, "I said—*give it back!*"

Philadini stiffened, his eyebrows twitched and he glowered at Finn, "We don't have time for this! Lead off, Goodhook."

However, when Goodhook still didn't move Philadini's mouth tightened. With eyebrows still twitching he tossed the book of spells to Finn. Satisfied, Goodhook finally set off and Philadini ran at his side. Almost everyone followed but Grindlebrook looked torn.

"Go with your grandfather." Androver said.

After she had scampered off Androver grinned at Finn, "Come on, you."

Maggie and Tom set off with him but Finn stayed put because the golden book had suddenly become much heavier. He gawped at it. It seemed different somehow.

"The pencil!" He shouted, "Something's different about the pencil!" The others rushed back and gathered around. "Look!" Finn said. "It's grown a sharp point and there's fine script along it." He pulled at the pencil and it came away in his hand.

"Ooh," Maggie said, "clever boy."

Tom had a good smirk on. Finn grinned. *Maybe, I didn't nearly die for nothing.*

Androver gave him a friendly slap on the back, "Well done!"

It almost knocked the wind out of Finn and momentarily he wondered how he'd ever managed to escape him that first day way back at Finkley Field. Then the book became heavier still. Suddenly, it flipped open. It looked just the same only doubled in size. He held it in both hands but then, with a powerful snap, it flipped open again causing him to drop it. It did another flip as it landed becoming bigger than a full sized text book. They all stared goggle eyed.

"Woah, amazing." Tom said

"Wait till I tell Philadini." Androver said.

The book doubled in size one last time, letters rose proud of its shiny gold surface and now it had real pages. Finn dropped to his knees and ran his fingers over the title.

"I wonder what those words say." Maggie said.

"Eh?" Finn said, "It says, 'Albinonus's Book Of Spells'."

Everyone stared at him.

"Are you having a laugh?" Tom said, "It's in some weird language."

Finn glanced at him then back at the book. The words on the front, indeed, were indecipherable script. "That's weird, I could swear it read 'Albinonus's Book Of Spells' just now."

Androver saw smoke filtering through the trees, "We must hurry."

Finn opened the book at random, its pages were made of thick creamy parchment and felt luxurious but they were blank. He opened it somewhere else and, again finding the pages totally blank, he fanned them from back to front—all empty. His shoulders slumped.

"I guess we need Philadini again."

A thick blanket of smoke drifted over them, blinding them for several seconds. Androver had a coughing fit, "We'd better get after the others." He wheezed.

"Wait a moment," Maggie said, "what's the pencil for?"

Finn had it scooped in his hand, examining it now, it had morphed into an iridescent blue pen and had acquired an exquisitely carved nib, "I'll give it a go—it wont take long."

Androver assessed the thickening smoke. All heard trees cracking and branches snapping and occasional red hot embers fell through the canopy. His eyes widened, *"We don't have time."* But Maggie lay a gentle hand on his arm, imploring him with her eyes. "Be quick, then."

Finn wrote, 'We need help' on a random page. No response. He added, 'to put out a fire'. No response.

Androver spotted flames licking a tree nearby, "Sorry Finn," Androver said, "I need to go." Then added quietly. "If I set on fire you'll never find the ravine."

Finn's brow knotted and he balled his fists, *"Albinonus told me it would work when I needed it!"*

"Calm down," Maggie said,"try asking for yourself."

Finn looked up at Androver, "If this doesn't work I give up."

"Hurry." The Attuk said.

Finn wrote, 'I need a strong spell to put a fire out.'

Blood red letters appeared underneath his request spelling out, 'Who are you?'

"Who am I?" He exclaimed, brow knotted.

Tom got down next to him, "Are you ok mate?"

Finn looked at his best friend in the whole world and pointed to the words, "But—that's what it says!"

Tom looked at the book, "It's a blank page, mate."

Maggie and Androver got to their knees too.

"Can you see something that we can't?" Androver said.

Finn pointed to the page, "It's there in big blood red letters, 'Who are you?' the damn thing says!"

Androver squeezed his shoulder, "Forget explaining to us—just do what it says."

He wrote, 'I am Finn.'

No answer.

'A Ring Bearer.' He added.

An instruction appeared in blood red, 'Hold your ring to the page and write your requirement.'

Smoke enveloped them again, Finn's eyes watered and he had a coughing fit. Androver jumped out of the way when a flurry of burning leaves trickled down. Then the crackling within the woods was augmented by a bang as a tree exploded. All flinched and Finn, squinting through smarting eyes, wrote awkwardly with his left hand whilst pressing the jewels in his ring into the page.

'I need a spell to put out a big fire!'.

The book replied, 'Don't be impertinent! Where?'.

Finn was unsure now whether his tears were because of smoke or frustration. He wrote, 'I apologise. All around me. It's very big.'

Nothing at first, then, after a long pause came the response, 'Hmm, I need to think about this one,' then the book clamped itself shut, halved in size, then halved again and again.

"*No!*" Finn shouted at it.

Maggie grabbed his hand, "What happened—what did it say?"

"I asked it for a spell to put out a big fire and it said it bloody well wanted to think about it!" He looked glum at Androver, "We'd better run, don't you think?"

"Lets go—and fast!"

Finn grabbed at the little golden book of spells, "Damn! I can't pick it up—it's got way too heavy."

Androver glared at him, "This is no time for jokes!" He bent down and snatched at it but it seemed stuck to the earth. *"What?* I can't lift it either!" Flames broke through the undergrowth and a blast of heat washed over them. "We can't leave it—but we can't stay!" Androver said. Sweat dripped off his forehead and the end of his nose, he wrung his hands whilst combing the area with his eyes and spotted something. "Quick, lets roll that rock over it—at least that'll be some sort of a marker."

They rushed to the rock and huffed and puffed it over Albinonus' Book Of Spells, but, without warning, the rock shot high into the air and Finn narrowly missed being crushed when it fell.

"Woah!" He gasped.

The book had enlarged itself to encyclopaedia size again. He dropped to his knees and tore it open at random.

'How dare you attempt to violate me!' Greeted him in blood red.

Bigger flames licked trees at the edge of Finn's vision. Androver was shaking now. Scribbling fast Finn wrote, 'I'm desperately sorry—I was trying to hide you.'

THE BOY WHO FELL THROUGH THE SKY

The book retorted, 'Hmm. Well, I'll let it go this time. If it happens again—I'll let you fry!'

Finn became desperate, 'Please help me!' He wrote.

'Is there plenty of water nearby?' The book asked in a flourish of red letters.

'Loads.' Finn scribbled.

'Very well then.' The book responded. 'Get angry, point around in a circle, and shout out in your loudest voice, '*Waterobiscurfiratic!*'.

Finn didn't need to get any more angry. The others stared at him as if he'd gone a bit lunatic when he stuck out his arm, spun on the spot, and screamed out the spell.

"WATEROBISCURFIRATIC!"

Shaking his hand because his ring was squeezing him madly, he checked the book and saw in huge blood red letters, 'Well done—*now —run for your life!*' Then it snapped shut, flipped itself smaller and smaller and smaller and jumped into his hand.

"Run!" Finn yelled.

"Follow me! Keep close!" Androver yelled as he dashed into the trees. With his eyes smarting he dodged floating embers and wraiths of flame and skimmed the tracks left by his Attuks.

They kept close.

Way ahead of them, Philadini and Goodhook were staring into the ravine. It was carpeted with thick and parched grass and clumps of bone dry bushes. Spindly trees grew everywhere.

"If that lot catches we'll all burn," Goodhook whispered, "and anything could attack us from atop those cliffs."

Philadini stroked his beard, "I could conjure up a protective circle but nothing like big enough for everyone—you're sure this ravine leads all the way to the Unfillable Lake?"

"Definitely."

They pondered the Attuks milling around them. All sweated profusely, some skittered about, assessing where the fire would come from first. They were over two hundred souls and most were willing to risk the ravine. Just then a tree crashed down not too far away.

"We could burn it clear." Philadini said.

"There's no time, we'll be on fire soon."

"Any sign of Androver or our young warriors?"

"Not yet."

A frustrated voice called out from the fringes of the Attuks.

"*Where are they!*" It was Grindlebrook. She stood at the periphery, biting her lip and staring hard into the trees. Suddenly, she shouted to her grandfather, "They must be lost—I'm going back!"

"Stay here!" Goodhook yelled. But she was already running off fast. "*You don't know where they are!*" He bawled after her. Philadini grabbed his arm. Goodhook rounded on him. "Unhand me!"

"I need you here!"

Someone screamed, a female. She had tried to catch Grindlebrook but a flaming branch fell on her and she was afire. A crowd of Attuks ran to her, and, not daring to touch her, ripped leafy branches off trees and beat vainly at her flames.

"Water!"

Those with a supply of drinking water threw it on her. She screamed, sizzled and smoked then passed out. The rest of the Attuks bunched up and pushed their way toward the ravine. Goodhook's brow furrowed, he bunched his fists.

Philadini grabbed him "Steady now, old friend." He said quietly, so no one could hear. "Grindlebrook is smart enough to outwit the flames—she'll find them." Then he released him.

Goodhook breathed in deeply, he stood straight and tall and waved his arms, "Hold fast!" He bawled. "We await the Ring Bearer!"

Meanwhile, Grindlebrook was speeding away. She ran, back-tracking as fast as she could and got maybe half way, when, at the corner of her vision, she saw a firebreather scamper behind a tree. She pulled up sharp, panting, and stared at it. If the firebreather sprayed her she knew she was dead. She was aware of their speed and cunning, she'd been present at kills, but never with less than a dozen Attucks. It might chase her, run to its clan or lie in wait. She made her choice. Silently, she stalked to the tree, and, with her heart leaping inside her breast, made a blind grab behind it, low, at root level. She got lucky, clutched its spindly ankle and yanked. The firebreather dug its tiny claws into the tree as she darted around the trunk and rammed its monkey-like face into the bark. Now if it squirted fire it would fry itself. She had it by the back of its head and a leg. It stank of dead things and foul sweat, causing her eyes to water. It was about waist high on her and wriggled like a snake. In one swift move she let go its leg and got her knee into its lower back. Now she had it for sure if she just kept pushing hard with her leg and clung onto its head.

"How many are you!"

"You're going to die!" It hissed.

"Not before you." She said with an eerie calm. "And slow and excruciating it will be—*I'm going to skin you."*

"Wait!" It squealed. "I can tell you that—there's a dozen of us—we're hunting small animals."

"You lie, wretched beast. Where are your friends?"

No answer.

With her free hand she ripped out her silver dagger and poked it into its ribs until blood flowed. "Ready to die?" The firebreather whimpered and writhed. "Ok." She said and began to slice. The firebreather screamed and thrashed which made her cuts go deeper. It ceased thrashing and groaned and mewed through clenched teeth—soon she had cut enough and began peeling its flesh.

"Aaaaaagghh—stop! They're at the ravine! I was sent to hunt stragglers!"

"Thought so." Grindlebrook's eyes turned to mist.

She dropped her dagger, simultaneously grabbing the firebreathers ankles and wrenched. Its claws came off the tree pulling chunks of bark with them. The firebreather tried to spray her with its flaming juice but Grindlebrook was quick enough. Howling a war cry, she swung it through the air, trailing a perfect circle of fire, and smashed its head against the tree. Its brains splattered over the trunk and it went limp. She spat on its body and, uttering a profanity regarding its breeding, she grabbed her dagger and took off at full pelt to stop the Attuks from going into the ravine. She belted along, narrowly dodging a blazing tree that fell in her path and, even when her lungs were bursting with the effort she didn't slow down. But she was too late, by the time she got back there was no one in sight apart from her grandfather. He was knelt with his head pressed to the ground wracked with sobs. The ravine was ablaze. Just then, a tremendous gust of wind flattened both of them and fanned the flames wilder.

Meanwhile, Finn, Maggie and Tom struggled for breath but kept up with Androver, who coughed and wheezed as he dashed through the hot air. Constantly, they had to wipe their eyes even though they did their best to duck the smoke. Once Maggie's hair got tangled in a spiky bush but the boys quickly got it unravelled for her. The heat was so intense that new fires were constantly breaking out, and at intervals, trees toppling down shook the ground. Twice they needed to leap over burning trunks.

Without Androver, none of them could have followed the tracks of the Attuks at the speed they ran, but he, being an expert tracker, couldn't miss the signs of hundreds of feet dashing through a wood. Rushing seemingly headlong, dodging sparks and flames and never looking back, he was, nonetheless, listening intently to the struggles of his charges and knew they were close. His only pause for breath came whilst they stopped to free Maggie's hair. Immediately fleeing onwards he caught a glimpse of a crumpled and bloodied firebreather sans head, he grinned to himself and wondered whose handy-work it was.

Suddenly, they were flattened to the ground by a tremendous blast of wind, which was followed by an almost equally tremendous roar as blazes all around were fanned into attack and devoured fresh dry brush. Picking themselves up they ran on, only to be flattened by another howling and unstoppable wall of wind. Again they got up and ran on, again they were flattened by another screaming squall.

"What was that bloody spell you incanted?" Maggie wheezed out.

"Something about water biscuits and fire in the attic." Finn said.

"*What*—?" Tom croaked between sucks and gasps.

Androver jumped to his feet, "*Don't talk, run.*"

They scrambled off the forest floor and bounded onwards. Eventually, when it seemed like their bodies should have already given up and been engulfed by fire, they caught sight of Grindlebrook and Goodhook. Through a shimmering haze of heat and smoke they could see that they were hacking furiously at bushes, trying to create a fire break around themselves.

When they glimpsed Androver bringing the young people, Grindlebrook and Goodhook fell to their knees, exhausted, dishevelled, and blackened, "It's no use," Goodhook gasped, soot smeared and blurry-eyed, "they charged the ravine, Philadini went in after—trapped now—I waited for Grindlebrook, we heard screams, firebreathers, ambush—I couldn't stop them—Grindlebrook searched for you—killed one—"

Just then, the most ferocious blast of wind yet flattened them all. But, unlike before, this time it didn't stop. It howled and whistled and blew and blew, fanning the blaze to its greatest roar, bending brush in half and toppling weakened trees. But then they were hit by the most immense deluge of water when, sucked up and transported by a screaming hurricane of wind, the whole expanse of spray from the Falls of Rhandoror unloaded itself. Masses of smoke surged out from the ravine and infernos everywhere hissed with rage. Water and more water dumped out of the sky in an endless torrent.

Finn burst out laughing, hands held high, vainly attempting to fend off the onslaught. "It worked!" He gasped. Soon they were floundering in a muddy swamp of ash and charred branches. Still the wind howled and moaned and water crashed down and down, and still they couldn't stand without being blown over.

"Get that bloody book out and tell it to stop before we drown!" Maggie whooped as she gave him a great big wet hug.

Then the wind died as quickly as it began, the sky cleared and the woods steamed rather than smoked. They picked themselves up and regarded each others bedraggled state.

Tom beamed, "That was some freaking storm—take that, Philadini!" He punched the air, but, seeing Grindlebrook's and Goodhook's troubled countenances he wiped the smirk off his face and together they tramped into the ravine.

It was dark, by the time the survivors sat safe and dry on the shore of the Unfillable Lake. By then almost half the Attuks were either missing or dead. Many more would die from their injuries during the night.

Once the Attuks were in the ravine, Firebreathers had torched their retreat whilst more torched the way ahead. They'd scarpered leaving a wall of fire advancing from either direction. Philadini had protected as many as he could, his spells holding back some of the flames, but he couldn't protect everyone. Goodhook was inconsolable. He sat shaking his head with Grindlebrook squeezing him tight. Later she recounted to survivors the capturing of the firebreather and Finn recounted the tale about Albinonus' book of spells. However, instead of becoming jealous of Finn's prowess, for once Philadini allowed himself to be fascinated.

"I did do something special, didn't I?" Finn said, once he had answered all Philadini's questions.

"Yes, you did something *very* special. All may have died but for you."

"Why did you lie to me in the tomb?"

"It wasn't about you, it was about Krukill. The Black Diamond gives her the power to see over huge distances and she can read minds. I didn't want her to discover you had acquired Albinonus's Book Of Spells, also, I admit I didn't think you would be able to make use of it, being a novice—I was wrong about that—I apologise." He offered his hand to Finn.

Finn took it, "Apology accepted."

Maggie and Tom watched Philadini like predators about to pounce.

"I apologise to you all." The magician said, then, seeing Grindlebrook hanging onto Goodhook, he said, "We'll have to cook ourselves tonight."

"There's no dry wood." Maggie said, with half a grin that quickly dissipated.

Philadini smiled ruefully, "Well, the River Rhand may lay beyond *my* powers of diversion, but I reckon I can manage a cooking fire." He wandered off to collect wood himself, rather than expecting others to do it.

"That was a breath of fresh air." Tom said.

A few Attuks had totally missed the trauma of the fire having travelled around the wood with the pacuns and the mucklebacks. Devastated by the loss of their fellows, they quietly unloaded the supplies needed for the night and wandered about with tubs of special balm, tending the injured as best they could. Afterward they organised a ceremony for the known dead. Some brave souls wanted to return to the woods and begin a rescue hunt but Philadini wouldn't hear of it.

"We search tomorrow." He said, "You know not what remains lurking behind those blackened trees."

After a hurried supper the three inseparables gathered blankets and found themselves a place to sleep. Exhaustion soon overcame them and, easing themselves into positions that had the least aches and stings from their bruises and scrapes, they slept.

Finn woke in the dead of night. Everyone was asleep apart from those on watch and two silhouettes by the campfire, Philadini and

Goodhook. They talked in whispers. Goodhook had his head hung low.

Finn turned over and listened to waves gently lapping onto shingle by the lakeshore. His body was spent and he knew he would soon slip back to sleep. Wearily drawing his right hand out of his covers he peered into the cool flames burning within the jewels of his ring. *Was it only yesterday morning when we stood by the tomb and I got chosen*? He thought back—yes, this is our second night. He squinted hard at the golden threads passing through the gemstones. Script was woven into them but way too small to read. He gave up and thought about how wonderful it would be to wake up in his cosy bed in the attic of Hattie's cottage and, with that thought, he drifted back to sleep.

He dreamed of jumping off a wall and floating down toward a moat with Tom and Maggie. They fell ever so slowly at first then accelerated faster and faster but, rather than landing in Finkley Field, they plunged into cold black and slimy water. Unseen scaly hands grabbed at him, yanking him down, down and further down. He struggled to break free but got torn away from Maggie and Tom and dragged ever deeper. His chest was bursting but he knew he couldn't take a breath or he would surely drown. Then he felt himself being bound with soggy ropes and rusty chains and finally, a heavy weight was placed on his chest forcing him into the ooze at the bottom of the moat. Only his eyes remained above it. He watched as three murky green lights descended, coming ever closer until he could see they were lanterns inside of which, fat cream candles covered in ancient script flickered and smoked. Maggie's severed head followed the lanterns down, sinking gracefully toward him until it came to rest on the ooze next to his head. She smiled at him, exhaling bubble after bubble. They burst, saying, "Finn, Finn, Finn." He opened his mouth to tell her that he loved her but it filled with gritty slime and after there was only black.

The Unfillable Lake

❦

Finn awoke with a start.

The Unfillable Lake lay just a stones throw away. He saw blood red predawn light slowly melting the night sky and fading the stars. For a few peaceful moments he resisted the flood of memories itching to engulf him. Stifling a yawn he turned onto his back. Then, wincing from his bruises, he stretched, looked up at his right hand and saw faint amber flickers pulsing out of his ring. Damn, he thought, it's all true. He lay there listening to water lapping onto shingle and managed to hold back his thoughts for all of twenty-seconds before the floodgates opened and his peace was flushed out by the terrors and successes of the previous day.

He tried thinking positively.

Waking up with the best friends I'm ever going to meet is quite special. Waking up with them on the shore of a stunning lake in a different world as a player in an enchanted fairytale is indescribably special. *But is it enchanted or doomed?*

He gave up positive thinking, turned over again and looked toward the campsite. No one was about except Androver. They waved to each other, then Finn got up, tramped to the shoreline and scrunched down onto shingle. He wrapped his arms around his legs, rested his chin on his knees and gazed out over the Unfillable Lake, waiting for the true dawn and Maggie and Tom to wake. However, the one to join him first was Grindlebrook. She squeezed his arm without speaking and settled herself onto the shingle beside him. Shivering a little from pre-dawn cool she wrapped her arms around herself like Finn. A while later the tip of the sun broke the horizon and flashed across the lake.

"How perfect is that?" Finn whispered

"Beyond perfect."

"I hope you can come with us, Grindly."

She squeezed his arm again, "Don't talk, just watch. There'll be merfyns about."

"What's a—?"

"Hi guys." Maggie said and plonked herself down on the other side of Finn. "Are you ok, Grindly?"

Grindlebrook had to lean forward to see her, "I'm very sad inside but I'm not hurt or burned thanks to Finn here and his magic."

"Might just have been freak weather." Finn said.

Maggie nudged him. "Take the compliment."

Tom turned up just then and sat next to Grindlebrook. "Morning." He grunted.

"What's up, grumpy?" Maggie said.

"Just a bit croaky."

A sizeable swirl disturbed the glass-like surface of the lake.

"Woah," Maggie said, "whatever that was it was big!"

Close by, the water humped and a long red fin glided in a circle then sank.

Grindlebrook shot to her feet, "Merfyn!"

The others leapt up.

Then, two long red fins sliced the surface heading straight for each other but slid out of sight before meeting. A few sleepy Attuks trudged to the shore to see.

"They're checking us out," Grindlebrook whispered, "it's probably best just to sit and—"

Three spiky green heads poked out of the lake right in front of them. They all shuffled backwards apart from Grindlebrook. "It's ok," she said, "they're our friends."

A merfyn raised a scaly green arm which had a lobster-like claw for a hand and snapped it, clack-clack-clack. Finn's heart thumped. The creatures had fat rubbery lips, needle sharp teeth and unblinking orange eyes. Triple gills either side of their necks opened and closed with a sucking sound and adorning their scalps were red spikes with black tips. They sank back into the lake leaving three rings on its surface.

"Woah." Finn and the twins breathed.

"Get ready," Grindlebrook said, "they might attack—they enjoy teasing young people."

To their left a merfyn leapt clear out of the water, describing an elegant arc. Its glistening green-gold body caught the early sun perfectly. *"Arrik-arrik-arrik!"* It squawked, as it soared through the air before making an almost splash-less re-entry. Whilst Finn was entranced by its slippery display, two merfyns rushed out of the lake onto the shingle and shook themselves, spraying water everywhere like wet dogs. They had four arms—two of which ended with webbed hands, a third had tentacles for fingers, the fourth having the claw. Tom and Maggie managed to scramble away but Finn got caught. The soggy creatures pounced on him, grabbed his legs and dragged him toward the water.

"Aaaaagghh!"

The merfyns had power in their legs and a mad look in their eyes. Finn screamed again, flailed out with his arms and dug his hands as deep as he could into the shingle but they dragged him onward, halfway into the water. Suddenly, one let go his leg and leaned over him, distending its jaws right in his face, *"Yaahk-yaahk-yaahk!"* It shrieked. Its cold lake-breath blew his blonde hair back, and it snapped its claws loudly, slid its suckered tentacles around his neck and began to squeeze. Right at that moment, the third merfyn launched itself out of the lake, shoved its companions off Finn and all three fell into a tangled heap of fins, scales and snapping claws. They 'arrik-arriked' away, shaking with mirth.

Grindlebrook was rolling about clutching her stomach from the pain of laughing. "Oh, Finn," she wheezed, "that was just so . . ." She burst out laughing again and behind her swelled a chorus of chortling Attuks.

Finn's heart thumped like a drum, Maggie and Tom gingerly shuffled toward him but flinched back when a merfyn glared at them and shrieked *"Yaahk!"* Then, with a sound like a fish would make if it could giggle, it flopped back into the pile of fins. Sodden, Finn dragged himself to Maggie and Tom to recover and catch his breath. None of them saw the funny side of it, but the Attuks did and it made for a break in their sombre mood.

Finally, the merfyns untangled themselves and the young people regarded them warily. Besides a long red dorsal fin, fins ran along the back of their arms and legs. They stood as tall a small man and had webbed feet with spikes for toenails. Arranging themselves into a line they sat cross legged and lay back the forest of red quills on their heads. Each extended a webbed hand and gestured them to approach.

"Their quills are poisonous," Grindlebrook said, "laying them down is a sign they want to be friends."

Maggie blew out her cheeks, "Grindly, *if you are setting us up—*"

"I'm not, the gracious thing to do is shake hands."

"I'm up for it." Tom said, puffing his chest out.

Finn didn't say anything. He just lay there soaked and gawping.

"It really is ok," Grindlebrook said, "they've had their fun."

Finn drew himself up into a sitting position, frowned at the merfyns, scrunched his waterlogged denims and watched. Tom went first. A merfyn offered him a webbed hand coated in tiny green scales. Tom made the tiniest flinch as he took its moist hand in his own and shook it.

"Hi, I'm Tom."

The merfyn opened its mouth in a flattened V shape and flapped its gills. "Arrik-arrik." It squawked gently, and nodded its head.

Tom nodded too. Then shook hands with the next and the next, each introduction mirroring the first. Maggie swallowed then went and presented herself to a merfyn.

"Good morning Mr. Merfyn, you scared me witless."

The merfyn nudged the one next to it. Its chest heaved in and out and its spikes and fins fluttered.

"It likes you." Grindlebrook said.

Maggie managed not to grimace and completed her salutations. Seeing no harm came to them, Finn ceased frowning and relaxed a little. He shrugged and went to a merfyn and offered his hand. The merfyn was about to take it but suddenly snatched its hand away and 'arrik-arriked' excitedly to the others. All three peered closely at his right hand then became silent and bowed their heads.

Finn looked to Grindlebrook for advice.

"They've recognised your ring." She said.

The merfyns remained with their heads bowed. Finn didn't know what to do. Just then Philadini joined them.

"They want you to forgive them, Finn. To attack a Ring Bearer is a disrespectful thing for them to do."

Finn decided right then that merfyns were a bit complicated. "Erm . . . I forgive you."

Slowly the merfyns raised their heads and gazed at him with mouths slightly open.

"Offer your hand if you wish," Philadini said, "they'll never attack you again, in fact, now they know you are a Ring Bearer, they'll probably fight to the death for you."

The merfyns nodded their heads and bowed.

Again Finn offered his hand to a merfyn. It gazed up at him, then grasped it. The merfyn's hand felt damp and cold but, although Finn squirmed inside, he managed not to frown. After bowing low over his hand the merfyn scooted across the shingle, dived into the lake and disappeared. Just as Finn had completed shaking hands with its companions it re-emerged from the lake and, flapping in its grasp, was a sizeable silver-green fish. The merfyn laid it at his feet.

Finn smiled for the first time that day, "Thank you."

Tom nudged Grindlebrook, "Can you cook fish?"

"I can cook anything." She grappled the hapless creature to the campfire, dispatched it, and began preparing breakfast.

The more time Finn spent with the merfyns the more he liked them and he began to see the funny side of their mock attack. He watched their fins and spikes become erect, retract, or flutter, depending on their emotions. One indicated by gesticulation it wanted to see his ring, and, when he held his hand out, it ran its tentacle fingers over it, subtly sucking its gems. It felt creepy. Then Grindlebrook called everyone for breakfast and the merfyns slipped back into the Unfillable Lake and they were gone.

"So what's the story about the Unfillable Lake?" Finn asked whilst chomping on a sweet piece of barbecued fish.

Philadini explained, "Ah yes, the Unfillable Lake, well, it's a bit of a mystery. Although it has four major rivers feeding it, plus many tributaries and streams, no water ever escapes it."

"That should be impossible."

"Yes, it should," the magician replied, "but, way down in the deepest parts of the lakes' bed there are faults—great gashes as the merfyns describe them. The water escapes through them. Long, long ago, the merfyns explored them and found immense underwater caverns and cave systems but were set upon there by invisible creatures. They are afraid to return, which is most unlike them—they love danger and adventure—so no one really knows where the water goes."

"It has to go somewhere."

"Precisely, and therein lies the mystery. It is also volcanic and—"

Just then Androver plonked two sacks next to Philadini. One clanked.

"Here are the sacks you asked for."

"Thank you, how is Goodhook?"

Rather than answering him Androver spoke to Grindlebrook, "I think your grandfather needs you."

Grindlebrook lowered her eyes and paused for a few seconds before turning to Philadini and saying very quietly, "I have to go with you." Then she left to join her grandfather.

Nobody said a word as they watched her have a heated discussion with Goodhook. Then she ran off in tears to sit by herself on the lakeshore. Goodhook paced about with head lowered, hands in his pockets, muttering.

"What are you going to do?" Androver asked Philadini.

For an answer the magician hefted the sacks, rummaged around in the one that didn't clank and fished out some garments.

"These smocks are woven with magic thread." He said. "They will protect our young friends from the searing heat of the Atta Desert." Reverently, he laid them out on the ground.

There were four of them.

Androver pursed his lips, "I see you've already decided."

Tom looked at the garments then at Maggie and Finn. *"Grindlebrook's coming with us!"* He said.

Maggie pursed her lips and reached out to the dull and baggy smocks. She stroked the material, "Hmm." Was all she said.

"They will assume whatever shape and colour you think up." Philadini said to her.

"Oh! Can I try one on?"

Philadini saw Goodhook was watching them. He gave out a deep sigh. "Maybe you should wait." He said. "Feel free to explore the other sack, but be careful, there are sharp weapons within. I'd better go speak with Goodhook."

They all turned to watch. Within seconds Philadini had his hands on his hips and Goodhook was flailing his arms about. Suddenly he prodded Philadini in the chest, yelled something and spat on the ground. Philadini held his hands wide and palms up talking fast but Goodhook stormed off. Philadini returned to the others.

"It's not good," he said, "I can't get through to him, he's overwrought—blaming himself for yesterdays deaths and madder than hell that I'm willing to let Grindlebrook come with us to the desert. He wants us all to go back into the woods and search for survivors though I'm sure he knows it's useless. There'll be firebreathers still lurking, maybe drunes too—it'd be stupid to risk it."

Androver grimaced but nodded, "I hate to say it but I reckon you are right."

"There's more," Philadini said, "he has outright forbidden Grindlebrook to come with us."

"What's to be done?" Androver asked.

"I'll wait until he cools off then try again. He'll never be able to stop her—you know how Grindlebrook is—she'd just follow us anyway, but he has to see it for himself—if I take her without his permission then—"

Tom jumped up. Maggie sprang up too and grabbed his hand, "Stay here, Tom I'll go sit with Grindlebrook." He pulled his hand away.

"Tom," Philadini said, quietly, "better a young woman."

Tom lowered his eyes and shrugged, "Ok."

Androver picked up the clanky sack, "Might as well get on with it." He untied it and spilled its contents onto the ground. They counted four sheathed swords, four daggers and two bows complemented with quivers of arrows. Also, filled with clear and coloured liquids, were numerous tiny phials with cork stoppers. A map fell out, followed by a compass and then a horn similar to Goodhook's.

"Strange tools for breaking into a prison." Finn said.

"You first need to learn how to kill a drune." Philadini said.

Silence.

Finn swallowed, Tom smirked. Androver scratched his head, "How did all that fit into one sack?"

"It's a magic sack."

Androver peered inside it, "There's something stuck in the corner."

He groped within and pulled out a thick golden tube adorned with exquisite script, "What's this?"

"It looks similar to what we call a telescope." Tom said.

Androver passed it to him. Indeed, the tube had lenses at both ends, but didn't extend like a telescope. Tom tried peering through it.

"It's blurred."

Philadini smiled, "See if you can work it out."

Tom studied the script, "Beautiful writing."

Finn watched Tom. The script on the object he held was the same as the script he had seen inside the tomb. He guessed it had been inscribed by Albinonus and he also knew what it said, but there was no way he was going to tell Tom. He wanted him to work it out for himself. Tom tried to focus on a burnt out tree.

"*Oh.*"

"What happened?" Androver said.

Tom kept squinting through it, "It became clear then blurred again but I'm not sure how." He stopped trying and studied the instrument. Running his fingers along the words engraved along it he felt a tiny vibration. "*Ah.*" He raised it to his eye once more. This time, by stroking the script on the side of the golden tube he got the tree to come into sharp focus. "Got it! It *is* a telescope."

"Well done." Philadini said.

Tom and Philadini smiled at each other. Finn beamed inside.

"Here, have a go." Tom said.

Finn took the instrument and looked out across the surface of the Unfillable Lake. He focussed it and clearly saw a fish rising way, way out from the shore. "Hey, this thing is really powerful *and* crystal clear."

Philadini clapped his hands.

Androver picked up the compass. "How does this work?"

"Oh that's a great little tool," Philadini said, "It always points to the Great Oak or maybe it's Albinonus's tomb, I'm not quite sure which, but, if you use it along with a map, you can tell which direction you are going in even if it's cloudy or at night."

"How far away from the Great Oak does it work?"

"Forever."

Androver's eyes clouded.

"That's got you thinking."

"I was once so lost someone very dear to me didn't survive—I wish I'd had this little magic tool with me then." His lips were pressed tight together as he picked up one of the four swords and unsheathed it. "Hmm, it hardly weighs anything."

"Careful, you could cleave a tree trunk with that."

"That is not possible."

"Try it." Philadini said.

Androver went to the nearest tree.

"Better work out which way it will fall." The magician called.

Androver adjusted his stance and hefted the sword easily with one hand. When he flashed it in an arc it sliced into the tree like it were cheese and with a mere half a dozen slashes he had cut a big V into the trunk. Hearing it splinter he jumped away in case it kicked back, however, the tree fell as cleanly as if it had fainted. He kept shaking his head over and over long after he had slid the sword back into its scabbard.

Finn picked up the horn and was about to blow on it but Philadini grabbed his wrist.

"That's a munkhorn—any note from that will carry straight across the Unfillable Lake. I think we can do without bringing any attention to ourselves."

Finn lowered it, "I never was any good at music anyway."

Philadini laughed, "No one is capable of playing music on a munkhorn. They only have five notes and all of them are out of tune with one another. Each note is a command. I'll teach you young warriors what they mean in a more appropriate setting."

Finn sniffed the horn, "Strange aroma, what's it made from?"

"Muckleback tusk."

Finn asked Androver, "Was that a munkhorn that Goodhook blew back at Finkley Field?"

The attuk nodded, "Yes it was, and I'm wondering how he is and where he's got to—I think I'd better have a wander about and make sure he's ok."

Not far away from his Attuks, in a small clearing shielded from camp by a clump of bushes, Goodhook was sat on a rock. It was a little private hideaway he'd discovered during a fishing trip half a lifetime ago. His elbows were set on his knees, his head was in his hands and

THE BOY WHO FELL THROUGH THE SKY

his eyes were shut whilst he pondered yesterdays horrors and todays dilemma. However, although he waited and waited and waited, no insights came. He sighed. On opening his eyes he had to blink several times because something was dazzling him. Then he gasped, and his heart did a grateful leap. Laying at his feet was The Book Of Writing That Cannot Be Unwritten. He fell upon it and ripped it open, but the words he read almost killed him.

'*Let Her Go!*' It commanded in big bold letters.

The instant he read it the book disappeared. He fell to the ground, curled into a ball and wept freely until Androver found him there.

Meanwhile Grindlebrook was sat on the lakeshore with Maggie's arm draped around her. They were gazing out across the placid waters. The Unfillable Lake was so big that the opposite shore lay unseen and its blue water met up with blue sky.

"I was *horrible.*" Grindlebrook confessed to Maggie. "It was so cruel of me to tell granddad I was leaving him and my Attuk clan after all they've done for me, and it seems much worse after so many of us died yesterday."

She broke down and Maggie hugged her tightly, "It may not happen."

Grindlebrook stared at Maggie through blurred vision, "I know you mean well, but I also know Philadini. He might be a bit of a snake but he's not poisonous *and* I know exactly how to charm him. It's easy for me. I can already see he's going to let me go."

Maggie frowned, "But you're Goodhook's granddaughter. It's surely up to him not Philadini."

Grindlebrook squeezed her, "Oh dear, dear Maggie, we're going to war! Philadini, for the moment, is our leader. Nothing matters now except keeping Finn alive. We have to have a Ring Bearer—it's the only way."

Maggie let go of Grindlebrook and stared at Finn chatting amiably with her brother and the magician, "But—but he's just a boy." She whispered.

Grindlebrook reached out and gently turned Maggie's face to hers, "You love him, don't you?"

It was Maggie's turn to have damp eyes, "I feel like I've known him forever, even before we met, which was like when we were three." She dabbed her eyes with her sleeve.

Grindlebrook squeezed her hand, she wasn't scared of much, but she was too scared to tell Maggie that she, too, was in love.

Meanwhile, Philadini gathered up the phials of coloured liquids. There were seven of them and one clear one, all about as thick as his thumb. He stowed them carefully inside his robes without explaining their purpose. "We need to make a move," he said, "as soon as Androver gets back with Goodhook we'll head along the shore to the boat. Tom, can you take care of the looking tool?"

"Telescope," Tom said, "That's what we call it back home, but they're not as clever as this one."

"Ok, that's what we'll call it then."

Again, Finn beamed inside as Tom proudly slipped it into his pocket. Then he helped to put the weapons and tools back into the sack which never seemed to fill up or become heavy.

When Goodhook returned with Androver Grindlebrook jumped up and ran to him.

"I need to be alone with my granddaughter," Goodhook said to Androver, "I'll meet you at the boat."

Androver helped to break camp and Maggie rejoined the boys. Grindlebrook and Goodhook set off hand in hand along the lakeshore with their heads bowed as if searching for interesting stones in the shingle. Soon, everyone fell in at a respectable distance behind them. Presently, the troop came across the mucklebacks but no one mounted up because the boat they were headed for wasn't moored too far away, and, it being such a beautiful morning, they preferred to walk. A little further along Goodhook and Grindlebrook halted and hugged each other tightly then walked on again. Androver explained to Philadini what Goodhook had divulged to him about the Book Of Writing That Cannot Be Unwritten. Philadini nodded with lips pursed.

"Good," he said. "it is so much better coming to him that way than from me."

Soon, a wooden boat, painted leaf green with a short mast, came into view. It was moored by a long jetty. The water around it was alive with merfyns. The nearer they got the more excited the merfyns became, many jumping clear of the water and all making quite a racket with their 'arrik-arriking'. Some came right out of the lake and slopped along the shingle to get a closer look at the Ring Bearer. Three of them 'arrik-arriked' extra-excitedly and Finn guessed they must be the ones who had scared him stupid earlier, however, it was quite difficult for him to tell them apart.

Goodhook came to Philadini. He looked worn out, "Has Androver told you what happened?"

"Yes, old friend. Would you like to sail with us to the other side of the Unfillable Lake? You can get some private time with Grindlebrook there and the merfyns will help you bring the boat back."

"Thank you. That would mean a lot to me."

They put their disagreement behind them, embraced, then helped with stowing supplies into the boat.

"Put those sacks and your weapons into the lockers," Philadini said, "we don't want any sharp objects flying around the boat."

"But the lake is flat calm." Grindlebrook said.

"You know as well as I do that it can change abruptly."

"He's right," Goodhook said, "come on, it wont hurt to give them up for an hour or two." He unhitched his half sword and dagger and dutifully stowed them. Reluctantly, Grindlebrook stowed hers too. Philadini kept a careful eye on the sacks of magic paraphernalia as they were locked away.

It was time to say goodbye.

Amidst a chorus of 'arrik-arriking' from merfyns eager to get going, Finn, Maggie and Tom went around the Attuk clan hugging and shaking hands and expressing their sorrow again for yesterdays losses. It was particularly difficult for Maggie to say goodbye to Androver.

"I wish you were coming with us."

Androver wiped an eye with his sleeve, "I'll never forget how brave you are, particularly, the way you tamed Loopy."

"Loopy! Oh my—I have to say goodbye to Loopy!" She scanned the mucklebacks, searching for him.

Androver smiled, "He's already gone. Your mucklebacks will meet you around the other side of the water."

Maggie fairly beamed at the news, then became still and frowned, "Androver, will I ever see you again?"

"Of course you will." He said, but his eyes misted up and he had to wipe away another tear.

"That is the kindest lie anyone ever told me." Maggie said quietly. She held her arms out and got a big squishy hug from him. "Goodbye, dearest Androver, and thank you, thank you, thank you—and promise me you'll look after Goodhook."

"Ha! That giant of an Attuk can look after himself without my help —he may be low at the moment but in a war he's magnificent!"

He turned away then, and, as Maggie watched his bulky frame walking off she saw him wiping his eyes with both his sleeves, it was only then she realised that she was blubbering too.

"Come on, Sis." Tom called from the boat.

Maggie was last to board. Everything inside the vessel was painted cream. She sat next to Finn on a bench which ran along its sides. Tom fiddled with the telescope, shifting position, focussing here there and everywhere. Goodhook and Grindlebrook settled near the prow and Philadini stood with hands on hips surveying the lake. The boat was over thirty feet long so there was plenty of space for everyone. Two merfyns leapt clean out of the water into the boat and hauled on the anchor rope. Hand over hand they heaved it aboard whilst Philadini coiled it. The anchor chain came aboard next and then the rusty anchor itself. Once they'd stashed everything neatly the merfyns dove back into the lake. Attuks cast off hawsers securing the vessel to bollards on the jetty.

"Why the anchor as well as mooring ropes?" Finn asked.

"It gets a bit hairy around here from time to time," Philadini said, "it's calm today so just relax and enjoy the voyage."

Then the Attuks shoved the boat away from the jetty and merfyns pushed it toward open water by paddling their webbed feet. The passengers waved a last goodbye to the Attuks lining the shore. In their black garb they again reminded Finn of a crowd of mourners at a funeral. None of them smiled as they waved them off. One or two wiped their eyes.

"Aw—they're crying." Maggie said.

Finn frowned, "I got them so wrong." He whispered.

Tom put the telescope down and waved goodbye to them, "We all did, mate." He said quietly.

"We have six oars." Philadini called out. "Who would like—"

Nine merfyns leapt out of the water and squabbled over who would row. Philadini looked like he didn't know whether to scold, applaud, or laugh. Playfully he thrust three of them overboard with an oar then stood grinning and calling time. However they didn't need him to establish a dependable rowing rhythm, and one merfyn scowled at Philadini but it looked good natured to Finn, so he assumed they were just having fun.

"I'll keep a watch forward until we make deep water." Goodhook said, and took up a stance at the prow with a foot on the bench and a hand shading his eyes. Grindlebrook sidled over to him and leaned her head against his leg. Philadini offered instructions to Tom.

"Whilst Goodhook watches forward could you be keeping an eye around and about the lake with the telescope? Just scan the surface and let me know if you notice anything unusual. When your eyes get tired, Finn or Maggie can relieve you."

"What am I searching for?"

"Turbulence."

Tom shrugged at Maggie and Finn then got on with scanning the lake.

The shoreline slipped away and the Attuks disappeared from view. Finn felt sad but excited too. Now, there was nothing to break the horizon. They were enveloped by flat calm water apart from being surrounded by frolicking merfyns. It was still morning but the sun was already hot. Everyone fell silent, lost in their own thoughts. The only sounds were creaking oars, puffing merfyns and splashes and gurgles from a strong bow wave that bustled against the hull. They were making good progress and the movement of the vessel caused a slight breeze which was welcome as the sky remained cloudless. Many merfyns swam with the boat like escorts and some younger ones gallivanted and splashed each other. Every so often, a merfyn from further off would launch itself high into the air, arcing or somersaulting, sometimes twisting. When they did that, they would catch the sunlight and glisten green, gold and red.

Finn and Maggie were kneeling shoulder to shoulder, hands on the gunwale, fascinated. Finn leaned into Maggie and felt a gentle push back. It thrilled him. He turned his head to hers at the same time she turned hers to his.

"Philadini!" Tom called, *"I think something's happening!"*

He pointed out across the lake and passed the telescope to the magician. Maggie and Finn jumped up and strained to get a glimpse of what it was he'd seen. Grindlebrook eyed the lockers that secured her weapons.

"Goodhook!" Philadini said. "Come take a look at this."

All the merfyns ceased rowing and rushed to the gunwale to check out what was going on. The boat, luckily, was very stable otherwise they might have capsized. Maggie and Finn strained to see what Tom had seen but the lake seemed flat calm to them for as far as they could see. Goodhook first scouted with naked eyes then, with lips pursed, surveyed with the telescope. The merfyns pointed and jabbered and one lent over the side *'arrik-arriking'* to those in the water. Others jumped into the vessel to get a better view. The boat slowed to a drift and everyone stared hard, searching the lake. Eventually, Maggie and Finn could just about make out a thin line cutting across the water in the far distance.

"Whatever is it?" Maggie whispered.

Goodhook lowered the telescope but kept looking forward, *"Turbulence."*

Philadini made urgent communications with the merfyns. They gesticulated wildly, their dorsal fins erect and their spikes fluttering and clicking as they 'arrik-arriked'. All pointed multiple arms in the same direction, making it clear they should row fast, away from the turbulence.

"Listen up," Philadini said, "I'm handing charge of the vessel to the merfyns."

Goodhook gave him a single nod.

Another three merfyns jumped into the boat and replaced Goodhook at the prow. With three lookouts they were able to scan forward and sideways simultaneously. The others rushed back to their oars and those on the port side heaved hard, turning the boat, then all six hauled in perfect time with all they had. The boat made way with increasing speed. More merfyns swam to the boat and helped to push, kicking their fins as busy as a paddle steamer. The boat glided through the water ever faster and its bow wave peeled away stronger and stronger, sparkling, hissing and noisier. Tom had the telescope again. He saw the line in the water mutate into urgent bubbling foam and, randomly, clusters of foam shot into the air propelled by some mysterious force from below. He shouted for Philadini to take another look. Soon the turbulent area became much larger, and even Maggie and Finn could now see it quite clearly without the telescope. Then erratic crinkles spread out and across the lakes' surface as fast as ice cracking.

All the while the turbulence became more and more ferocious at its centre and between it and the boat, violent swirls appeared.

The merfyns shouted instructions amongst themselves but always in an orderly fashion. Those in the boat rowed like fury, refreshed regularly by another six powerful merfyns who would leap out of the water and time the swopping of oars perfectly so that their direction never veered off course. Those pushing the boat relentlessly thrashed their fins as if their own lives depended on it.

Then, small whirlpools about a foot in diameter appeared right across the lake.

"It's going to be a big one!" Goodhook said. Philadini nodded ruefully. Maggie pressed herself closer to Finn.

"What's a big one?" Tom asked.

"There's no time to explain," Philadini said, "better put the telescope away in case it drops into the lake."

Tom stuck it in a pocket and buttoned the flap.

Currents began rushing this way and that, dividing the water. Towards the centre of the turbulence large waves formed and ripped into one another tearing themselves apart.

Then, 'the big one' happened.

Foam, bubbling and spurting at the heart of the turbulence changed colour from cream to black and billows of steam, peppered with solid debris, exploded out of it. This mad contaminated spume continued for half a minute or so then, suddenly, a huge red and black tongue of almost molten rock sizzled out of the lake and, like a giant red hot poker, thrust itself upward for maybe a thousand feet. The crew and passengers gasped as one and watched helplessly as the devilish tongue licked the sky then splintered into cascading and amorphous lava bombs. The huge searing globs rained down, exploding on contact with the water, leaving giant and smoke filled water blisters which popped releasing noxious sulphur-tainted smoke. However, the boat was just beyond range and everyone let out huge sighs of relief. Glancing about, Finn saw that everyone was wide eyed and gripping the gunnel as tight as himself.

But, it was far from over.

Whilst the merfyns valiantly propelled the vessel onwards they were chased now by an angry sea laced with ugly black foam. Circles of bigger and bigger waves were rushing out from the epicentre and the whirlpools were spinning ever and ever wider, becoming treacherous watery cyclones. The merfyns at the prow shouted to those in the water and three more jumped into the boat, unlashed the tiller and hung onto it, guiding the vessel between the holes in the water and keeping the waves stern on. Just then Finn spotted a headland on the opposite shore of the lake but the boat was heading parallel to it.

"Shouldn't we be heading for land?"

His words came out far louder than he intended. Philadini patted his shoulder.

"The merfyns know best."

Seconds later, a massive whirlpool, rotating at a dizzying rate and as big as the boat, opened up exactly where Finn thought they should be heading. The merfyns put on a spurt but the whirlpool followed their course as if hunting them down. They battled with waves and currents to escape the maelstrom but, steadily, it gained on them. Finn and Maggie gripped the gunwale, their knuckles white and not a single smirk had appeared on Tom's face for some time. His ice blue eyes were stretched wide. Grindlebrook, meanwhile, clung onto her grandfather's belt as he leaned over the side watching the progress of the whirlpool. Minute after minute the merfyns strove to row and thrust the boat further from the vortex but, bit by bit, they were losing and it edged closer and closer until the gap separating them was a mere boat-length. It was twisting madly and sucking at the vessel which was being dragged into an orbit around it, and, still, that watery cyclone was growing ever stronger in magnitude and savagery.

Finally, at the very last moment, hundreds of merfyns, leaping like flying fish and coming from all directions, flashed across the lake to their aid. With the help of so many fresh bodies the merfyns managed to gain some water between the boat and the whirlpool and, by swopping places frequently, they edged the boat away from the grip of the merciless and swirling black hole. Everyone cheered and cheered them on until they were delivered to calmer water.

Just as they thought they had been liberated, the young people, including Grindlebrook were overcome by an intense and eerie whistling. It was a high pitched note, shrill and screaming at the far edge of the audio spectrum, way too high for an adult to perceive. Finn, Maggie and Tom's brows were tightly knotted and they clasped their hands over their ears, attempting to block out the penetrating screeches. Goodhook, recognising the signs, grabbed Grindlebrook and fell to the deck holding her tight beneath him.

Although he heard nothing Philadini knew what must be happening, he stared in horror, recognising all too well the meaning behind their discomfort.

"*Drunes!*" He yelled.

He thrust his way through the clutch of merfyn rowers and, diving with staring eyes and grasping fingers, he flailed his arms in an attempt to grab the Ring Bearer. But he was too late. Finn was wrenched from his clutches by a huge stinking drune. The rust coloured wrinkled beast had snapped its claws tight around Finn's arms and yanked him over the side of the vessel. Finn shrieked in pain and outrage as the infernal thing glided him, with his feet skipping across the surface of the blackened water, straight to the massive thrashing whirlpool and dropped him into its gaping maw. As Finn plunged he saw above him a perfect circle of blue sky and two drunes dropping Maggie and Tom, screaming and writhing, into the whirlpools' funnel after him. Dark water raced and seethed, spinning crazily around them as they plummeted. The last thing Finn saw, before a swirling black mess tore him under, was a fireball shooting across the eye of the whirlpool.

He crashed spinning and helpless into the terrible grip and surges of the vortex. It mauled and slashed at him, and, down, down it dragged him. Then, he felt multiple hands grasp at him and soggy ropes and chains being wrapped around his arms and legs as he was tugged deeper and deeper. His chest was bursting but he fought the desperate urge to take a breath, so staving off his certain death for a few moments longer. No light penetrated this far, and, in blackness he came to rest on squishy ooze on the bed of the lake. Finally, a heavy weight landed on his chest forcing him into it.

His nightmare had come true.

Still, he held his breath, hanging on until his consciousness slipped away and then he floated in a black dream without thoughts, slowly drifting this way and that. All he was aware of were vague pains with no centre. The dream seemed to last for hour on hour when he could do nothing but drift and drift. By and by he could make out three faint green shapes sinking toward him closer and closer. They looked like lanterns. Each contained two orange flames illuminating strange ancient script. Then Maggie's severed head appeared and hovered above him, calling out, *Finn, Finn, Finn.*

He lay there on the edge of death until suddenly he felt himself sucked upward and, like a lift rocketing into the sky, he rushed into glaring sunlight. Blinking, he saw Maggie's head peering over Goodhook's shoulder. All he could see of her was her wet head dripping water onto his face whilst Goodhook, in his black garb, pumped his breastbone for all he was worth, causing his chest to feel like it would cave in. Suddenly, Finn vomited a thick spray of evil smelling black sludge all over Goodhook then coughed up another couple of lumps of the stuff. Goodhook simply laughed instead of chastising him.

"He's back! Finns back!"

Three panting green faces grinned at him with razor sharp teeth and thick rubbery lips. Finn guessed the merfyns blazing orange eyes and green-gold scaly skin were his lanterns and strange script. Tom punched him playfully right where the drune had clawed him causing him to grimace and cough again. But he didn't care, in that moment seeing Tom and Maggie alive meant everything to him. He struggled to get up but he'd got jelly muscles and floundered back onto the deck.

"Take it steady." Goodhook said.

"What happened to the drunes?" Finn managed to groan.

Goodhook pointed to a huge sparkling vulture perched on the prow. "Desert vultures ripped their wings to shreds and when they fell to the lake the merfyns dragged them into the deeps."

Finn raised a hand and waved a weak hello to the desert vulture. It spread its wings, showing off its magnificent metallic plumage and fairly dazzled him. "Thank you." He croaked.

The desert vulture nodded its head, gave a shake of its wings and uttered a friendly squawk. Goodhook helped Finn up to a sitting position, resting his back against the lockers. Grindlebrook sat with him.

"The merfyns saved you all." She said, "There were four drunes, the last one grabbed the anchor and dropped it into the whirlpool. It missed Tom and Maggie but tangled you up. Merfyns cut the anchor rope with their teeth to save the boat being dragged into the whirlpool and got you out of there as quick as they could."

Finn gazed at Tom and Maggie huddled together, "Can you help me over there, please?"

She helped him across the boat. His arms stung madly and bled a little where they'd been wrenched by the drune's claws but he managed not to cry out. Tom helped him down between him and Maggie.

"First blood to the vultures, Finn," Philadini called out, "we thought we'd lost you for a moment there."

Finn gave him a thumbs up.

"Are you ok?" Maggie said. "You were gone for ages."

"I think so, apart from hurting like crazy."

"Loads of merfyns grabbed us," Tom said, "we were back in the boat in no time—but it was well scary!"

Finn peered at Tom. *That's the first time in my whole life I ever heard him say he was scared.*

"Philadini shot loads of fireballs at the drunes," Grindlebrook said, "but missed them every time. He nearly got a desert vulture though."

"Well, how many drunes did you shoot down?"

"I'd have got all four if you hadn't made us stow those bows and arrows away." She said, grinning.

"Arrik-arrik-arrik!" Chortled a merfyn, slapping its leg and making strange gurgles with its gills.

Finn laughed. "Just listen to them bickering instead of applauding the vultures and the merfyns."

"Oh, let us have a bit of fun, you." Grindlebrook said, and threw a cloth at him.

Then, with a wink at her grandfather and Philadini, they attempted a mock attack on the young people but ended up piled in a heap on the bottom of the boat, because, right at that moment, the boat bumped into the shore, knocking them flying.

They had made it across the Unfillable Lake.

Everyone stood, except Finn, who was unable, and cheered the merfyns.

"Arrik-arrik-arrik!" The merfyns exclaimed and snapped their claws in the air.

Tom and Maggie helped Finn disembark after the others had piled out of the boat. None gave a thought to the four drunes sleeping in their watery grave.

∽

That night, when everyone had eaten and they were relaxed around the campfire, a desert vulture related its tale of chasing the drunes. Even the merfyns became still whilst it strutted about, shook its wings and lifted single flight feathers, here and there, for emphasis. Since the ceremony of the ring the vultures had scouted a massive area but they had only found five drunes. They had been hiding out in a gorge between the desert and the Unfillable Lake. The drunes had been fast, only one was downed at the gorge and might still be alive. However, the vulture affirmed that its wings were in tatters. It ended its story with news that a band of orgils was heading their way.

At this, a merfyn sprang to its feet, 'arrik-arriking' and shaking its tentacle fingers and snapping its claws. It explained to everyone, with help from Philadini's translation, that the orgils came to the lake regularly to catch fish in order to feed those incarcerated in Uderzandu Prison. The merfyn made it clear that they would have killed the orgils long ago but were worried the prisoners might starve. A hush had fallen at the mention of the prison. Grindlebrook was first to break the silence.

"Ha! Orgils are easy." She spat on the grass. "Even I have no fear of them."

"What's an orgil?" Maggie said.

"Enemies," Goodhook said, "they're fierce, big and strong but not very clever."

"How many are they?" Philadini asked.

The desert vulture counted with its flight feathers indicating there were about thirty of them then scratched a diagram in loose soil of their whereabouts by using its beak and claws.

"Hmm." Philadini mused but didn't elaborate.

A sudden thought occurred to Finn. He stiffened and patted his pocket, then relaxed—Albinonus's book of spells was still there. He checked his wounds. The grazes he had acquired from his shackles in the tomb had almost healed thanks to the help of the special balm, but, his whole body ached from his ordeals. He felt under his T shirt and found grazes made by the drunes' claws. He showed them to Goodhook who anointed them for him.

Later, whilst watching the campfire and waiting for sleep to come, Finn wondered about the drunes. *If they picked us out because they know who we are, the skies are going to be full of them.* His ring gave him a reassuring squeeze. He pulled his right hand out from under his blanket and gazed into the cold flames flickering within its gems. Soon he fell into an exhausted sleep.

He awoke with a start in the middle of the night. Everyone was asleep except Grindlebrook who was taking her turn at watch. She smiled at him and motioned for him to go back to sleep. He snuggled down and rested his head on his arm. *But for the merfyns I would be lying at the bottom of the Unfillable Lake being torn apart and eaten by whatever lurks down there.* He looked again at Grindlebrook and she motioned him to shut his eyes. *She's so much more than I ever thought she was*, he thought. Soon, he fell asleep and began dreaming of unknown monsters.

From out of a very dark place in his mind a vile beast leered at him through dull and yellow eyes. Its face was matted with sticky red hair, and a spike, dangling bloody saliva, flicked in and out of its mouth. Then, when a stench similar to bat guano filtered into his nostrils the hackles on the back of his neck stood up as erect as bamboo because he'd realised he was no longer dreaming. He gasped and his blood chilled to icy slush as he watched the huge and ungodly thing advancing toward him in grotesque jerks.

The Orgils

"*It's dead Finn.*" A familiar voice called out of the dark.
But the monstrous hairy beast was still towering over Finn and dribbling lumpy blood onto his chest. He shuddered, squirming back to avoid as much of the hot globs as he was able.

"*It's dead Finn.*" The voice repeated.

The massive thing lunged for him—Finn spun away and got tangled in his blankets. It just missed him however, its hulking head crashing to the ground right next to his own. It lay still. Finn stared at it then upward and there sat Grindlebrook smiling at him from atop Loola, her muckleback whose triple tusks dripped blood.

"It's dead Finn," Grindlebrook said, for a third time, "it's an orgil. Wake the others and follow the lakeshore."

She turned Loola and galloped off. Finn watched her disappear into an early mist. He attempted to wriggle his already expanded vision of Grindlebrook into the new role of monster killer, failed, threw off his blankets and shook Maggie and Tom awake.

"*Get up! Get up!*"

"But—"

"*Get up! We're being attacked by orgils!*"

"What—?"

"*Get up! Now!*"

They struggled out of their blankets, rubbed sleep out of their eyes then gawped at the fallen orgil.

"Grindlebrook killed it." Finn said.

"Eh?" Tom said.

"Well, maybe her muckleback spiked it, but she was riding it."

Tom stared at the monsters body, Maggie ran her fingers through her hair, trying to fuse her simple picture of Grindlebrook with the bloodied, huge and hairy creature, "Finn, you're bleeding again."

"It's orgil blood. Come on."

Still not quite awake, Tom and Maggie ran after Finn through wispy mist and gloomy half-light to the lakeshore. Screams and splashes told them which way to head. Finn charged onwards, scrunching over shingle into thicker mist and keeping the lake hard to his left. Briefly, Tom and Maggie paused and glanced at each other—this was a Finn they had never seen before. They followed on again, rounded a bend and the mist parted.

Bathed in red dawn light, carnage awaited.

A huge shoal of merfyns was attacking a crowd of orgils who floundered in the shallows of the Unfillable Lake. The orgils, three times the bulk of a human and twice as high, swung out with heavy clubs and stabbed at the merfyns with barbed fishing spikes. But the merfyns were fast and flashed through the hairy mob, biting at their legs and avoiding their lunges. They went for their tendons and every so often an orgil would topple to a bloody but fast end.

A flock of desert vultures, circling overhead, were cawing madly. Five Mucklebacks, two riderless, three of them ridden by Goodhook, Philadini, and Grindlebrook, herded the orgils, keeping them knotted together knee deep in the water. Any that made a break for it got speared by muckleback horns. Maggie recognised Loopy, and swallowed as he made a kill.

Beyond the skirmish the lake was shrouded in mist to head height making the battle look like it was wrapped in cotton wool. Soon there were fewer orgils. They fought on as best they could, bellowing and roaring whilst the merfyns shrieked and tore and the mucklebacks herded them ever deeper into water reddened by their blood. Steadily orgil after orgil buckled to its fate squealing, choking and clutching at their last moments.

The young people hurried past a fallen orgil but the battle was won almost before they reached the fray. Finn stared into the eyes of the last orgil as it was dragged under. It seemed to reflect his gaze with sadness as well as fear as it surrendered itself into bloody water boiling with merfyns. Bits of it floated to the surface just as he stepped onto a mess of guts at the water's edge. He bent double and vomited. Maggie took his arm and pulled him away.

"That was *horrible*." She said.

Bloody and hot, Grindlebrook rode passed them, *"Orgils,"* she called out in a derisory tone and spat, "told you they were easy to kill."

She jogged her muckleback along the shore until she reached clear water, there she dismounted then waded out and swam keeping just this side of the mist. She rubbed herself down and drank. Once clear of blood she re-emerged dripping lake-water and lit up by a petrol dawn. The beautiful light tinted the cotton-wool-mist with pink, orange and lavender tones. Grindlebrook's eyes were fixed on her grandfather and as soon as he dismounted she ran to him. Finn and the twins found themselves a grassy hump on which to sit, set a little way back from the lake.

"Grindly's not quite who I thought she was." Tom said in a whisper.

Finn and Maggie remained quiet, watching her. Meanwhile, Philadini got off his albino muckleback and chatted with merfyns by the water's edge. The mucklebacks, now riderless, wandered along the shore, paddled into the lake, then rolled about washing off the battle. A while later Philadini came and sat with the young people.

"That was pretty freaky." Tom said.

Maggie screwed her face up, "Freaky? It was gruesome. Tell me that's the end of it."

"Who knows?" Philadini said. "The thing is, once a fight starts it goes its own way. You have to go with it and be vicious or you die. What happened is what happened. We did what we did and we won. Put it behind you. We need to move on."

He went off to talk with Goodhook. Grindlebrook came and joined the young people. Her hair was exactly the colour of wet red grapes. She blew droplets of water off her nose then sat next to Maggie and patted her leg, "You ok?" She asked.

Maggie peered into her hazel eyes. The killer was gone and the Grindlebrook she knew was back. Maggie frowned and gazed forward. The mist was dissipating and as far as she could see long, red dorsal fins cut the water, "I—I guess so. It was horrific."

"Not as horrific as losing—but orgils are stupid—you could kill one."

Maggie flinched at the thought.

"They can't be completely stupid." Finn said. "The one that stole into camp almost killed me."

Maggie stared, mouth agape.

"That's not how it happened," Grindlebrook said, giving Maggie's arm a squeeze, "it was already dead but its head was stuck on Loola's tusks, she was just wandering around trying to shake it off. Finn, you explain—I'm going for another swim—it's hard to wash off the stink of battle."

Grindlebrook jogged to the lake, splashed through the shallows then dived forwards and disappeared. Tom's eyes followed her. At first he grinned waiting for her to resurface, then, after thirty-seconds or so he stood, shielding his eyes from the sun and peered hard, searching for her. After another twenty-seconds he walked fast to the lake but, just then, she reappeared much further out. His shoulders relaxed, she saw him on the shore and laughed.

"Maggie?" Finn said.

"Yes?"

"Grindly's turning out to be a bit awesome."

Maggie nodded, "Yep, and I reckon she's got Tom tied up in knots —I've never seen him like this before. Now, tell me, what happened?"

"Well, I woke up and saw this wild monster's head . . ."

∼

When Grindlebrook finished her swim everyone got together for a pow wow.

"Why didn't you tell us the orgils were coming?" Maggie said.

"We didn't know," Philadini said, "merfyns came to the camp deep in the night and told us the orgils were at the lake and also that our mucklebacks had been spotted not too far away, so we waited for them to turn up. An orgil scout saw them, then us, so we had no choice but to attack."

Maggie turned her attention to the mucklebacks frolicking in the water, "Loopy doesn't want to know me today."

Tom patted her leg, "Get a grip. Loopy's been busy protecting you."

Maggie was quiet for a moment but then she pulled a face at the desert vultures who were ripping into an orgil carcass. Suddenly, as if spooked, they all took off cawing madly and flew toward a hill set a little back from the lake.

"Pass me the telescope please, Tom." Philadini said.

Tom lobbed it to him. Philadini squinted at the vultures.

"What is it?" Tom asked.

"I think it must be that injured drune the desert vulture told us about last night. It's scrabbling up through scrub on that hillside—dragging itself by its arms."

He passed the telescope back to Tom, "Yeah," Tom said, "something's wrong with its leg and its wings are tattered."

He passed the telescope to Finn who saw the hill came to a point, almost like a cone. He watched the drune struggle to its brow and wave at something. Then the desert vultures were upon it. The drune staggered and covered its eyes but they got at its neck and it fell, bashing around in the dust and trying to push them off, "The vultures are making a real mess of it." He was smiling as he lowered the telescope.

Maggie scrunched her hands into knots, *"Finn—y*ou're worrying me."

"But—we were nearly killed by drunes yesterday."

"It's no reason to gloat—you're being bloodthirsty."

"Maggie, stop right there!" Philadini said. "Get used to it—for us to live they have to die."

Her brow knotted and she opened her mouth to speak but caught Grindlebrook's expression. Instead, Maggie stalked off toward the lake without even acknowledging Philadini had spoken, then paced up and down the shore. The vultures returned, and, with beaks bloody and eyes fiery, squawked their news to Philadini.

"There are orgils beyond the hill," he explained, "the drune was waving to them and they ran off in the direction of the Atta Desert."

"How many?" Goodhook asked.

"As many as we have killed already."

"We'd better get after them."

Philadini fished his pipe out, primed it and got it going nicely, all the while regarding Goodhook, "No, I think not. Not far beyond that hill there's a canyon that leads to a bottleneck. Lets not take the bait. We'll break camp, say our goodbyes and thanks."

Without waiting for a response Philadini headed back to the camp. The others sat silent for a while then Goodhook sighed, "Come on, Philadini knows best." They collected Maggie, broke camp then Goodhook showed them something they didn't know about mucklebacks—a pouch on the chests of the females which were so neat they'd not noticed them before, "It's where they carry their young, they let us pack our things in there. Sometimes they carry injured warriors."

"Joey pouches." Maggie said. When Goodhook looked puzzled she added, "That's what they call them in Australia—erm home—I mean in our world."

Goodhook nodded, then he looked at Grindlebrook, gave out a big sigh and led her away from the others.

"Philadini?" Maggie said.

The magician took one look at her vexed expression and nodded.

"I know what you're thinking. They are saying goodbye and you believe the chances aren't very good for Goodhook making it back across the Unfillable Lake alone, yes?"

Maggie's eyebrows were pinched so much her nose wrinkled, "Why did you let him come?"

The magician shook his head and sighed again, "I can't get it right all the time."

Maggie looked ready to gouge his eyes out.

"Ok, ok, so Goodhook can't come with us into the desert because he'll set on fire and he'll die crossing the lake if a bunch of drunes turn up. Right?" She nodded. He sat down and patted the grass. Warily, Maggie sat too. "I've allowed my best friend to walk into mortal danger. What would you do?"

"That's not a fair question," Maggie said, "because I would never do that."

"Just supposing," he said, and glanced at Finn, "you did it by accident?"

Her eyes became fiery, "*I wouldn't do it!*"

"Good answer. Ok, so what's to be done now? Now that I have been stupid and got Goodhook into this mess?"

"*You have to help him.*"

The magician looked troubled, "Yes, but what if whatever choice I make kills him anyway."

Maggie suddenly saw in his eyes that he really cared. Her shoulders drooped. She looked at Goodhook hugging his granddaughter with tears rolling down his cheeks and found it too hard to bear, "I can't choose. Why can't we simply travel at night?"

"Clever girl! That is exactly what we're going to do." He fished inside his robe and pulled out a map he had retrieved from one of the magic sacks, "Would you like to navigate?"

Maggie looked at the map, then at Philadini, then back at the map and burst out her biggest grin since landing in Finkley Field, "No," she said, "definitely not—I could get lost on my way to the village shop. But I thank you from the bottom of my heart. Can I be the one to tell them, pleeeese?" Philadini beamed at her and nodded. She sprang up and ran toward the Attuks, stopped dead in her tracks, ran back to Philadini and pecked him on the cheek, "Don't let it go to your head," she said, 'but I just saw something to actually like about you." She ran off again and gave them the news.

Finn watched Goodhook hug Maggie and saw Grindlebrook jumping up and down. *She's half warrior, half girl, and she could have slit my throat easily, anytime she liked.*

"Tom?" he said.

"Yeah?"

"Your girlfriend's a bit scary."

~

WHEN THEY WERE PACKED AND READY TO DEPART EVERYONE SAID GOODBYE and thanks to the merfyns. Their spikes fluttered and their fins flapped and they gave everybody soggy hugs. Then Loopy plodded to Maggie and lowered his head so she could pull on the hairs between his ears. He blinked his big green eyes. "How dare you ignore me?" She said, still wearing the grin that had stayed on her face ever since Philadini had said Goodhook could come with them.

Meanwhile, Grindlebrook spoke to Loola and she agreed to carry both her and Goodhook. Then, once everyone had mounted up, they set off, keeping the lakeshore to their left. When they were almost out of sight, the merfyns 'arrik-arriked' mournfully. Everyone halted to give them a final wave. Finn felt a pang at leaving them so abruptly, but Philadini had insisted it was imperative they head off immediately. The desert vultures however, ignored everyone and tore away at orgil carcasses.

After following the shore for some time their route led away from the Unfillable Lake and Philadini called a halt. The sun had already reached its zenith. They stocked up on water and, whilst the mucklebacks drank, Finn and Tom skimmed flat pebbles across the surface of the lake. Tom was best at it. Maggie and Grindlebrook sat on a rock a little way off watching them whilst Philadini and Goodhook huddled over the map. By now the mist was long gone. Finn scrabbled about looking for more pebbles then stood staring out across the water.

"I think I might have upset Maggie." He said.

"That's not difficult." Tom said.

"Hah! Yeah, I know, but, the thing is I *enjoyed* watching that drune getting savaged so maybe she's right and—"

"Nah mate, I enjoyed it too—I hate those things."

"What's happening to us? I never used to be like that. I mean wanting to kill things—creatures—even if they are bad—and are they truly bad, I mean those orgils never stood a chance did they?"

Tom had a smirk on.

"What's funny?"

"You are. Stop worrying, I'm loving it."

Finn kicked pebbles into the water and Tom went back to skimming them. He got one to go way out. A merfyn poked its head above the water checking out what was going on. It raised its claw and snapped it a few times. They waved back. Maggie and Grindlebrook waved to the merfyn too.

"I love the merfyns," Maggie said, "but, they're so *savage*."

"They're special," Grindlebrook said, "I knew you'd like them—they *need* to be ruthless though, we all do."

Maggie made a sweep of her hand across their view, "Actually, this damn lake gives me the creeps." She shivered even though it was hot and wrapped her arms around herself. "It's stunning, majestic even, but, I'm scared stiff of it."

Grindlebrook put her arm around her and rested her head on hers, "When the drunes grabbed you yesterday I couldn't see, because Granddad was shielding me, but I knew what was happening. I wanted to die instead of you. It's not your fight, you shouldn't have to be part of it."

Maggie pulled away and stared at her, open mouthed.

"*Grindly!* You should never say such things. You are such a precious soul. I can't even imagine not knowing you now, even though it's only been days since we met—and—and—I'm sorry we misjudged you."

Grindlebrook stared blankly out over the lake, "Oh Maggie, I've been so lonely. I've been lonely for years and years . . . for all my life really, so, I don't *ever* mind the thought of dying because I'm the only young Attuk left so there's nothing for me to live for. I know that might sound ungrateful, but I'm not, it's just the truth. Don't tell any one though, will you—particularly granddad? Another truth is, I'm angry. So, so, *angry,* and, *boiling with hate.*"

"Grindly! That can't be true."

"*It is!*"

Grindlebrook scowled and took several deep breaths. When Maggie tried to speak she pressed a finger to her lips, "I need to tell you something." Maggie listened. "Towards the end of the great war, Krukill cursed our clan and murdered all the Attuk children. I know they are all dead. I can feel it. Granddad saved me. I'm small now but I was *really* tiny then. He drugged me and strapped me to his chest. When I awoke he fed me with drugged food. He hid me under his coat like that for months pretending to Krukill that he was a big fat useless drunk. I—I—can't remember it but he told me all about it. Now, since we've been cursed no one can have children, so I'm the last one and there's nothing for me to live for. If we don't kill Krukill and become human again our race will be gone forever. *It's her that I hate so much!*" She drew a deep breath and gazed wistfully at Tom. "Oh, Maggie, you are so lucky having Tom and Finn. They're the best boys you could wish for. Ever."

Maggie sat there open mouthed, her mind in a whirl, but, before she could even start to form a reply Philadini called out, "*Time to move on.*"

The young people returned to their mucklebacks and, once mounted, the magician turned his huge albino into a tight, thickly wooded valley. For a while they skirted around tree trunks, climbing steadily upward. Everything was green and dim under a thick canopy of interlocking branches. Birds chirped but, although Finn searched, he never saw one. He sniffed woody aromas and his stomach rumbled—he was ravenous because Philadini had refused to hang around waiting for breakfast. They plodded on. The trees closed in, winding their trail ever tighter and tighter and branches snapped and younger trees got bent or uprooted as their mucklebacks forced a way through. Eventually, the trees began to thin out and the sun came through in patches. Finally, they passed beyond the wood and their mucklebacks zig-zagged up a steep rocky slope and finally they arrived at a viewpoint. Everyone looked back toward the Unfillable Lake. From that height they could just make out the opposite shore. Way over to their left rose the triangular hill where the drune had died. They turned their mucklebacks and gazed at what lay ahead. A parched horizon. In between was green brush thinning out to brown scrub. They dismounted. The dark mouth of a cave was nearby.

"We rest here until nightfall." Philadini said. "Unpack what we need and send the mucklebacks into the valley to graze."

He walked into the cave and disappeared. When they'd unpacked Goodhook sat in the entrance and hung his head. Grindlebrook joined him and lay her head on his arm. Tom went and sat cross-legged in front of him. He waited until the big Attuk lifted his head, "It's good that you're coming with us."

Goodhook sighed a big sigh and looked glum, "Thank you. I wish—"

"*Ignito!*" Incanted a voice from within the cave.

"Come on—let's go inside," Grindlebrook said, "I'll rustle up some lunch."

"Perfect." Tom said.

She skipped into the cave and everyone followed. The cave was cool and refreshing and they found Philadini sat in a comfortable sandy chamber. He had lit fire torches. Finn ran a hand over the rock. A tiny insect scurried away. Some sort of spider, he thought. Everyone sat in a circle.

"Ok," Philadini said, "at the minimum there is a band of orgils heading to Uderzandu Prison with news of this morning's skirmish, and, there may be more drunes about. I know we saw four at the Falls of Rhandoror—but we can't assume they are the ones that were killed at the Unfillable Lake."

"Not forgetting those at Finkley field." Tom piped up.

"Exactly," Philadini said, "good point. We can hope they don't know our intentions, but, it feels to me like we are being hunted. Now, who wants to take first watch?"

Maggie's hand shot up, "I'd like to do something useful instead of moaning."

Philadini grinned, "Good. Pay special attention to the triangular hill where we saw the drune killed. Something may come to view the corpse and it won't be a merfyn." A vision of the last orgil to die, and it being savaged by merfyns, sprang into Finn's mind. *It seemed more like a victim than an enemy,* he thought. Philadini then led Maggie to three rocks near the cave that leant against one another forming a hide. Its shade prevented the telescope from reflecting the sun. Maggie marvelled at the telescopes' magnification and clarity.

Philadini went back into the cave, "Goodhook, we need to talk, let's take a stroll and check on the mucklebacks, you three should attempt to get some sleep." Grindlebrook looked concerned. "We won't be long." Philadini said. After they were gone she sat shaking her head.

"Hey Grindly, no adults!" Tom said smirking.

Grindlebrook gave him a pinched look until he stopped smirking and began to fidget. Finn tried to think of something to say to break the tension.

"Thanks for not killing me." He said to her.

Grindlebrook looked perplexed.

"Huh?" Tom said.

Just then, Maggie rushed into the cave.

"*Drunes!*" She exclaimed. *"Loads of them! They just poured out of the ground in a huge black cloud!"*

The Atta Desert

Finn flinched, and, digging his fingers into the sand he gawped at Maggie. Tom flinched too but Grindlebrook remained calm. Holding a finger to her lips, she crept to the mouth of the cave and lay flat, peered out, then motioned them to follow. The three inseparables instinctively accepted her as leader and crawled to her. Although it was a long way away they could still make out a mass of drunes swarming above the triangular hill.

"Well done, Maggie." Grindlebrook said.

"Must be over a hundred of them." Tom murmured.

The drunes landed, and almost covered the hill, peppering it to rust.

"Telescope please, Maggie." Grindlebrook said.

Maggie's hand shook as she passed it to her.

Finn squirmed himself flat on the ground, "What about Goodhook and Philadini?"

Grindlebrook grunted but didn't say anything. Finn rested his chin on his hands and waited. After carefully scanning everywhere she could see, Grindlebrook passed the telescope to him but he fumbled it and struggled to get it to focus, then, suddenly, he got a sharp image of a drune's face. It's big red eyes appeared to be boring straight into his own, startling him. "Woah! One's looking this way." Pulling the focus back a bit, he watched the drune turn in every direction then point toward the lake. All the drunes followed its gaze. Finn puffed out a sigh. *"Phew.* It didn't see us, they're looking toward the lake now. There'll be merfyns about."

"Drunes don't attack merfyns," Grindlebrook said, "they get drowned." As if to contradict her, the drunes took to the air, circled once then dived toward the Unfillable Lake disappearing from view. "Nobody move!" Grindlebrook said, "Finn, keep scanning." They lay silent, waiting, Finn could feel the tension mounting, Grindlebrook spoke first. "I hope granddad—"

"Got them!" Finn said. "They're chasing the desert vultures."

He offered the telescope back to Grindlebrook, "No, let Maggie see."

Finn passed the telescope to her and Maggie's hand was steady now but Tom was getting fidgety at not getting a turn, "Patience, dearest brother." Maggie said, then watched the chase, "The vultures are leading them away." She scoped around, "The corpse is still on the hill."

Grindlebrook got up and brushed herself down, "They don't go in for burying their dead. Tom, would you like to take the next watch?"

"Sure—*boss*—wanna join me?"

Grindlebrook frowned at him, "No, as soon as I think it's safe I'm going to fetch granddad and Philadini."

Tom pulled a face but took his turn on watch.

A short while later, as soon as Grindlebrook had fetched them, Philadini went with Maggie and joined Tom at the lookout, "Where did they appear from?" He said

"Over there," she pointed, then hugged herself at the memory, "they funnelled out of the ground like a hoard of bats."

Philadini stroked his beard with one hand whilst fishing out his pipe with the other, "That, is exactly where that bottleneck is I wanted to avoid. Those orgils that the desert vultures told us about *were* attempting to lead us into a trap."

Leaving Tom on watch, they went back into the cave.

"Philadini?" Grindlebrook said.

"Mmm?"

"Having to travel at night is all my fault, if I hadn't insisted on coming we wouldn't be in this situation."

"Hush Grindlebrook, if we hadn't been resting here, awaiting nightfall, we might have been in plain view of those drunes anyway."

Her brow knotted, "But, granddad and me—we should go back—we can travel by night on my muckleback, she'd carry us anywhere, Loola loves me."

"No, you'd never make it—not with over a hundred drunes wandering around the skies. You are both staying with us." She persisted but Philadini ignored her pleas, and, puffing on his pipe he took out the map and studied it. Eventually she gave up and Philadini asked Goodhook to come take a look. Philadini rested his finger by a place on the map marked, 'Stirianus's Oasis', in a remote part of the desert. Their eyes met. "That's where we're going to head for." Philadini said.

Goodhook's eye's bulged, "Stirianus's Oasis? You can't be serious!"

"Never been more so."

"But—"

"The drunes are gathering, it's convinced me."

Goodhook's expression was appalled, "But Stirianus is a drunk!"

"He's also the second most powerful magician on this world."

Grindlebrook piped up, "What's happening?"

"Philadini wants us to go to Stirianus's Oasis!" Her grandfather said.

Grindlebrook looked aghast, "What—?"

"Now listen to me," Philadini commanded, "Stirianus took the key to Uderzandu Prison off Krukill's turnkey, right after he relieved him of his head. I saw him do it myself during the last battle of the great war so, if we can get him sober, we stand a chance."

Finn's ears pricked up, "Chance of what?"

Philadini drew on his pipe and contemplated him, "Getting you lot to Itako."

Finn beamed at him, "Where the trail starts!"

"Huh?"

"The trail of the *'lost ones'*."

"Oh that," Philadini said, "I was thinking more of getting an army together."

Finn frowned, *"I want to search for our parents."*

Maggie shook her head, "I just want to sit on my basket swing watching clouds."

Grindlebrook looked exasperated, "Oh, you lot—I'm off to check on Tom."

THERE WAS NO MOON WHEN THEY PREPARED TO START OUT THAT NIGHT. It was quite dark and a light breeze blew. Finn ran his hands over the rock hard hide of his muckleback. *I bet he could fight off a drune, no trouble—I must think up a good name for him.* Everyone mounted up. No one talked because Philadini had said don't if you don't need to, so, for company all Finn had were the plodding footfalls and grunts from five heavy mucklebacks picking their way toward the desert. Occasionally they rustled against vegetation or bushes. Above him, the sky was star splattered with intricate sparkly patterns, but they didn't give out much light. He wondered if somewhere up there someone was gazing back or even if Earth was up there revolving around one of the stars. *Where has it gone?* He looked about, his eyes were more accustomed to the dark now and he could make out the others. All of a sudden he realised he was enjoying himself. He raised his right hand to see the fire-glow from his ring, sucked in a few gulps of crisp night air then relaxed back into the loping sway of his muckleback.

Goodhook was perched on Loola's seat, Grindlebrook was sat right behind him on the highest part of her hump. Goodhook had the magic map which provided its own inner glow in darkness. Although he was good at map reading he was also an Attuk, a child of the desert, so the map was just a reminder for him rather than an essential. He passed it to his granddaughter so she could follow their route. Grindlebrook was the only Attuk who could never be at one with the Atta Desert because she had been too young to know it on that terrible day when Krukill cursed all the surviving Attuks, thus enabling their homeland to burn them alive.

The vegetation was thinning out and Finn guessed they must be near the desert. Sniffing the air he thought he could sense it becoming drier. He was glad Goodhook was with them and thought back to their first contact way back in Finkley Field when he'd kicked Goodhook in the face and he almost laughed at the absurdity of it. He trusted him completely now, and was sure Maggie and Tom felt the same. Soon, the first moon rose and gave enough light for the mucklebacks to pick up the pace a bit. Finn had been expecting sand dunes to appear but the terrain remained flat and hard. When the second moon rose, big, bold and creamy-white, the extra light gave the mucklebacks even more confidence but Philadini insisted there was to be no getting into the high perches or travelling any faster. They must be mindful of hazards, he said. Hour after hour they rode on with no stops for food and Finn became hungry and lacklustre. Just before dawn, rocky outcrops appeared and within them they located several caves. They dismounted, stretched their aches away and settled into one of them. The mucklebacks found a larger cave a short distance away. After making a hot drink and a simple meal everyone soon fell asleep, apart from Goodhook who insisted he take the first watch.

Finn awoke in the middle of the day instead of the middle of the night. He made his way past sleeping bodies to the cave mouth. Philadini was now on watch.

"Hi." Finn said.

The magician motioned him to sit, then pointed and whispered, "Watch that hole over there."

Finn plonked himself down onto sandy soil and waited. Soon, a small spray of green hair poked up out of the hole. Finn raised his eyebrows and started to get up for a better look but Philadini pulled him back down. More green hair sprouted, followed by a forehead, then black eyebrows, then two unblinking slate-blue eyes. Philadini waved. Whatever it was shot back into the hole.

"Desert gronk." Philadini said, "We're camping on top of their home, they live in small clans beneath the desert. That was a young one, they're very shy but the adults are noisier than children. If we wait quietly it will eventually come right out. Can't sleep?"

Finn yawned, "I've slept but I always wake up for a while. Are gronks friendly?"

"Oh yes, *too* friendly sometimes. They'll come and speak to us when they are ready but it might be a while because they like to sleep late. Go get some more sleep yourself, we have another long trek ahead of us tonight and they'll still be around when you wake."

Finn retreated into the cave. Getting right under his blankets he peered into the fires within his ring. Tiredness fuzzed through his body and he slept. Hours later he was shaken awake by Maggie.

"Wake up, you're missing the fun."

He yawned and stretched himself awake. Grindlebrook was cradling a young gronk and adult gronks were crowding the cave.

"Philadini!" One of them exclaimed in an important voice. "What is the meaning of you coming to *my* desert without asking the desert vultures to inform me?"

"Er . . . I . . . well it was like—"

"Like what?" The gronk said, jamming his hands on his hips.

"*Like it was a secret!*"

"So—you've got secrets from me, have you, Mr Philadini?"

"Listen here, you disrespectful little gronk, we have come here to break into Uderzandu Prison—and *I'll thank you to keep quiet about it!* Now, be civil and introduce yourself to my friends."

"No one tells *me* what to do in my own desert. *Humph!*" The gronk made as if to leave but spun around wearing a great big grin, "Good to see you, you old rascal of a magician. Well, come on—out with it— who are these mysterious heroes you are going to break into Uderzandu with?"

And so everyone met Houni, head of the gronks. His wife, slightly taller than him, was called Mindal. They stood about hip high with impish faces, bandy legs and luxurious green hair. Houni explained there were twenty-five families living below them and another hundred or so living around the area. They wore leather garments and some carried small spears. One, smaller than either Houni or Mindal, had three dead snakes hanging from his belt.

"I see you've been hunting, Himso." Philadini commented.

"Yes—plenty of food around here, would you like to eat snake with us tonight?"

"That would have been a pleasure, but we are travelling through the night as it's not safe for Attuks during the day." Himso frowned at Goodhook. Mindal, who was his mother, gave him a clip on the back of the head. Goodhook muttered something under his breath but let it go. Philadini, switched his attention back to Houni, "Did you know there were drunes about?"

"Yes, and I've heard they are gathering at Uderzandu—a couple of morkuns too. You'll get quite a welcome there."

Philadini visibly flinched, "*Morkuns?* So—I suppose there will be magicians about?"

"Three hunter-magi," Houni said, "your old enemies, Dhagan, Mongrix and Whorpus."

"Hmm. Might have known, well, there's no point worrying about them just yet. Listen, we're going to pay a little visit on Stirianus, is there anything we need to know?"

"Well, he's still drinking his magic juice—a lot of magic juice actually, but, your way should be clear, just watch out for the usual—shifting sands and burning valleys. Can I have a ride on a muckleback before you go?"

"Are you sure? You broke your arm last time you tried it."

"*Houni!*" Mindal exclaimed. "You are not getting on to a muckleback *ever again.*"

"Aw, Mindal, you're no fun." He said, but gave her a playful squeeze.

The banter between the gronks and the magician amused Finn and when they left just before sundown, he was sad to see them go. He watched them disappear back into their hole and pull a flat stone over it, "I really like them." He said.

Maggie grinned, "Me too. They're funny and strong and timid all mixed up."

Tom smirked, "I wonder what snake tastes like, I was well up for that."

Maggie pulled a face, "Why am I not surprised—"

"Time to make a move." Philadini said.

"Before we go," Maggie said, "what are these morkun thingies?"

Philadini raised his shoulders and sighed, "We need to—"

"Maggie is entitled to know." Goodhook said.

Philadini pursed his lips, "You're right, but, there'll be plenty of time to talk when we're safe inside Stirianus's Oasis."

"Don't you mean *if* we get inside?"

"We'll get in."

With that Stirianus left the cave and whistled for Sulan, his massive albino. The young people glanced between themselves then at Goodhook.

"What's going on?" Finn said.

It was Grindlebrook who answered, "Morkuns are hunting beasts and really dangerous. The only ones who can control them are hunter-magi, and, they're all allies of Krukill."

"What's a hunter-magi? Maggie said.

"It's just a fancy name for magicians who enjoy hunting and killing." Grindlebrook said.

"So, what are they doing at this Uderzandu place?" Tom said.

Grindlebrook frowned, "They must be hunting something, maybe—"

"Us?" Maggie said.

Grindlebrook looked to her grandfather, "Hopefully not but—"

"We need to go!" Philadini yelled from outside the cave.

Goodhook took a deep breath, "Grindlebrook, kindly ask Philadini to step back inside would you?"

She was back almost immediately, "He's already mounted up on Sulan and he won't come."

"Go tell him that if he doesn't I'm going to tell our friends exactly who Stirianus *really* is."

Grindlebrook grinned. Within half a minute Philadini was back, "Look, I was going to tell them—it just didn't seem to be the right time."

Maggie had her arms folded and her eyebrows pinched, Tom was smirking but Finn had Albinonus's little golden book of spells held high, "Remember what happened when you lied to us about this?"

Philadini contemplated Finn then took a deep breath, "Stirianus is Krukill's brother."

"What!" From Finn, Tom and Maggie.

Long silence.

"Hunter-magi!" Maggie said. *"Explain properly!"*

Philadini shrugged, "Dhagan, Mongrix and Whorpus are the hunter-magi Houni had news of. They're evil magicians and allies of Krukill—but, with Stirianus helping us, we should—"

"Don't leave anything out." Goodhook said.

Philadini sighed, "I won't—Stirianus is addicted to a magic potion he concocted. He's a drunk."

Maggie glanced between Goodhook and the magician, "For how long?"

"Over seven years. He's totally incapacitated by it."

"Is that all?"

"That's it." Philadini said.

Maggie paused for a long moment, "Thank you." She said, finally. "That wasn't so difficult, was it? Now, shall we get on with it?" She marched out of the cave followed smartly by Finn, Tom and Grindlebrook. *"Magicians!"* Maggie exclaimed under her breath.

Goodhook and Philadini stared at each other, then, smiling, Goodhook raised his eyebrows, bowed and held a hand out just like a maître d' would when directing patrons, "After you, old man."

Philadini stomped out, "Less of the old man, if you please."

A short while later, Goodhook and Grindlebrook led off again on Loola and they made careful progress until the first moon rose, when the mucklebacks upped the pace. Finn's mood started off as tetchy but the ride under the stars was wonderful and soon lifted his spirits. He speculated about why they would have anything to do with Krukill's brother but gave up, after concluding everything always turned out different to what he imagined. He made his mind up to tackle Philadini for more information at the first opportunity. When the second moon appeared the mucklebacks again wanted to speed up but Philadini said hold back. They trotted on, making steady progress further and further into the desert, still over hard terrain, and, not long before dawn, were rewarded with their first glimpse of Stirianus's Oasis. Its perimeter was marked by random sparkling lights and looked as if a constellation of stars had floated down to the surface of the desert. Everyone halted their mucklebacks to take it in.

"That, is one beautiful destination." Maggie said quietly.

"Yes, it is." Philadini said, also in a low voice, "Stirianus certainly has style. There are caves nearby, we'll rest there and prepare a meal."

Finn was about to suggest they gallop the last bit but decided he was in no hurry to meet his enemy's brother, besides, he was ravenous. They found the caves, settled themselves into one of them and the mucklebacks into a larger one. Philadini gave him the first watch and he hunkered down just inside the cave mouth and watched the stars fading rather than keeping his eyes on the oasis. He reasoned that it was ok to watch them because any drunes would come at them from the sky. Soon a line of pale pink light crept up where the sun would rise and Grindlebrook brought him a hot drink plus a hot oatmeal wrap. He thanked her and chomped on it. She yawned, glanced at Stirianus's Oasis, then gave his shoulder a friendly squeeze before slipping back into the cave. As dawn advanced the stars became less and less distinct and Finn lowered his gaze to the perimeter of the oasis. His heart jumped when he made out tall black shapes prowling around it. He rushed into the cave and shook Philadini awake.

"Stirianus's Oasis is surrounded by drunes!"

Philadini blinked a couple of times, got up, strolled casually out of the cave and held his hand out for the telescope. He checked out the black shapes with it then handed it back to Finn. "Black eagles—the most ferocious bird in the Atta Desert. You met one at the Ceremony of the Ring back at the Great Oak. They're Stirianus's guards."

Finn dropped his eyes, "Oh. Sorry. I should have checked properly before disturbing you."

"Do not be, you did the right thing—keeping watch is difficult but I wouldn't let you do it if I thought you lacking." He went back into the cave.

Finn settled down once more and continued his watch. He leaned back against the rock, propped his elbows on his knees and, by the light of the encroaching dawn, studied everything more carefully with the telescope. He picked out a lazy trail of smoke curling way over the horizon and a short while later followed the flight of a flock of shimmering desert vultures. They alighted at the oasis, drank and preened, then flew on. He was cheered by seeing them again and wondered if they were the ones that the drunes had chased. He hoped so. For all his searching he didn't get a glimpse of Stirianus himself before Goodhook arrived to take over the watch.

"My apologies for slowing the journey."

Finn felt for him. How things have changed since Finkley Field, he thought, "No worries, I'm just glad you're here."

Goodhook smiled a big Attuk smile, "Thank you, that means a lot to me."

He sat and accepted the telescope but Finn didn't make a move to go, "What are our chances?" He asked.

Goodhook sighed and ran a hand through his untidy white hair, He succeeded in making more tufts stick out, "I wish I knew. Look, I was once a man of the desert, but I always stayed well clear of Uderzandu Prison because I never heard of anyone going in there and ever coming out again. However, The Book Of Writing That Cannot Be Unwritten said your task was to liberate the cousins from it, so it must be possible. Does that help?"

"Who are the cousins again?"

"Three magicians."

More of them! Finn thought, "Good ones?"

"In theory, get some sleep."

"Ok, see you."

His blankets were laid out for him between Maggie and Tom. He snuggled under them and in his mind he conjured up images of bickering magicians firing powerful spells at each other. It's all about them, he thought. Take the magicians out of the equation and this would be a fantastic place to be. He turned on his side and for a while he watched Maggie sleeping. Her face was illuminated by flickers from a fire torch. She's worth fighting for, he thought, and so's Tom and Grindlebrook, and mum and dad. *I'm sure they're in this world somewhere.* He snuggled further down, right under his blankets, and peered at the fires within his ring. Soon his eyes became heavy and he slipped into a deep slumber. Many hours later he was woken up by Maggie stroking his hair.

"Wakey, wakey, supper's ready, or should I say breakfast."

With sleep-filled eyes he gazed up at her and got a lovely fuzzy feeling. Stretching his arms he yawned, then sat up. Suddenly, he felt a heavy weight placed firmly in his lap. The golden cover of The Book Of Writing That Cannot Be Unwritten was reflecting into his eyes. Philadini jumped up, surprisingly sprightly for a three hundred year old.

"Open it! Anywhere!"

Finn ripped it open and read, *"Your enemy is strong. Success is unlikely."*

Finn felt his stomach go queasy.

"Turn the page!" Philadini said.

Finn hurriedly flicked the page over, *"Read the message within your ring."*

"Again!"

But The Book Of Writing That Cannot Be Unwritten simply vanished.

"Oh . . . that is just so frustrating." Finn said, and thumped his leg. "Was I too slow?"

Philadini sighed and shook his head, "No, you did well, 'The Book' gave a similar message hundreds of years ago, before the fall of Tallakin—one of the old empires. It appeared only once during that reign saying, 'The answer lays inside the ring', but the riddle was never solved and a benevolent regime destroyed."

"Has it ever said 'success is unlikely' before?" Finn said, quietly.

No one answered and they sat in silence for a while, everyone lost in their own thoughts.

Suddenly Tom perked up, "Give me your ring." He said. Philadini and Goodhook made a move to stop him but Tom held up a hand, "Hang on, I'm not going to try and wear it—I've got an idea that's all."

They relaxed. Finn threw off his blankets and stood up, he twisted the ring off and dropped it into Tom's outstretched palm, "There you go, mate." He trusted Tom and didn't care if they didn't.

Tom squinted into the gems studying the fires within. "I reckon we could use the telescope as a projector. We'll need to douse the fire and the torches and move further into the cave. When it's absolutely dark we might be able to see something."

"What's a projector?" Philadini said, looking worried.

"It's a contraption from our world. The thing is, if we are in complete darkness and hold the ring to the eyepiece of the telescope it may make the writing inside the gems bigger by picturing it onto the wall of the cave."

"Are you trying to make a weapon?" Philadini asked. "That ring has strange powers."

"No," Tom said, sighing, "you must know there's minuscule writing inside the fire gems. I just want to make it bigger so that you can read it, that's all. Look, I'm not being condescending but we know about things in our world that are cleverer than what you have here—even if we don't have any real magic—just let me give it a try—it might work."

Philadini looked to Maggie. She raised her eyebrows, "It's all true," she said, "it's worth a try."

Philadini paused then nodded. He went to the mouth of the cave. Grindlebrook was on watch and surveying Stirianus's Oasis with the telescope, "Anything?"

"No, only a gronk. He's wandering about inside the perimeter of the oasis, he just seems to be doing a few chores. There's no sign of Stirianus."

"He'll be there." Philadini said. "Will you be ok staying on watch a while longer?"

"Of course."

"Good, let me have the telescope. Tom wants to show us something with it." Grindlebrook passed it to him wearing a quizzical expression, but, Philadini being Philadini, didn't offer an explanation. He took it into the cave and gave it to Tom, "I must say, Tom, you have me curious. Ok, watch your step everybody—I'm not familiar with this particular cave." They doused the fire and all the torches but one which Philadini used to navigate deeper into the cave, "Ok, we should have gone far enough—*Ignito-Deisistus!*"

They were plunged into total darkness.

"Erm . . . there's a problem," Tom said, "could you light the torch again please?"

"I thought there might be. *Ignito!*"

The torch obediently burst back into flames. Tom held up the ring. It had morphed back into a plain gold band.

"That was a bit dumb of me."

He gave it back to Finn. As soon as he slipped it onto the second finger of his right hand it formed five little lumps which grew into three sparkling gemstones and two opaque ones. Everyone gathered around to watch the intricate transformations. Once the flames within the stones had reignited Philadini snuffed the torch again and the cave was plunged back into complete darkness. When their eyes had adjusted everybody saw three tiny fires glowing in the gems.

"Ok, hold your hand still, mate." Tom said. Finn held his hand as steady as he could and Tom fumbled the telescope into place, resting the eyepiece directly onto the fire gems. Three orange circles projected through it onto the wall of the cave. But they were blurred and flickering. "It's working!" Tom said. "Try to hold your hand steady." Tom managed to almost focus the orange circles but the images jumped about too much.

"This is marvellous!" Philadini croaked, sounding all choked up. "No one has seen this before, *ever*. Try kneeling down—if Finn places his hand on the ground that should steady it." They did so and when Tom stroked the telescope and got it into sharp focus, three flames danced clearly on the roof of the cave. More important than that though, there were words in ancient script picked out perfectly. However, so were two large and unblinking green eyes, "Uh, oh." Philadini whispered, "I don't think those eyes are within the ring—I think it's a wortzdag! *Ignito!*"

His torch burst into flame and threw its light onto a gooey black mess stuck to the roof of the cave. In a blink, the oozy stuff morphed into a huge bat-like creature which hissed, showing off vampire-like teeth. Maggie screamed but Goodhook was fast, he whipped his half sword out, leapt up, and with one swift slice decapitated it. The creature's body flopped down upon them, slain, but still jerking. Maggie though, continued to scream, but further away now. The others scrambled themselves from beneath the wortzdag and saw her being dragged along the ground by a thick black cord coiled tightly around her legs. She flailed her arms around, shrieking for help and grabbing out wildly but her fingers just flaked through loose sandy soil. She was drawn to the lip of a crescent shaped hole and tried to brace herself across it but failed and got yanked into it.

"*Skorpikan!*" Goodhook exclaimed.

Finn forgot himself. He charged to the crescent hole and dived straight into it. Tom shot after him.

"*Grab him!*" Philadini yelled.

Goodhook grappled with Tom and they fell to the ground in a bundle. Grindlebrook, alerted by Maggie's screams, ran into the wild scene, jumped on her grandfather and pulled at his hair, "*Leave Tom alone!*"

Meanwhile, Finn had landed at the bottom of a deep hole. It had become tighter the further he dropped which broke his fall somewhat. He hit dirt and got a mouthful. Coughing and spluttering he felt about with his arms and found a gap, and in pitch dark, dragged himself into a cramped tunnel.

"*Ignito!*" He incanted, but although sparks flew out of his ring there was no fuel to ignite.

Rustling sounds ahead and Maggie's muffled wailing almost drove him into a frenzy, but he just about controlled it. *Must keep my wits, there's no way the adults can follow.* He pulled himself onwards. Dirt filled his hair and got down the back of his T shirt. He kept on incanting the only spell he knew and by the sparks he created made his way forward until the tight burrow suddenly opened out. He heard Maggie whimpering close by, but then her voice became drowned by intense buzzing, something like a furious swarm of bees.

"Maggie?" He wheezed into the dark.

"Finn? Thank heavens! H—h—help me."

'*Ignito!*' Finn incanted once more. This time with anger rather than trepidation. Fat sparks flew out of his ring, careering this way and that. One landed on Maggie's leg and set the hem of her dungarees alight.

She screamed again. At the same moment another spark found fuel off to his right. An eerie red glow spread, then burst into flame.

The mad buzzing stopped and Finn saw horror.

They were in an underground chamber. Maggie was wrapped from knees to waist by a thick, slimy cord protruding from the abdomen of a hideous black insect half again as big as her. The cord prevented the fire in her dungarees spreading above her knee but the pain caused her brow to knit tight and her top lip to tremble. She sobbed. The giant insect glared at Finn with four shiny black eyes. Its devilish mandibles snapped and clicked and it dribbled something green and sticky. Its huge scorpion-like claws, looking powerful enough to snip him in half, flexed open and shut. The thing raised itself on its back legs like it was about to strike.

Finn's legs gave up and he fell, whacking the wind out of himself. From the fire, crackling merrily to his right, high pitched squeals issued. He chanced a glance. So did the giant insect. It was a nest. Within it, baby skorpikans were burning. Acrid smoke mixed with sickly insect stinks hit his nostrils and caused his eyes to weep. Their mother buzzed a high pitched rasp something like a chain-saw in a frenzy and a red stinger thrust in and out from the end of her fat abdomen.

Finn somehow pulled himself up and faced it. His ring was squeezing him incessantly as if it was scared. He prayed for purple, red and green smoke to appear or a genie or something—anything.

Maggie screamed the loudest and longest scream of her entire life as the skorpikan leapt into the air dragging her behind it. Its wings hummed a deep and mournful sound as it flew around and around its chamber, attempting to save its frantic offspring, but they burned and popped. Maggie got bashed against the ground repeatedly. Then the mother skorpikan gave up her rescues and hovered near the still burning nest glaring at Finn. She snapped her black claws, screeched an ungodly screech, extended her stinger and went for him. Finn knew he was going to die, but still, he made a fist and held his ring as far forward as he could demanding it bring them reprieve. No coloured smoke turned up but he did hear a familiar click and scrape followed by a whoosh and a formidable flame.

"*Chew on that!*" Roared Tom, as he launched himself at the skorpikan with his aerosol blazing.

Too late to turn, the skorpikan flew straight into Tom's savage flame and was engulfed. Its wings fried instantly and it crashed and raged. Tom darted around and around the thrashing insect, burning and burning it whilst deftly avoiding its attempts to sting him. Smoke like a plastics fire billowed out of it whilst he maintained his thumb pressure until his aerosol was spent and the thing was fried to a crispy hulk. The only recognisable thing left of it was a pair of shiny black pincers. He grinned whilst Maggie and Finn panted and wheezed huge sighs of relief. Tom tossed the empty aerosol can into the air, booted it cleanly into the ravaged nest of burnt baby skorpikans, and, in fading red light, smirked his best ever smirk.

"Told you it would come in handy."

Finn and Tom unravelled the now limp black cord from around Maggie's legs, being careful of her injuries. She was badly bruised and covering one shin were weeping blisters. One leg of her dungarees was charred and holed up to her knee. She grimaced throughout the process but didn't cry out.

"Always meant to cut 'em off." She said and managed a little smile.

They hugged tightly, wiped sweat and muck off their faces then Tom led the way back along the tunnel with the aid of the last of the fuel in his Zippo. Maggie crawled in the middle and although her bruises ached and her blisters stung she didn't cry out once. Awaiting them Philadini's magic rope dangled yellow and sparkling. There was no room to turn so Tom groped his lighter back to Maggie then tugged on the rope and got hauled up. Even though he stank of smoke and sweat and was covered in dirt Grindlebrook hugged him tighter than she had ever hugged anyone in her life. Maggie got drawn up next and Goodhook helped her limp to the side of the cave. She sat there shaking with her back resting against it. Last was Finn. As his head popped out of the hole he tossed the empty lighter to Tom who caught it with one hand, flicked its wheel a few times trying to ignite it then shrugged and stuck it in his pocket.

"It'll make a great souvenir." He said.

After Philadini helped Finn out of the hole the three inseparables told their tales. Everyone hugged and congratulated them then Goodhook, holding the fire torch at arms length from his body, led them back toward the cave entrance. Maggie leaned on Grindlebrook and made her way as best she could. Then, when the big Attuk turned the last corner, he stopped dead in his tracks.

"What is it?" Philadini said.

"Three huge stinking drunes," Goodhook whispered, "they're peering into the cave."

The Crystal Coffins

❦

Krukill slept fitfully.
She awoke with a start in the middle of the night, and, rubbing her forehead, was surprised to find it covered in a thin film of sweat. She lay unmoving between gossamer silk sheets for a long time weighing up scraps of information. When she sensed dawn approaching she arose, tugged back heavy velvet drapes, and stood watching daybreak seep toward the valley. The fresh light charmed a sparkling and frozen landscape, brushing the glittering snow with a swathe of orange and lavender. On a whim she threw on a black fur cloak and headed for the depths of her fortress. Her pace was brisk. She descended ever lower, past the dungeon where the drune had spent its last hours, and on, deeper still. Her breath fogged. At the far end of a final and empty corridor she passed through an apparition wall, faced a thick metal door and rubbed her hand over its ice-dewed surface, making sure her seal was intact. A gruesome death awaited any that dare tamper with it. Of course, there was always Verko—her mark might not deter *her* contrary and perverse whims, but it was undisturbed. Her apparition wall being transparent from the rear she took a last look behind, because Vrix, being her guardian, might have deigned to follow, *he*, could track in silence through any terrain. The passage remained clear.

She held her hand to the door and uttered a quiet incantation. It swung open. Stepping inside, she snapped her fingers several times and fire torches spluttered into life illuminating four crystal coffins seated on stone plinths. The crypt was cold and damp. A drip of water splashed onto one of the coffins. She prowled around them. Each contained a body, vaguely visible through misty crystal. She stopped by one, snapped off a minuscule ice stalagmite that had begun to grow upon it, then dropped to her knees and wiped the side of the coffin, however, the mist was on the inside and the body within remained indistinct. She made a quick decision. Resealing the door she searched for a drac and commanded it to summon Vrix.

In a bedchamber, way above, Verko stirred. She opened an eye and saw Zilla asleep by a fire still smouldering from the previous night. Turning onto her back she wondered how she could possibly amuse herself for another day in the Southlands. Today, her mother was bound to confront her about Dulgo, and she might have to wait an age before killing someone else. She got up and summoned a servant, "Is my mother awake?" She snapped.

"I will enquire, your highness." Keeping a sharp eye on Zilla, the servant backed out of her bedroom. When the servant didn't return quick enough Verko stomped to the door, wrenched it open and almost stumbled into Vrix, "What are *you* doing outside my door!" She hissed.

He paused mid stride and met her black eyed stare, "I was merely passing . . . your . . . highness, I have been summoned by *her majesty*."

Verko looked him up and down. Because he was her mothers favourite, she had often searched for a reason to hurt him but he was a clever animal and never gave her an excuse. Curtly, she nodded her head and he resumed his search for his mistress.

He didn't find Krukill in her chambers. It was a little game she played. She would summon him and not tell the messenger where to find her. He checked the kitchens and caught a glimpse of her through a window. She was out in the courtyard. He negotiated the two passages separating them, however, when he went out into the frosty air, he saw that a servant had Krukill's attention and was pointing through the fortress gates. Vrix slowed and followed them as they walked across the drawbridge, then off the track and further on, all the way to the edge of the precipice. Vrix held back until the servant had finished his gesticulations and received a promise of reward. When the servant left he glanced at Vrix with gloating eyes. Vrix merely smiled inside then approached his mistress.

"There was an incident here yesterday?" She said.

Vrix said nothing and closed his thoughts down. Krukill watched him. He waited, curious as to whether she would attempt to read his mind. Once, years ago, she had searched deep within his being, looking for the reasons he refused to be rewarded for his gallantry. He was pleased today when he felt no fuzzy slicing within his head. She was being respectful. It was one of the reasons she had his loyalty. He spoke in the calmest voice he could muster. It came out as a deadly growl, "Dulgo fell over the precipice. He has been replaced. Your fortress is secure."

Krukill reached out her hand, touching his furry forearm, "You're upset. He was your friend, yes?"

"He was."

She nodded, watching him. He lowered his eyes. After a while, when he didn't expand, she spoke, "Follow me." She led him back into the fortress, along stone corridors, down a spiral stairway, onwards and down again until finally they reached her apparition wall. She paused facing it, took a glance behind at Vrix, then walked through. He flinched then followed. They stood by the metal door beyond which lay the crystal coffins. "Before I take you through this door, I need you to swear this stays between you and me."

He flared his bear-like nostrils and flashed his killing teeth, "I always learn something interesting when you ask me that."

She laughed, "Well, go on then, my huge, hulking, animal hero. Swear to me."

He bowed his head low knowing this was just playing another game—she already had his allegiance, even in the face of death. He licked his chops, "I swear, my lady." He growled.

She gravely nodded her acceptance. Rituals out of the way she incanted the door open and relit the torches. Vrix needed to stoop to enter. Once inside, he stood up straight and stroked a paw-hand through his thick mat of hair whilst his eyes darted around the room. Then he circled the four crystal coffins before crouching and peering into one of them. Like Krukill, he attempted to wipe away a fine film of mist on the crystal. When he realised it was on the inside his eyes widened, his ears pricked up and he stared at his mistress.

"They are alive?"

"Very much so." She pointed to a long handled and robust silver axe hanging on a wall, "Vrix, my old friend, you and I are going on separate journeys. I want you to promise me that, should I fail to return, you will come to this chamber, take that silver axe, smash these coffins one by one and behead the occupants."

He looked between her, the axe and the coffins, "One by one? They are dangerous?"

"I don't know."

"Who are they?"

"Do you swear you will do it?"

He knew instantly they were going to war. He also knew that this time her request was no idle ritual. Further, he knew they would fight separately, but he didn't know why. He didn't like it, "Why the mystery?"

She smiled and leaned against one of the coffins. It made a grating sound and shifted a couple of inches. They both stared, fascinated, whilst the misty red haired figure within shifted its position, turning over before settling again.

"I wouldn't ask if it wasn't important but I doubt it will come to that, we will be reunited soon and then we fight shoulder to shoulder."

"Much better. But, why do you think there is even a chance you may fail?"

Krukill doused the torches, led him out, sealed the door then fished a silver key out of her robe. Pressing it against her mark on the door she murmured an incantation over it then held it out for him. Just as he was about to accept it she swiped it away.

"Do you swear!"

He stepped back and puffed his barrel chest out, "I am merely curious. The task is somewhat . . . somewhat unusual."

"Vrix?"

He scratched his ear, "Who are they?"

Anyone but *he* would be dead for this questioning of her. She knew that he knew it. But, even though she trusted him more than any other, still, she searched his eyes before speaking, "I bartered them in return for sparing the life of a miserable runt of a magician who irked me."

"So, they have, perhaps, a *special* value?"

"Much higher to me than the runt knew."

"Ah, and who—"

"I learned of their coming from The Book Of Writing That Cannot Be Unwritten."

"Intriguing, and who—"

"Their names are Keith and Jane Gibson, and Angus and Susie Finkley."

"Finkley's!"

Her mouth curled up at one corner, she had him now, "They are the mothers and fathers of those who have dared enter Finkley Field."

Vrix bared his killing teeth right to their roots—exactly what she wanted to see.

"And now, my most loyal drac, do you swear?"

He made a wide sweeping bow, "Most graciously, your majesty!"

She dropped the silver key into his paw hand, turned on her heel and left Vrix there. Through the apparition wall he watched her sashay up the stone corridor, more than a little amused, and, *very* confident he was capable of carrying out her request should it become necessary. He made his own way at a slower pace, returning to the edge of the precipice, and, once there, paid his last respects to Dulgo—his best friend, his only true friend. *Dead.* He kept his face to the valley. No one should see his tears. He cursed Verko over and over even though he knew it could never work.

Vrix possessed not a single shred of magic.

Stirianus's Oasis

Goodhook gripped the hilt of his half-sword. "If I can just entice them in—"

"Not on your own." Philadini said, whilst stepping around the corner. All three drunes hissed, "Stay back, young people!"

Tom and Grindlebrook took a peek. The drunes leaned in a little further. One flexed a claw and its big red eyes flashed darker, another pawed the ground, flicking its skinny tongue around its jaws and left it hanging, the third crouched, its muscles tensed ready to pounce. Their stink washed over everyone. Goodhook's nostrils twitched then twitched again.

"I've got to see." Finn whispered.

He and Maggie dropped to their haunches and peered between the legs of the others. Maggie let out a little whimper as a blister burst.

"Wait for my signal." Philadini whispered to Goodhook, then stepped forward and spoke out in his most pompous manner, "*I, am Philadini, descendent of Albinonus, High Lord of Nowhere Land.*"

The drunes craned in even further. Just then Finn's belly rumbled so loudly that one heard it. It stooped to get a look at him and Philadini saw his chance. He flashed his arms wide and incanted.

"*Akafeblaze!*"

He couldn't miss at that range and his fireball flew at the drune and fried its head. Its legs collapsed and the drune crashed to the ground. Shrieking madly, its companions fled the cave and took flight.

Goodhook raced after them and hurled his half-sword spinning through the air, severing a wing of one of them. The drune squealed and flapped its other wing in a frenzy as it tumbled to the ground. Grindlebrook ripped out her dagger and circled the smelly and thrashing beast opposite her grandfather. She watched its eyes and at the same time felt the heat of the sun searing into her. On Goodhook's signal they pounced, he going for its heart with his dagger and she the throat, but the drune squirmed and writhed and they both missed. It lashed out at Grindlebrook with its long hooked talons but she was too quick for it.

Finn was there now. He eyed the hilt of Goodhook's sword sticking out of the thicker part of its wing. His heart pounded with the urge to help. Tom nudged him. They glanced at each other and nodded.

"Let's grab it and hold it fast!" Finn said.

Emboldened by killing the skorpikan they leapt in and, seizing its good wing, hung on grimly whilst Maggie hobbled around it and threw herself onto its broken wing, pinning it tight beneath her thus enabling Grindlebrook to grab her grandfather's sword and do a proper job on its neck. In the same moment Goodhook rammed his dagger into its heart. Purple blood fountained and the drune made a few frenzied last kicks then expired. Panting, everyone stared at one another.

Meanwhile the third drune was high in the sky, and Philadini was letting go fireball after fireball at it but all missed, "They're almost impossible to control." He said.

Goodhook rolled his eyes, took out his munkhorn and blew the note for attack. The black eagles guarding Stirianus's oasis heard it and responded. A flock of them first flew toward them, then, when they caught sight of the drune, changed direction and pursued it.

"*That*, was the messiest drune kill ever." Goodhook said. "One of us should have been able to deal with it."

Grindlebrook lowered her eyes. She nodded.

What's he talking about? Finn thought. But Tom smirked, "I want to learn how to do that."

"Tom!" Maggie exclaimed.

"You've come on a long way since Finkley Field," Goodhook said, "we'll teach you how."

The attack call of the munkhorn had also roused the mucklebacks.

They charged out of their cave but halted abruptly when they saw the drune was already dead. They plodded to the corpse and sniffed at it. Meanwhile, the Attuks got out of the sun and retired to the cave. Maggie limped after them.

"Let me see your burns." Goodhook said. Maggie pulled her charred dungarees above her knees. One leg was worse than the other. Grindlebrook sat with her and put her arm round her. "I'll grease your blisters with some balm." Goodhook said. "They'll heal quick enough. Have you any other injuries?"

She shook her head, "Just bruises."

"Oh Maggie, you're so brave." Grindlebrook said.

Maggie flipped her hair back and stared at her. "Me? Brave? You've just chopped up a drune's neck and call *me* brave when all I did was pussy around and lay on its injured wing? Finn and Tom are the brave ones. And remember, I got captured by the skorpikan, that's all, I didn't actually *do* anything. It was them who came after me and saved my life—proper heroes they were. Actually, they've always been my hero's, forever."

Grindlebrook squeezed her hand. "You're all our heroes."

Goodhook anointed her shins then they sat back and relaxed, waiting for the heat to go out of the sun. When dusk fell, lights began twinkling like stars around the perimeter of the oasis.

"Time to descend on Stirianus." Philadini called out to them.

"What about that message Finn got from the Book Of Writing That Can't Be Unwritten?" Maggie said.

"Cannot—not Can't." Philadini said, his expression like a teacher correcting a favourite pupil. "We'll get chance to see what's written inside the ring soon enough, now Tom's found the way. Right now I want to get us inside Stirianus's Oasis because we don't know yet whether the black eagles caught up with that drune that escaped us—if it alerts that massive flock you saw . . ."

Grindlebrook helped Maggie get onto Loopy. He gave a low growl when he saw her wounds, so, once everyone else had mounted up and they rode on, she told him about her adventure with the skorpikan. His ears flew about when she got to the bit about Tom burning it to a crisp.

Stirianus's Oasis turned out to be further away than it looked, growing ever bigger the nearer they got. They were further delayed by having to negotiate around a large area of sinking sands. The second moon was appearing by the time they finally arrived at the perimeter of the oasis, which was marked out by an ethereal yellow line connecting bushes, full of luminous insects. It was these masses of insects that had caused the bushes to appear like lights from the distance. Huge black eagles were strutting along Stirianus's magic boundary, guarding it proudly, and they eyed everyone haughtily. The magnificent birds were even taller than the adults. Finn could hear muffled singing and guessed it must be the magician himself.

"Ok, dismount," Philadini said, "but do not attempt to cross that yellow line." Finn got off his muckleback and went toward one of the bushes. "*Stop!*" Philadini shouted. "Something very unpleasant will happen if you get too close to that bush." Finn heeded Philadini and retreated. "Now we wait. Better Stirianus invites us in than I meddle with his magic."

Finn sat on a rock with Tom, Maggie and Grindlebrook whilst they waited. Tuneless singing wavered in the background. It was coming from a dwelling which would have resembled a lighthouse but for a large overhanging upper tier that caused it to look like a giant mushroom. Finn gazed up at the tall white structure wondering why he hadn't noticed it through the telescope whilst he was on watch. Meanwhile, their mucklebacks lined up along the magic yellow boundary sniffing the air and staring longingly at the still and dark water of the oasis. Some black eagles gathered into a bunch in front of them and eyed them with stony stares. Just then a gronk stuck his head out of the doorway at the base of the white building and glared at them.

"Oh look," Philadini said, "here comes Stirianus's pet gronk—now he *is* a piece of work."

"*No visitors!* And that includes you, *Philadini!*"

"Is that so, *Amelious gronk?*"

"That, *is so!*"

The gronk strode up quickly, halting just the other side of the ghostly yellow line. Scowling, he folded his arms and tapped his right foot. He was about waist height to Philadini, had a wispy moustache, lank green hair and shifty green eyes.

"Nervous are we?" Philadini said.

"I am not nervous—I am irritated."

"How sad, I thought you might have been having fun—there's a lot of singing going on."

Amelious sneered, "Stirianus is always happy with *my* company—unlike the mood that comes over him every time you turn up. Now, *if you will excuse me,* I have things to attend to." He turned to leave.

An edge crept into Philadini's voice, "Just a moment, you ignorant little gronk, I have an invitation from Stirianus—it says he needs my help, *urgently.*"

The gronk bristled, "Stirianus would give you no such thing—all he needs is me and his medicine."

"Like to keep him drunk do you, you insignificant little gronk? Gets you the run of the place, does it?"

"I've no idea what you are talking about. Now either show me your invitation or be on your way."

Philadini turned to Goodhook, winked and held out his hand, "The directions, if you please."

Goodhook fished inside his jacket, pulled out the magic map and passed it over. Philadini unfolded the self-illuminating parchment.

Amelious clamped his hands on his hips, "Hah! That's just a map, it's not an invitation."

"*This,* is a magical map. I extracted it from the Tomb of Albinonus because Stirianus sent a black eagle to the Great Oak to ask me for it. It is all the invitation we need. Now, you either let us in or I will get my friend Finn here to set that tapping foot of yours on fire. He's a budding magician so he doesn't have much control—you might lose your leg."

"*You wouldn't dare.*"

"Finn—*burn this gronk*—he's a disgrace to his race."

Finn looked quizzically at Philadini. The magician gestured he should do it. Finn raised his hand and pointed at the gronk's foot.

Amelious hissed at him, "You can't do magic, you're just a scared little boy."

I'm way bigger than you are, Finn thought. But he lowered his arm and checked out Philadini again.

"*Do it!*" Philadini hissed with a slicing edge to his voice.

"*Ok!*"

What's he angry with *me* for, Finn thought? He raised his right hand again, pointed at the gronk's foot, and opened his mouth to incant. This time Amelious noticed Finn's ring. His eyes widened and his eyebrows shot up. He gasped then ran to the building.

"*Stirianus! Stirianus!* You've got visitors!"

The singing stopped and a muffled voice called out from within the mushroom-shaped house.

"Fetch grog more!"

Amelious stared back at everyone from by the house. He took a step inside the doorway, thought better of it, then vanished behind the dwelling.

Philadini laughed, "He's all front that gronk. Well done, Finn. Now lets see if we fare any better with his master."

Cussing sounded from within the white mushroom house and a shaky shadow passed from one window to another as someone descended. Finally, the door creaked fully open.

"Who it is?" A wobbly voice called out.

"I've brought some friends, Stirianus," Philadini said, "I thought we might have a party."

There was a pause. Then a tall robed figure tottered out of the house.

"Philidily?"

"*Yes*, and I've got friends with me."

"Hang while on I my get boots."

Soon Finn got his first proper glimpse of Stirianus. He was a dishevelled and drunken version of Philadini wearing a crumpled hat, big boots, and drink stained robes. He zigzagged to the boundary, peering first at Philadini then at his company. Matted hair dangled over his shoulders and his nose was even longer than Philadini's. His eyebrows grew thick and bristly above milky brown eyes and he clasped a bottle to his chest as if it were precious.

"Wait till you swig a have of this. Made myself it—scrapings put of muckleback horn in—makes the all difference."

"I can't wait." Philadini said.

"Come you forwards lots. I cant shadows you in the see."

Maggie kept back, holding her nose.

Stirianus perused his visitors, "Be fun should this!"

He made passes with his free hand above his magic boundary, incanting the same spell over and over until he eventually found the correct word order. Instantly, the ghostly yellow line vanished and they were in. The mucklebacks trotted straight to the lake for a drink and a swim whilst Stirianus fiddled with words until he managed to re-engage his magical protection.

Amelious scowled at them from the shadows. Finn gave him his best stare and pointed at him with his right hand. The gronk shrank back behind the building and Philadini winked at Finn. Black eagles gathered around watching everyone intently but when nothing untoward happened they returned to patrolling the yellow line from bush to bush.

Stirianus draped an arm around Philadini, as much for support as friendliness, and everyone followed as they bumped up several staircases and entered a large room full of mystical artefacts and empty bottles. Their host pointed haphazardly to doors leading onto a huge balcony then wandered off, muttering something mixed up about bottles and a gronk. Everyone filtered out through the doors and gawped at the huge double moonlit view.

"Wow—it's so beautiful." Maggie said.

The balcony encircled the whole living area giving rise to the mushroom shape of the house. Finn walked with Maggie to a rail and they stood together, closer than they needed. Her warmth quickened his pulse. Below them their mucklebacks splashed in dark water, then they took a tour with everyone around the broad balcony, marvelling at the vastness of the views. Above them masses of stars sparkled and sweet night air blew over them from the wider desert.

Back with more drink, their host lurched around the living room, then commenced bashing dusty cushions. When he was satisfied his pigsty looked welcoming he loped onto the balcony.

"In come and drinks a have with me!"

Reluctantly, everyone went inside and found a perch. Stirianus eyed his guests, grinning lopsidedly. He raised a bottle, finished it with one long swig and lobbed it over his shoulder. Grindlebrook and Maggie glanced at each other and shook their heads imperceptibly. Philadini opened a couple more bottles and pretended to drink with Stirianus who'd been drinking all day so he was easily fooled and it only took two more bottles for him to pass out.

"Right," Philadini said, "Finn, you come with me, we'll go sort out that waste of a gronk, Amelious; everybody else get some rest, tomorrow is going to be *very* tricky. We'll need to be fresh and sharp if we are to get the better of Stirianus. You'll find that the bedrooms are in the basement, and don't mess with any of those instruments, Stirianus does nasty magic."

Finn wanted to hang out with Maggie and tried to catch her eye but she was head to head with Grindlebrook. *Magicians,* he thought, and tramped after Philadini. Once outside, they soon found the unsavoury gronk hiding in a hollow within an old cactus.

"Amelious gronk," Philadini said, "because you are a disgrace to your race I am going to set you free."

A muffled voice replied, "What do you mean, set me free?"

"I'll show you."

He grabbed the gronk by his ears and dragged him squealing out of the cactus and then to the magic boundary.

"You cant throw me out there—I won't survive—drunes will get me."

"Cowardice becomes you, Amelious, of course you can survive out there, you're a gronk, go dig yourself a hole."

With that he picked him up by his grubby green hair and leather thong and tossed him over the magic boundary. He was unharmed because its job was to stop anything entering but didn't prevent anyone leaving.

"*Please,* Philadini, let me back in—I promise I'll treat you very nicely."

"No you wouldn't, you despicable lying excuse for a gronk, consider your employment terminated. Come on Finn, I've had quite enough of him." They left Amelious to fend for himself and went back indoors. The living room was now empty, apart from Stirianus who was snoring peacefully. Philadini stroked his beard whilst he pondered their host. "Go search a room out for yourself, Finn, I need to stay up and have a good long think and a smoke."

Finn left him there and renegotiated the staircases. Descending further, he discovered a rabbit warren of rooms was below ground level. He soon came across an empty one and slid gratefully under fluffy and richly embroidered covers that lay on top of a wonderfully comfortable sleeping platform. Instantly snug, he realised how much he had missed a bed as his head sank into mildly scented pillows. He pictured the view of the desert from Stirianus's balcony and in no time drifted off to sleep. For once he didn't wake up during the night and he awoke the next morning feeling completely refreshed. He stretched then got up and, whilst climbing the staircases back up to the living area, he overheard Stirianus pontificating loudly about his favourite brew.

"The best thing about that new magic grog of mine is you don't get hangovers—shall we have one after breakfast?"

Finn walked into the living room. Everyone was there. He took a seat.

"Great idea," Philadini said, "but first, let me re-introduce you to another of my friends."

"Hello, I'm Finn."

"Are you? You don't look like Finn to me."

"Erm . . . I really am Finn."

"Well, never mind," Stirianus said, "everybody has to be somebody, I thought you were Tom. Now, as I was saying, Philadini, this new grog is really quite special."

"Tom's my best friend," Finn said, "he's sitting over there, you met him last night."

Stirianus glared at Finn who felt his whole body quiver as if somebody was shaking him like a saltcellar. "I have only just met you," Stirianus said, "and already you have an annoying habit—you interrupt." Turning away, he continued, "The thing is Philadini, if we don't have a drink before midday it gets really boring around here. Now, where is that pesky gronk of mine. *Amelious!*" He shouted down the stairway.

"He left." Philadini said.

"What do you mean, 'he left'?"

"He said the drunes were coming and it wasn't safe with you anymore."

"Drunes! Not safe! Pah! That gronk has lost his head—drunes are no match for me!"

"He also said you hadn't paid him for over a year and if the drunes didn't get him the morkuns would."

"Morkuns? I hate morkuns!" Stirianus shouted, "The trouble with you, Philadini, is that every time I see you, you make me so angry I have to throw you out. *Now,* I need a drink *before* breakfast!"

Philadini leaned in, "There are hundreds of drunes gathering at Uderzandu Prison, morkuns too. I came here to warn you that huntermagi are with them—your old enemies, Dhagan, Mongrix, and Whorpus. They'll be coming to collect you. It'll be pretty dreary in Uderzandu, and, there'll be no grog. Ok, everybody, we had best be on our way." He got up and made to leave.

"Hang on, hang on," Stirianus said. "what do you mean they're coming to collect me? And where are you going?"

"Well, there is no way I am sticking around here with hunter-magi and morkuns about. I can't beat them on my own. We're off to Itako. The Itakans will welcome us and we can hide out in the Dark Mountains. They have good grog there too."

"Yes, I see. But collect me? What are you talking about?"

"Houni the gronk told me Krukill wants to lock you up. She thinks you're a problem and reckons you're an easy target because you've taken to the drink."

"What! Krukill? Me? Easy target? Are you winding me up, Philadini? Because if you are—" He jumped up, his formidable side really shining now.

Philadini remained seated and draped an arm over the back of his chair, "Please—sit, cousin, all you need to do is stay off the grog and you will be just fine."

Stirianus went very quiet. The expression on his face chilled Finn who tried to look inconspicuous by sitting on his hands. No one spoke. Then, without warning, Stirianus whirled around, stalked out of the room and jogged purposefully downstairs. Philadini grinned, reached inside his robes, and, taking out his selection of potions he chose one that contained a clear liquid and gave the phial to Tom, "Now Tom, I'm sure he has gone to get more grog. He won't suspect you, so shake a couple of drops of that potion into his drink when I distract him. *No more*—I only want to knock him out, not kill him."

Stirianus returned with his arms bursting with bottles. He dumped them on a knee high table then relaxed into a deep sofa, took a good long pull on a bottle then filled a goblet with the rest. He grinned at Philadini, "You nearly had me there but I don't believe a word of it. I know what your game is—there are no morkuns or drunes or Dhagan and his mates, are there? It's just a ruse to get me to go on that old hair brained scheme of yours to free those pesky cousins of ours from Uderzandu. Blah! Well, they can stay locked up for a millennium for all I care—it'll be the making of them. Now, let's just have a drink and forget about them. It's not possible anyway. I made sure of that."

Philadini sat forwards and steepled his hands, "Listen, Stirianus, there really *are* drunes about—we killed two only last night, and Houni the gronk has seen morkuns. Surely the desert vultures have told you?"

"I have Amelious shoo them away—they're far too bright, and, pompous with it—sparkling about everywhere looking for someone to impress. They might dazzle your eyes but when it comes to personality they're a bit—erm—flat. Get my drift? Moreover, I don't like happy creatures! Come on, have a drink with me. We can have some fun today." He refilled his goblet and took a slug. Apart from his slurping, silence consumed the room.

Finn squirmed inside. *I've got to say something*, "But we need your help!" He said.

"Can't be done—have a drink everybody—there's plenty of goblets and loads of grog."

Finn got to his feet, "Why do you say it can't be done!"

Stirianus peered at him then slapped his sofa as if swatting an insect, "Because, *I* say it cannot be done, young man! Now, stop being impertinent and have a drink with me and be civil. I've welcomed you into my home and I am beginning to wish I had not."

Finn bit his lip then pressed on, "But, why not? I have to free the cousins! The Book Of Writing That Cannot Be Unwritten told me I must," he glanced at Tom and Maggie before adding, "if we are ever to have a chance of finding our parents again."

Maggie and Tom lowered their eyes and Stirianus caught their discomfort.

"That's a pretty little story—*Finn*—that's your name, isn't it?" Finn nodded. "Well, Finn, you are out of luck because I threw the key to Uderzandu Prison into the middle of the Unfillable Lake years ago. It's gone forever—you'll never find it, and you can't free the cousins without it. *That's for sure*. Now, sit down and have a drink with me."

Silence.

Maggie and Tom passed a worried glance between themselves then at Finn who glowered at Stirianus. Goodhook and Grindlebrook's shoulders sagged as they watched the smelly magician take a swig from his goblet then refill it. Philadini though, sat stroking his beard, eyes afire, then, seeming to make a decision, he thrust his hand into his robes. Stirianus, suddenly alert, rammed his goblet down and leaned forwards, hands hovering at the ready, intent on the other magician.

Philadini grasped what he was searching for, plucked it out of his robes, and waved it at Stirianus.

"Is this the key you're talking about?"

He lobbed a silver object onto the table. It was about the size of a cigar tube, covered in script and with complicated gears on one end. Goodhook recognised it instantly—it was the exquisite tool that Philadini had entrusted to him years ago.

Stirianus jumped backwards as if avoiding a deadly snake, "Where did you get that!" He demanded hoarsely then made to grab it but Finn was quick and swiped it away, "Give me that key!" Stirianus bawled and went for him.

"Stop!" Shouted Philadini, jumping between them. "It's not yours! Albinonus would be ashamed of you."

Whilst Stirianus glared apoplectically at Philadini, Tom slipped a couple of drops out of the clear phial into his goblet.

Stirianus tapped Philadini's chest, *"What would you know about what Albinonus wanted, you meddling fool?"*

Philadini backed up, "I won't fight you Stirianus. *We*, are going to break into Uderzandu Prison and free the cousins. *And*, I repeat, there really are drunes and morkuns about. The merfyns killed thirty orgils at the Unfillable Lake a couple of days ago. We helped them. Dhagan, Mongrix and Whorpus will come after you, and, so will *Krukill*."

Stirianus shook with rage, he seemed ready to incant Philadini into oblivion, "I'll ask you one last time—where did you get that key from!"

"The merfyns saw you throw it into the Unfillable Lake. You were raving drunk. They retrieved it and gave it to me to look after."

Stirianus screwed his face up and remained pointing and staring at Philadini. Finn fully expected him to incant some abominable spell, but, all of a sudden, he relaxed, sat down and took another good long swig of his grog, "Wait 'till I get my hands on that stupid gronk." He said, then grabbed at his stomach and stiffened. His eyes grew large and he made a fumbling lunge for Philadini but missed and dropped to the floor like a wet rag.

"Phew." Philadini said. His hands were shaking.

Goodhook held out his hand palm up and Finn dropped the key to Uderzandu Prison into it.

"So that's what it is."

Philadini slumped into a chair and said in a shaky voice, "I knew it would be far safer with you. He wasn't very happy to see it again, was he?"

"You clever old magician." Goodhook said.

"Less of the old, if you please."

"*Naughty* magician, *I* think!" Grindlebrook said. "You lied to us that Stirianus had the key to Uderzandu Prison just to persuade us to come here with you."

"No, I said he filched it from Krukill's turnkey, I didn't say he still had it, did I?" Grindlebrook pounced on him and bashed him with a cushion. Philadini flopped back and let her whack him a few times then he exclaimed "Enough! The result was worth the subterfuge."

Grindlebrook desisted and grinned at him, "You should be beaten more often!"

"Phew," Philadini said again, and wiped his brow. "Control your granddaughter please, Goodhook."

"If I could do that, we wouldn't even be here."

"Hmm, well, I'm glad you did come. Ok, listen up, Stirianus will sleep for a couple of days and we'll have a lay day. The only job we must do today is destroy all his stock of magic grog, and, don't drink any!"

As it turned out, several days went by before Stirianus woke up. Everyone's bruises, blisters and cuts were healing and the three inseparables spent their time being taught fighting skills. Philadini dug out the sacks containing the weapons he had borrowed from Stirianus's tomb, rigged up a thick awning to keep off the sun, and Finn, Maggie and Tom got some intense training in swordplay, unarmed combat, and archery. Grindlebrook and Goodhook taught them whilst Philadini used his magic to enable them to assimilate skills quickly. They learned fast. Maggie turned out to be best at archery, Tom at swordplay and Finn became all round good at everything. They had to be super careful with the weapons as they were incredibly sharp and Goodhook made them start with sticks, teaching them safety and defensive moves first before he would allow any of them to even pick up a real weapon. The black eagles and mucklebacks became their audience and formed a circle around them, cawing or grunting whenever someone accomplished a new deft move. Grindlebrook laughed at their first efforts, later she grinned, then, when they became more proficient, pursed her lips and nodded appreciation. She surprised Tom with her swordsmanship, particularly her ability to whisk his sword out of his hand at will. The better he got the more he thought he would be able to beat her but he never did. He never lost his smirk though, and saluted her with his sword at his every failure. The last thing Goodhook taught them was the theory of how to defeat a drune, alone, with only a sword. Throughout, Finn was hoping to be taught more spells but the days passed without Philadini's input.

∼

ON THE THIRD MORNING STIRIANUS AWOKE. HE PROPPED HIMSELF UP WITH one hand and scratched his head with the other. The first person he spoke to was Philadini.

"*You*, are cunning." He croaked. He stretched himself, loped out onto his balcony, grabbed the guard rail and shook his head a few times as he gazed out at the desert. Philadini followed him and motioned the young people to do likewise. Goodhook and Grindlebrook stayed out of the sun but watched from the doorway. All waited in silence. Suddenly, Stirianus rounded on Philadini, but, instead of looking ominous his expression was benign. "I suppose I ought to thank you." He said, now in a clearer voice. "How long have I been drunk?"

"A tad shy of eight years."

"Is that all? I thought it was longer. Oh well, it was impossible for me any other way. After Krukill murdered my wife I found a day lasted too long. I needed to kill it." He paused, perusing the landscape like he was checking no one had meddled with it, then ran his eyes over his guests, "Ok, tell me about this harebrained scheme of yours so that I can pick it to pieces."

Philadini fished out his pipe and primed it, "Like I said, we are going to break into Uderzandu, free the prisoners and take them to Itako."

Stirianus snorted, "And what do you expect to achieve with that bunch of layabouts and criminals. The last time—"

"Hear me out."

Stirianus rolled his eyes, then a flash of something caught his attention. "Come here." He said to Finn in a gentle voice. Finn felt butterflies in his stomach, *what now?* He approached. Stirianus offered him his hand but when Finn accepted it the magician grabbed his wrist with his other hand and yanked him close. "Who are you really! Who gave you that ring!" He demanded, eyeball to eyeball.

Finn squirmed, attempting to break free, "Let me go!"

"Stirianus?" Philadini said.

Stirianus let go of Finn and glared at the other magician, "You've got some explaining to do!"

Philadini grinned, sucked on his pipe, blew a perfect smoke ring and followed it by blowing a perfect smoke sarcophagus which glided through the middle of it.

"*Well!*"

"I was coming to that."

Stirianus's eyebrows twitched like he was attempting to tie a knot with them, "*Explain! Now!*"

Philadini hauled in the fish, "Finn, show Stirianus the little trinket that Albinonus leant you."

When Finn held up the little golden book Stirianus's eyes nearly popped out of his head.

"*My book of spells!*" He snatched it off Finn.

Philadini cleared his throat, "*Whose* book of spells?"

Stirianus held the book tighter, "Don't be impertinent!"

Philadini tapped his pipe on the railing. Ash floated down and out of sight, "The *temporary* guardian of the book is always whomever Albinonus chooses to lend it to, however, the important thing is that we have more going for us than a bunch of chancers from Itako, don't you think?"

Stirianus glared at him but Philadini simply twinkled his eyes at the superior magician. Slowly Stirianus's expression transformed from a maddened scowl into a broad grin, "Well you—sly—old—sorcerer! You knew you had me before you even set foot into my home!" He burst into laughter and turned his attention back to Finn. "Give me a proper look at that ring." Grinning now, Finn held up his hand. "What can you do with it?"

"Not a lot. Set things on fire, put them out again, and one time, purple, red and green smoke flushed out of it and saved my life."

"Saved your life already, has it?"

"Finn's being a tad modest," Philadini said, "what he actually did was outwit the demons and statues in Albinonus's Tomb, met Albinonus himself and inveigled his book of spells away from him then used it to divert the entire Falls of Rhandoror to put out a raging forest fire, thus saving the Attuk nation from extinction.

Stirianus beamed at Finn, "That's more like it! There's no need to be humble around here. Killed any drunes yet?"

Finn shook his head, "Er no—fact is—I don't feel like I'm a proper magician. I just got lucky, I think."

"*Lucky?*" Stirianus said. "That ring has *believing magic* imbedded into it. Of course, the ring helps the wearer perform a few simple spells *but*, it's what you can think up and believe that it excels at."

"Why don't proper magicians wear it?"

"Doesn't work, my boy. Doesn't work at all. That ring was crafted to enable mere mortals to vanquish evil sorcerers. *Believing magic* is a balancing order of magic, no less. It's a very old form of magic, none have ever fathomed its secrets because the talent that forged it died with the ancients."

"What happened?"

"Cataclysm! *Colossal* cataclysm—nowhere was safe. *The Nothing* appeared for the first time and the ancients, thinking the answers to all destiny lay within it, walked into it and disappeared forever—well, that's how the story goes anyhow."

"So they might still be in *The Nothing*."

Stirianus took a step back, "You, are a strange boy. Easily led. You need to toughen up." He turned to Philadini. "I'm starving. Let's have breakfast. I'll get the gronk to rustle something up."

"Amelious gronk really has gone."

Stirianus started then shrugged, "Did I really not reward him for a whole year?"

Philadini grinned, "I made that bit up—it might have been longer."

"Hah! Actually, I never did take to him. Sleazy sort of character."

Just then, Grindlebrook called out from the doorway, "I've cleaned the kitchen and I can prepare breakfast."

Stirianus smiled at her then deposited the golden book of spells back into Finn's palm, "Look after that for me would you?" Everyone followed him inside. After breakfast they spent the rest of the morning filling Stirianus in, each telling their part. Then he gave everyone a tour around his domain except Goodhook and Grindlebrook who stayed out of the sun. The mucklebacks ignored everyone and lazed by the oasis in the shade of palm trees that had elongated russet leaves and sprouted strange purple and orange fruit. "Ok, now I've shown everyone around, show me some of your magic, Finn"

Finn dutifully incanted *'Ignito!'* and set fire to a bush.

Stirianus waited for more. Finn shrugged.

"Is that the extent of your spells?"

"'I'm afraid so."

Stirianus glared at Philadini, then relaxed, "Oh well, you've made some sort of a start. Let's see how quick you learn—here's a spell for smashing or exploding things." He pointed at a large rock.

"Exakraak!"

The rock dutifully exploded with a loud crack.

"*Woah!*" Tom and Maggie exclaimed.

Finn chose a rock and pointed at it with his ring hand, "Exucroak!—erm, no I mean Exa—exa—what was that spell again?"

Patiently Stirianus taught him the spell. Finn got quite frustrated trying it over and over before he began to get the hang of it then, finally, after getting a couple of stones to jump about, he managed to split a small one into two. Stirianus sighed.

"I thought so, *you*, are a slow learner."

Finn looked downcast.

"Don't be upset. Slow learners are the best. They are the most imaginative and the most creative. You are going to be amazing."

Finn looked up. He positively beamed, *"No teacher ever said that to me."*

"Well, your teachers can't have known very much—you are going to be great—all you have to do is believe impossible things and get angry."

"Philadini got me well angry before I did my first fire spell."

"Exactly! It's one of the most important lessons. You will have to get *really* angry to do big magic."

"But you didn't get angry when you exploded that rock."

Stirianus nodded, "That, is because I'm a real magician, *you* are a Ring Bearer—it's going to be different for you. But it's also going to be special. *Very* special. I'll show you one more spell, we'll need a volunteer, Philadini?"

"I thought you said a volunteer." Philadini said.

Stirianus grinned, "He's very astute, my cousin. Come on someone, oblige me by running around whilst I knock you off your feet."

"Sure." Tom said and ran off.

Stirianus pointed at him and, in a casual voice, incanted, "*Skatangle!*"

Tom got whacked straight off his feet. He rolled in the dust but came up smiling.

"That was fun."

Stirianus frowned, "It's a good thing you're not a Ring Bearer—this is battle magic—it's not meant for amusement."

Tom did one of his best smirks, "I bet you've used it for fun plenty of times."

"Don't you be impertinent either!"

Tom bowed theatrically. Finn grinned at Tom from behind Stirianus's back but wiped it off when the magician turned. Then Finn spent quite some time practicing the '*Skatangle*' incantation. It took him a lot of attempts and Tom needed to stand still before he even managed to cause him to stagger. Eventually he worked out a way to get angry quickly by imagining Philadini lying to him about Albinonus's Book of Spells, *"Skatangle!"* He incanted with force and knocked Tom flat. It sent tingles right up his ring arm to his shoulder.

"Hah!" Stirianus exclaimed, "Well incanted, my boy! Ok, that will do for today—lets have some refreshments." Philadini regarded him warily. "Don't worry, I'm aware you destroyed all my grog, and I thank you."

They went indoors. Grindlebrook had watched Finn's progress from a window on the staircase, "He's doing great." She whispered to Maggie.

Maggie beamed then frowned, "He's such a gentle soul."

"What are you guys whispering about?" Tom said.

But they wouldn't tell.

Everybody went into the lounge. All the debris from Stirianus's drinking lifestyle had been cleared by Goodhook and Grindlebrook. Stirianus looked pleased, "Thank you for tidying up. Now, about your plan, Philadini, there may be a large number of prisoners in

Uderzandu besides our cousins, so, if we are to free them all, we are going to need a lot of mucklebacks."

"We were intending a surprise attack." Philadini said. "We only have the five."

"Surprise is good but I think time is too short for a prolonged journey to Itako. If Krukill turns up, anyone on foot will be easy prey and we'd need to carry a lot of water and food. No, I think I'll get some black eagles to fly to the River Rhand and ask all the mucklebacks they can find to head to Uderzandu. As for us, we leave at first light, Goodhook?"

The big Attuk started at being addressed, "Yes, Stirianus, how can I be of assistance?"

"You are out of your element with your curse in this hot environment. You and your granddaughter must travel by night and make your own way to Uderzandu whilst I lead the others by day."

Goodhook seemed taken aback, he paused for a long moment but then acted professional, "Where will we meet you?"

"Do you have a map?"

"I already know the desert."

"Yes, but have you actually been to Uderzandu Prison?" Goodhook shook his head. "Ok, get the map and I'll show you how to stay safe." Goodhook fished it out and unfolded it on a table. Everyone gathered around. Grindlebrook held tightly onto her grandfather's hand and she and Maggie kept swopping glances, both wore pinched expressions. Stirianus placed a long finger on his oasis then tapped the map making sure Goodhook paid close attention then traced out his suggested route, "Keep clear of these burning valleys and make sure . . . " Once Stirianus had fully explained the route, and advised Goodhook of potential hazards, he quizzed Grindlebrook, "Can you look after your grandfather?"

She pulled herself up straight, "Of course I can."

"I believe you. What are you doing here by the way?"

She stood on her toes to gain more height and glared at Stirianus, "I belong here!"

He studied her for a moment then said, "I believe you again—what can you do?"

"I can ride a muckleback like the wind, I have the eyes of a hawk, I can fight with swords, daggers and spears, load and shoot a crossbow and kill anything in sight with a bow and arrow and . . . and . . . and I'm pretty good at cooking too."

"That, you have already proved. Would you like to prepare supper tonight?"

Grindlebrook skipped off to the kitchen to check on ingredients.

"You won't find her lacking in fighting skills." Goodhook said. "She's a feisty one."

"I already worked that one out." Stirianus said, then switched his attention to Tom and Maggie, "And what are you two bringing to the party?"

Maggie cocked her head to one side. Tom was about to speak but she trod on his foot, "Bringing?" She said, in her most indignant tone whilst staring straight into Stirianus's eyes. "*Bringing?*" She repeated, louder this time. "We've been virtually kidnapped! We're only here because I was stupid enough to persuade Finn to play a game of dodge the Attuk. The way I see it, it's your job to deliver Krukill to us so's he can get that bloody Black Diamond off her. After that, I'm expecting *you* to get the three of us back home to England! Humph!"

Stirianus's brow knotted and he was about to speak his opinion about Maggie's attitude when Philadini clapped a hand on his shoulder, "It is our fight not Maggie's—nor is it Tom or Finn's. Our job is to protect them not expect them to die for us."

Stirianus stared for a long moment at Philadini then relaxed. "I see." He looked Maggie up and down. "You are a brave young woman. There are not many who would dare stand up to me. I apologise—sometimes I get caught up with my enthusiasm. I give you three my word I will do everything in my power to protect you. There is a problem though."

Maggie folded her arms, "And what might that be?"

Stirianus lowered his eyes before replying, "If the magic of Finkley Field has been destroyed there is no way for you to get back home."

He sighed and sat down, Maggie placed herself in front of him and clamped her hands on her hips, "Why, am I not surprised? *Damn you magicians!* You're so full of yourselves. It's your bloody sister who started this whole thing off. Give me an Attuk any day!"

She stomped off to the kitchen. Grindlebrook smiled a welcome, "Hi, Maggie. Would you like to help me prepare supper?" Maggie burst into tears and fell into her arms. Grindlebrook hugged her tightly. "Whatever is the matter? Has Finn done something to upset you?"

"No, it's not him, it's—oh, I'm sorry for being like this—it's just that —just that—oh, I love you so much, Grindly, but—*I just want to go home!*"

"Tell me everything." Grindlebrook said. "I want to know just, well —*everything*—all there is to tell about your world."

Maggie stepped back, "I could just see you there—you would be amazing. Everybody would love you so much. You'd be famous too."

"What's famous?"

"Famous is . . . famous is . . . erm, not very important, actually. Oh Grindly, you have such a way of cheering me up. You're a very special person—Attuk, I mean."

"Do you really mean that?"

"Yes, I really do." Maggie stayed in the kitchen telling a wide eyed Grindlebrook all about England. She stuck in a story about Merlin, and witch burning too, just to give it a bit of authenticity. Then she got to describing folklore, mentioning werewolves and vampyres. Suddenly, Grindlebrook's eyes lit up.

"Vampyres! We've got loads of those here, werewolves too!"

Maggie blanched and had to sit, "What, you have *real* vampyres!"

"Of course they're real, I mean they can't die, can they? But there's none out here in the desert—werewolves never come here either."

Maggie stood up and stared unseeing through a window that gave out onto the desert.

"Oh my . . . " she whispered to herself, "oh my . . . "

Beyond The Oasis

The following morning Finn noticed that Stirianus looked much better.

Fresher too, he thought when he sniffed gently. His cloak looked crisp, his step was brisk and the smelly drunk had completely disappeared. Further, the milky film clouding his eyes had dissolved, leaving them bright and a deep nut-brown. Finn watched him present Goodhook and Grindlebrook with chameleon cloaks. When they hunkered down beneath them they resembled a pair of rocks on the flagstone floor. Next, Stirianus produced a simple blue and green amulet.

"This is a water finder." He said to Grindlebrook. "It's a very simple tool, the blue part always gravitates towards water. It becomes completely green if there is none nearby. Can you see that right now the blue portion is pointing to the oasis and green away?" Grindlebrook nodded. "If you ever run out of water and blue is pointing down, you'll need to dig."

She slipped it on, *"It's beautiful!"* Wherever she waved her arm, blue always remained on that portion nearest the small lake. *"Thank you."* She showed it to Maggie who was enthralled.

Finn though, was frowning, I have to say something, he thought and cleared his throat, "Do we *have* to travel separately?"

"Yes, we do," Stirianus said, "and try not to worry for them, drunes and suchlike have little interest in Attuks. It will be far safer for them on their own."

Finn scratched his head and glanced at Tom and Maggie. He saw they looked troubled too. "But drunes killed four Attuks at the Falls of Rhandoror and what about all those that got burned by the fire breathers?"

"They most likely got attacked because the drunes wanted to get at you," Stirianus said, "and, firebreathers never go into deserts, it doesn't suit their style of hunting—am I not right, Goodhook?"

"What Stirianus says is true. Neither bother us, it's you they are after."

Finn put his hands in his pockets and hunched his shoulders up. *It's all my fault.* He felt his cheeks burn and crumpled into a chair and hugged his legs into himself.

Maggie frowned, watching him, then glared at Stirianus, "It was your bloody sister who sent the drunes, wasn't it!"

Stirianus stared back at her but when Maggie held his gaze he lowered his eyes, "I'll call my muckleback." He said, and went out onto his terrace.

Tom went to Goodhook, "Be safe, and . . . and thank you." They shook hands.

"Yes, thank you." Maggie said and went to hug him too. "Thank you both. Right now I feel very humble. It's a terrible price you've had to pay to help us."

Goodhook was about to speak when a noise like a foghorn caused everyone to flinch.

"Relax," Philadini said, "it's only Stirianus calling his muckleback. His munkhorn got cracked years ago and he hasn't crafted another. I think only he could make it sound quite so dreadful though."

Moments later Stirianus returned, "Cincin, my muckleback, will be here soon enough."

"We can't leave just yet," Finn said, "we still haven't looked inside the ring."

Stirianus raised his eyebrows, "What's this you've been keeping from me?" Philadini filled him in. "You should have told me before," Stirianus said, "no matter, it's no reason to delay. Come on, I'll show you what we need to pack."

Everyone looked glum except Philadini and Stirianus. Finn pulled himself out of the chair and got on with it.

A while later, when they were almost ready to go, Stirianus's muckleback was spotted galloping toward them across the desert. She was kicking up quite a dust cloud. The young people saw that she was jet black and as huge as Sulan, Philadini's pure white muckleback. They also saw, when she got somewhat nearer, that she looked enormously powerful. Finally she slowed to a trot then stepped over Stirianus's magic boundary.

"Love's the desert, my Cincin does," Stirianus said, whilst bashing her rock hard flank affectionately, "she came to see me often, all the years I've been drunk. I think she had more faith in me than I did."

"How did she get across your boundary?" Finn asked.

"How very observant of you, my dear boy, that's only for me to know—I can't give all my tricks away now, can I? Otherwise half the creatures in the Atta Desert would be clomping around my lovely lake."

Tom and Grindlebrook went and sat together in the shade of a palm tree, by the side of the small lake, to say their goodbyes.

"He's going to miss her." Maggie said to Finn.

"Maggie—"

"Finn, nothing that has happened is your fault—you didn't want to come here, remember?"

"But—"

"Shush—this is all about the bloody magicians."

Goodhook was hot and wheezy but he braved the sun for a bit. He stuck close to Philadini, helping him load up Sulan's joey pouch, and spoke of Stirianus.

"Do you think we can trust him?"

"As far as any magician can trust another." Philadini said.

"No, then?"

"We have the same agenda so I think he'll do the right thing when it counts."

"That will have to do then. Look out for the young people."

"I will, you watch out for Grindlebrook."

"With my life!"

They embraced then Goodhook got out of the sun.

Stirianus went to discuss his plans with the black eagles and sent some off to the River Rhand to enrol the mucklebacks and others to scout for drunes. Philadini meanwhile, dug out the magic smocks he'd borrowed from Albinonus's Tomb. He called to Tom and Grindlebrook to come to him, gave them one each, then gave the other two to Finn and Maggie. Then he gave each a sword sheathed in tooled leather scabbards. "You'll need the smocks from now on. They will cool you in the day and warm you at night but I must ask you to never draw your swords unless you are told. Understand?" They nodded solemnly. Then Philadini gave a bow and two quivers of arrows to Grindlebrook, "You have always been the finest archer."

"Thank you!" She beamed at Philadini then held them high in the air to show them off to her grandfather.

It was time.

Maggie and Grindlebrook hugged forever. Finally Grindlebrook pushed her away tearfully and helped her climb onto Loopy. Goodhook came outside Stirianus's abode again and tossed a pot of balm up to her, "Your blisters should heal without needing more so it's just in case."

"Thank you. I can't tell you how much I want you to come with us."

"Just you trust the magicians, Maggie Finkley." Grindlebrook said, loud enough for Stirianus and Philadini to hear.

Maggie frowned, "I'll try." She whispered.

The heat got too much for Grindlebrook and she rushed indoors holding hands with her grandfather, "See you at Uderzandu, Tom!" She called from the doorway. Tom waved and gave her a grand smirk.

Then Loopy set off without being prompted but paused at the magic boundary, "It's ok Loopy," Maggie said, "it's only nasty if you try to break in." Still, Loopy waited until Stirianus had crossed it on Cincin and Philadini on Sulan before he tested the ghostly yellow perimeter line with his foot. "Scaredy cat." Maggie said. Loopy waggled his ears and snorted then trotted across it. When nothing happened his ears flopped and he did the muckleback equivalent of a shrug.

Not far beyond the boundary Finn looked back. Stirianus's mushroom shaped home had disappeared, "Where's your house gone?"

"It's still there," Stirianus said, "I can see it."

Finn called to Maggie, "Can you see it?"

She looked back, "No, I can't"

"Nor me." Tom said.

Soon they were over the horizon and the oasis was gone.

Finn's magic smock resembled a long, off white shirt without buttons. It was crumpled but comfortable and was keeping him quite cool. He wished it looked more like the clothes a bedouin would wear. Instantly, it transformed into what he was picturing, "Woah!"

"Wow! How did you do that?" Tom said.

"I just thought it and it happened."

Maggie gawped.

"Think of a colour." Philadini said.

Instantly, her cloak turned the shade of summer clouds. "Oh my, now that *is* fun." She changed it to primrose then red, then switched to stripes then checks then an ochre top and a pleated then a flowing skirt. "Well, I suppose that means I have to allow that magicians do have their uses." Philadini grinned.

Tom and Finn happened to turn their smocks to black at the same moment, *"Woah, check out the dark thoughts, man."* Tom said.

"Let's go denim." Finn said, "One, two, three!"

They amused themselves like that until each settled on their own theme. Finn chose black, Maggie cream pants with pale blue buttons and a flowing silk blouse, Tom chose midnight blue with a single star on his cuffs and a small crescent moon on his chest.

The desert spread away from them, flat in every direction, here and there though, stood massive wind-sculpted rocks. A while later Finn got a whiff of something dead, then smoke from Philadini's pipe wiped it away. Presently, they came upon endless hot gravel and their mucklebacks wheezed and grunted, scrunching through it, feet sinking deep, hour after hour. Their super tough hide protected them, but it was hard going, even for a muckleback. The backs of Finn's hands began to itch and he saw they had turned pink so he tucked them under his cloak. Looking up he got dazzled by the murderous sun so he pulled the hood he'd fashioned down over his forehead. Squinting about he saw mirages ahead and smoke off to his left.

"There's smoke over there."

"Burning valley." Stirianus said in a quiet voice. He didn't need to call out as everyone was bunched quite close. "They're dotted around the whole of the Atta Desert but I doubt we'll need to cross any. The fires are caused by jubas bushes; their leaves are exquisite to taste and also have a beguiling fragrance, but, you can't trust a jubas bush, as the saying goes. They lure the unwary with their hypnotic scent, then as soon as they nibble or pick the leaves the jubas bush explodes and cooks them alive. By nightfall they have all burned out and fresh young jubas shoots devour the prey they have cooked. By morning there is no trace of their macabre feast."

I'm not sure I believe that, Finn thought.

The day turned out to be uneventful. They got beyond the gravel sea and pressed further and further into the desert and camped under the stars.

Next morning Stirianus led off across rock desert. Once they had to ride through a canyon and Finn's nerves got frayed expecting drunes to leap out from behind every boulder or from every crevice, but none showed up. Beyond there the land opened out again, the sun scorched down and his muckleback moved slowly, saving strength by plodding with a fixed rhythm. Soon, the terrain in every direction became blurred, cloaked by mirages so thick it seemed they were caught in one giant seething cauldron. Still, the heat soared.

"I love this," Stirianus said to Philadini, "mirages make me feel so at home. When were you last out here?"

But Philadini didn't answer. He was straining forwards, shielding his eyes with his hand and peering into the mirage up ahead. He halted Sulan and said, "Pass me the telescope would you please, Tom." Philadini then stood on the seat of his albino muckleback and squinted through the eyepiece. Everyone had halted, wondering what he had seen. "Take a look at that mirage," he said, pointing, and tossed the telescope to Stirianus, "there's something moving about in there."

Stirianus focussed on it, "I can't see anything." He looked about and chose Maggie. "Would you mind taking a look for us?"

He passed her the telescope and she stood, slightly unsteady, on top of Loopy's hump. He turned his head to look at her. "Don't move!" The mirage shimmered, vague and ghost-like, so she couldn't be sure whether she had the telescope focussed or not. "It's hard to tell," she said, frowning, "but, I think there might be something within it, I thought I saw several things, like they were sort of swimming about, but then nothing." She played with the focus a bit more. All of a sudden she jerked back.

"*Ughh!*"

"What did you see!" Philadini demanded.

Maggie was shaking and sat down hard onto Loopy's hump. "A—a huge mouth and—and a great big long tail—there's something *horrible* in there."

Everyone had there eyes fixed on her except Stirianus who searched about, "I think I know what that might be. There's a hill poking through the mirage over to our left. If we look from up there the sun will be behind us so we should get a better view."

Maggie held the telescope out to him with a trembling hand, "Please—you look—I don't want to."

Stirianus eased Cincin to Loopy and took it, "Don't fret," he said, "we can keep you safe."

Finn rolled his eyes. *Yeah, sure,* he thought, *as if we ever feel safe—well, maybe Tom does.* He got to thinking about Itako and the trail of 'the lost ones'. *There's so much we don't know yet,* he mused, and then grappled with other possible meanings but came back to the same conclusion—*it has to be our parents.*

They rode to the hill, got off their steeds and climbed it. From the summit, even with the naked eye, everyone got glimpses of some monster thrashing about within the mirage. Stirianus was using the telescope. What he saw made him grip it so tight his hand shook.

"What is it?" Finn said.

"A mangsnake! It's a desert mangsnake and it looks like it's dying—we must try and save it."

Finn did a double take, "Aren't they dangerous?"

"Extremely, and huge, sometimes over fifty feet long, but I recognise him."

"Him?"

"It's definitely Strinku—I raised him from an egg—I could draw his markings in my sleep—we must hurry." He ran to Cincin. *"Come on."* He shouted.

Finn and everyone else rushed to their muckelbacks, got into the high perches and charged after Stirianus. When they got there the mangsnake was huge—well over knee high on the young people at its thickest point, and much thicker again in two places where its skin had been punctured; thereabouts, it was swollen to over waist height. Its wounds were oozing something yellow and sticky and just there its skin had turned blue-black. Elsewhere, from head to tail its body was covered in multi coloured bands and, if it were still, it would have resembled a gigantic stick of rock. Wherever Finn moved, the mangsnake seemed to keep its eyes on him, so he stayed well clear and just gawped. *It's big enough to swallow all of us!* For a while the mangsnake would lie still, then tie itself in knots, then be still once more. Finn got a queasy feeling when Stirianus went right up to it, just as if it was his favourite dog, and stroked its head. Everyone else hung well back. When it became stiller Stirianus went and studied the punctures in its body, and, whilst he did that, Finn walked the length of it with Tom, at what they thought was a safe distance away. Pacing with their feet, Finn counted sixty-one steps, Tom sixty-three. There was an off smell, like bad feet, when they passed its wounds.

"I'm pretty sure Strinku has been bitten by morkuns." Stirianus said. "What potions do you have, Philadini?"

Philadini got out his small collection and Stirianus studied them and grunted. He asked Maggie to search out a bowl from their stores and then he poured a measured amount of water into it. Next he added careful amounts from several of Philadini's phials and mixed everything up with an elegantly whittled stick which he produced from the folds of his cloak. He sniffed at his concoction and shook his head. Going back to Philadini's phials he muttered under his breath.

"What's the matter?" Philadini asked.

"No wungwort."

"Goodhook's balm has got wungwort in it." Philadini said.

Stirianus glared at him, "Where's that Attuk when you need him?"

"But you sent him—"

"Don't remind me!"

Maggie stepped forward. "Is this what you need?" She said, flourishing the tub of balm Goodhook gave her.

Stirianus's eyes flashed wide and he snatched it from her, ripped the lid off and sniffed. She frowned and looked ready to scold him but before she could say a word he jerked his head up and smiled, "Thank you, and pardon my rudeness, but there's not much time." As if in response, Strinku flailed up clouds of dust, rolled, squealed and gasped, then tremors wracked his whole body. Stirianus shivered, even though it was searingly hot. He quickly scraped a big dollop of mustard coloured balm out of the tub and flicked it off his fingers into the bowl. It splashed a little of his concoction out. He stirred the balm into the mixture, slowly at first then more and more vigorously, incanting all the while. "It'll start frothing if it's going to work." Nothing happened. He gazed into it, then at Strinku then back at the puce coloured liquid. "It will have to do."

Finn's ring meanwhile, was driving him nuts, squeezing him incessantly. Then it gave him a vicious squeeze harder than it ever had before. "*Owwwwch!*"

"What's up, mate?" Tom said.

"The bloody ring's trying to chop my finger off!"

"*Give it to me!*" Stirianus yelled.

"Eh?"

Stirianus opened his eyes so wide the whites turned red at the edges and his head shook. "*Don't argue with me, boy.*" He said in a whisper so cold it made it seem like a declaration he was going to slit Finn's throat. Finn yanked the ring off and handed it over. Stirianus kept staring at him but the ring suddenly distracted him by jumping out of his hand into the bowl. Instantly, the concoction frothed up like a popped bottle of champagne. Stirianus grabbed it up but then had to wait because Strinku went into another fit of spasms and thrashing. When he settled once more he remained panting deeply. Stirianus went to him and raised the frothing brew up to his big orange eye, Strinku blinked at it a few times then his diamond shaped pupil enlarged.

"Drink this, old friend." Stirianus said and lowered the bowl to the ground. The mangsnake kept his eyes fixed on the magician whilst he sniffed the brew, his tongue flicking this way and that, testing the air above it before slipping into it. Strinku seemed to like the taste and tucked in with vigour. Stirianus watched him slurping until the magic potion was half gone at which point it stopped bubbling. "There's a magic ring in there, don't swallow it, or, *I might have to kill you.*"

Strinku spluttered and coughed then raised his head and sneezed. He looked half guilty, half murderous and, for a moment, he seemed ready to strike the magician, his neck actually making a couple of jerks in Stirianus's direction. Then he ripped open his huge jaws revealing a pair of curved, footlong, and needle sharp poison teeth. A single drop of green juice dripped from the tip of one tooth but then his mouth closed and creased to a sly smile. The mangsnake burped and the ring fell out of his jaws and plopped into the magic potion. It began frothing again.

"Thought you had." Stirianus said.

Soon Strinku had finished up Stirianus's magic medicine and Finn's ring sparkled at them from the bottom of the bowl. The mangsnake blinked at it and Stirianus stroked his giant scaly head.

Finn stared at the ring. *I might have been off the hook if he hadn't burped it back up.*

"Sleep now," Stirianus said, "give the potion chance to do its work." Strinku lay his head down and closed his eyes. Stirianus retrieved the ring and gave it back to Finn, "Thank you."

Finn was about to say something about Stirianus's attitude but just then Strinku lifted his head once more, yawned, blinked, then opened his eyes wide and took a sweep around, nodding one by one to all present. When he paused on Maggie she began to lose herself in his huge eyes and felt her knees quivering. Finally, in a deep majestic voice the mangsnake spoke, "Thank you—thank you—everyone—a haw, haw, haw—hic!" He wavered there, trying to keep his eyes open for a few moments longer, then they rolled up and his huge head crashed to the ground, bashing up a cloud of dust.

"Is he dead?" Maggie said, looking like she didn't know whether to be sad or relieved.

Stirianus squatted and prised up an eyelid, "No—he's unconscious. Now we wait." All at once he became quite overcome. He wiped his forearm across his eyes then walked off and sat alone with his head lowered and shoulders slumped. Everyone stayed at a respectable distance. The mucklebacks had already dozed off, being unconcerned at the events unfolding, it offering them no opportunity for adventure. At times Strinku would wake and knot up but, as the day wore on, less and less. When he had been still for a long time and was snoring steadily Finn and Tom gathered the pluck to go stroke his scales. Each one was bigger than their hands.

Presently, Stirianus checked on Strinku again. "Well, he's still alive." He said. Finn saw that the magicians' eyes were red once more, but this time from tears. "We might as well make camp," Stirianus continued, "we're not going anywhere until I know he is either safe or dead so lets get ourselves as comfortable as we can."

By evening Strinku was coming around but his head however, remained resting on the ground. Stirianus sat cross legged in front of him as they whispered private words to each other. After a while, Stirianus said in a normal voice, "I want you to meet somebody." Strinku lifted his head unsteadily and perused his entourage. Stirianus gestured Finn should approach. Finn swallowed and glanced at Tom who gave him a smirk and a little push of encouragement. He wobbled a little as he approached the giant mangsnake.

"And who are you, young man?" Strinku said in the deepest, most sonorous and dignified voice that Finn had ever heard. It more than rivalled Goodhook's.

"I'm Finn."

"Ah!—*Finn!* I was the first to hear your name on the wind. Mangsnakes are often told secrets by mysterious means. Your name was spoken to me on a breeze no other could hear and I already know of your task. I must say though, ahem, I expected someone a tad, shall I say—*bigger?*"

Finn shrank a little smaller. Stirianus tapped Strinku on his snout, *"Be polite,* Finn is a Ring Bearer and he allowed me to use the healing power of his ring to save your life."

Finn frowned, *who is he to tell others to be polite?*

"Really?" Strinku said and purred like an enormous cat. "Come a little closer, *Finn.* I wish to better see this ring of yours." Finn sidled up to the mangsnake. Gingerly he held his ring up and Strinku hissed, but in a friendly sort of way, a bit like how a steam train sounds when coming to rest. Then he blinked and spoke. "I thank you for your gift of life." He said and bowed. "Ahem, may I offer you a far lesser gift?" Finn was already lost in the hypnotic gaze of his eyes and merely nodded. Strinku gently lowered his head atop Finn's whose knees shook and he had to fight an almost irrepressible urge to make a dash for it. Maggie held a hand to her mouth and didn't breathe but Tom just grinned. Then Finn felt like his thoughts were being stirred up with a big fat spoon. It went on for a half-minute or so. "You will now be able to converse with any snake for the rest of your life." Strinku declared. "That should be fun for you when you return home."

Finns legs went all wobbly again, "Er, thank you, erm, Strinku—you are the first person—erm creature—I mean snake—oh, I don't know what I mean. Do you think we will ever actually be going home?"

"Of course you will. Why ever not?" He glared at the magicians. "What have these sorcerers been telling you?"

"That Finkley Field is broken." Strinku did the mangsnake equivalent of a frown, Finn pressed on. "I mean the magic's gone—I mean stayed—Krukill's smashed it—oh I think my brain's gone wrong—I can't say what I mean."

"A haw, haw, haw—hic." Strinku sniggered. "You'll be just fine soon. It's only mangsnakey words searching for places to live in your mind. They'll push your thoughts around for a while." Then Strinku narrowed his eyes at Stirianus, "What is Finn trying to tell me?" Stirianus explained. "That *is* poor news." Strinku declared. "What is to be done?" When the magician had no answer Strinku blinked over and over again, then closed his eyes for a long moment. "I don't think I'm fully recovered," he muttered, then said to Finn, "perhaps I should go for a lie down—a haw, haw, haw—hic. It's been such a pleasure to meet you, I wish I could shake your hand. Now, I think I should sleep some more, but, before I do, who are these other people?" Philadini waved to him, "I recognise *you*—you're one of those pesky magician types."

Finn sniggered at Philadini's discomfort, *I'm beginning to like this Strinku*, he thought, "This is Maggie and Tom," he said, "they're my best friends in the whole world—erm, your world—erm, everywhere, I mean, I think."

"Hello." Maggie said, she gave a tentative smile but stayed where she was.

Strinku bowed to her, "Charmed."

Tom came right up to him, "Hi." He said to Strinku with a smirk.

Strinku flicked his tongue out and Tom reached out to shake it but Strinku whipped it back in and winked at Maggie. She flinched. "A haw, haw, haw—hic, well hello Tom—how very brave of you, young sir. I'm most honoured and pleased to meet you."

Greetings complete, Strinku slithered off to a patch of soft sand and curled himself into a lumpy turban shape, leaving only his forked tongue and one eye poking out. He made quite a big turban, way taller than either magician. By sunset he was breathing steadily and had had no more fits of the twists.

Later, whilst the mangsnake slept, Stirianus told the story of how they met, "About a hundred years ago, I was travelling through the desert on a quest to learn more of its mysteries, when one night I was neglectful, camped too close to sinking sands and got swallowed up. Apparently, a mangsnake saw me get pulled under and dragged me out unconscious. I knew none of this and woke up in a den full of the mangsnakes' friends and relatives—a most interesting way to wake up, I can tell you, however, they helped me instead of eating me, and I've been fond of them ever since. Years later, I came across a dead mangsnake. She'd been killed by morkuns and her nest had been violated and all her eggs eaten except one. She must have managed to bury it before she was attacked because just a fraction of it poked out of the sand and the morkuns had overlooked it. I dug the egg up and Cincin carried it in her safe pouch until we got home. Months later it hatched and I named the baby mangsnake, Strinku, then nursed him and taught him until he was robust enough and wise enough to be released back into the desert—one of the family, he is to me. He never truly grew up though, he's still cheeky and disrespectful."

Astute, more like, Finn thought.

They lit a fire and Philadini took first watch. Finn, Maggie and Tom found a sandy spot and settled down for the night. They were quiet for a while. Maggie was first to speak.

"Freedom doesn't come for free." She said.

"Eh?" Finn said.

"I was just thinking, freedom is an illusion. Here we are, out in a beautiful starlit desert with a huge mangsnake and a couple of magicians, all for free. But it costs us our freedom and happiness to do it, maybe our lives. So, I'm thinking, everything costs something, or a lot, so it's never free. There's always a price on everything even if it's not money."

"Have you been on Stirianus's grog, Sis?"

She gave Tom a friendly thump, *"You know what I mean."*

They were quiet again for a while, then Maggie sang the refrain softly, over and over, all the while poking a finger in Tom's ribs, "Freedom don't come for free, freedom don't come for, mmm, freedom . . .mmm" She had a good singing voice and Finn felt warm and fuzzy listening to her, Tom put his fingers in his ears but had a good smirk on. Meanwhile, Strinku slept on with one eye open. Soon, the three inseparables slept too.

Stirianus woke Finn deep in the night for his watch. The second moon was up so he found it was quite light. Strinku remained comatose and turban-like. In between checking the wider desert Finn gazed at Maggie sleeping. At the end of his watch he lay next to her, stroked her hair and kissed her cheek.

She stirred, "I love it when you do that."

"Which?"

"Both."

"We should get some sleep." He said.

"We already are, aren't we, stupid?" She replied dreamily.

Soon Finn drifted off.

He was brought out of his slumber by a fly on his face. Without opening his eyes he tried to shoo it away with his hand but it kept returning. He heard sniggering and opened his eyes.

"*Aaaaaaaaaghh!*" He screamed, and sprang away—Strinku had been tickling his face with his forked tongue.

The mangsnake was grinning the widest grin he'd ever seen, "A haw, haw, haw—hic!"

The whole crew were in fits of laughter.

"Woah—it's not safe being the last one to wake up around here."

"Oh Finn—" Maggie said, "that was just priceless."

Finn frowned then relaxed a bit and gazed at the huge mangsnake, "How are you, Strinku?"

"Ahem. Almost fully recovered, thank you." He showed off his wounds which had stopped oozing yellow puss and had completely knitted together. "It was morkuns!" He said as proud as if he'd killed them.

"Morkuns, eh?" Stirianus said. "Well, come on, tell us your little story, but be quick, you've held up a very important journey."

"Little story? *You* don't know how lucky you are you found me!"

"Oh? And why would that be?"

"That would be because we mangsnakes know all about your *very important journey*—and, I only got my wounds because I was brave enough to explore Uderzandu Prison for you."

That got their attention. Stirianus raised his eyebrows, "You wily old—"

"Who are you calling old? You've got hundreds of years on me, a haw, haw, haw—hic."

"Come on, Strinku," Finn said, "just tell us about it, *pleeease*."

"*You*, are a very important young man. Polite too—I like that." He jerked his head up and hissed at Stirianus. "Not at all like this pesky magician."

"*Strinku!* Have you no gratitude?" Stirianus said.

"Not really—but what I do have are six mangsnake brothers and sisters spying for you inside Uderzandu Prison as I speak."

"What! Have they seen—"

"I was speaking to my friend, Finn." Strinku said. Both Stirianus and Philadini rolled their eyes. Strinku flicked out his tongue at them, "Ahem. Now, Finn, this is what we've seen—besides a couple of morkuns, there are more than a hundred drunes, an odd wortzdag or two, plus maybe fifty or sixty orgils—oh, and three magicians—hunter-magi I believe they are called—I nearly forgot to mention them. A haw, haw, haw—hic."

He had Stirianus's full attention now, "How did you get in?"

"There's an old manghole that leads right inside—look, I'll draw a plan for you." He slithered to a patch of sand and marked out the route that led right to the heart of the prison with his head. Everyone crowded around. He filled in details with his tongue until they had all they needed to know.

"That's very good." Stirianus said. "What's this squiggly patch at the end?"

"That's a maze which, I think, leads to where your friends, 'the cousins', are locked up."

Stirianus raised his head and stared at the snake, "You think?"

"*Yes—I—think!*" Strinku said, holding his head higher than the magician's, which wasn't particularly difficult for a fifty foot mangsnake. He let out a hiss. This time he wasn't smiling.

Stirianus backed up a bit, "I didn't mean to offend you, is the maze hard to crack?"

Strinku hissed again, "Do you forget it was a snake that created the first riddle?"

"Erm—"

"*Magicians!*" Strinku fairly snorted out.

Stirianus clamped his hands on his hips, "Have you forgotten *who* it was who raised you?"

"*That,* is your biggest problem. You are like a father who thinks he is more intelligent than his children—such folly and such arrogance!

Unfortunately, arrogance, unlike wounds, is mostly incurable. Now listen, there's a malevolence in that maze—something truly depraved is lurking in there and I didn't wish to meet it—no, that is not quite accurate—I didn't *dare* to meet it and I," here Strinku paused and raised his head even higher so that he towered above everyone, *"am no coward!"*

Stirianus bowed to him, "You most certainly are not." He said, more respectful now. "Did you get a glimpse of it?"

"Only a shadow, a despicable thing even so, and it throws fire."

"And those three magicians, can you describe them?"

"Ahem, a tall skinny male with dark hair and a long nose, shorter than yours though, a woman with skulls hanging off her belt, and a squat male."

"Dhagan, Mongrix and Whorpus." Philadini said.

Stirianus nodded, "Definitely."

"Satisfied?" Strinku said.

"They're not the magicians we're wanting to spring out of there."

Strinku regarded Finn and sighed, "I hear Ring Bearers have more brains than magicians. Have you noticed that?" Finn grinned and Strinku continued. "They are sooo annoying, can't do riddles, lie constantly, and they're never happy with the help you give them, familiar?" Finn grinned more, Tom smirked and Maggie clamped a hand over her mouth to stifle a laugh. Stirianus paced about with his arms folded muttering something about morkuns messing up twice. "What was that?" Strinku demanded.

Stirianus stopped pacing, fiddled with his cuffs and looked like he was struggling to keep a scowl off his face. Finally, he shrugged, "I suppose you had better come with us." He said.

"Try and stop me—*a haw, haw, haw*—*hic*. I want to get one of those morkuns on my own, I'll show it who the biter is."

"Why were you all the way out here anyway?" The magician asked. "You're a long way from Uderzandu."

"I was, ahem, on my way to your tiny little *pond* to tell you of the words I heard on the wind but, in my good-natured haste to warn you, ahem, I became careless and got tracked. I escaped down an old manghole but not before I got bitten by morkuns for all my valour." He suddenly peered very closely at the magician. "You've stopped drinking, haven't you?"

Stirianus flinched, "Is there no creature in this desert that minds its own business!"

"Don't get all huffy with *me*, it was you who was doing all the drinking, and, you should know that mangsnakes have to know everything. Shall we go now? Having a friendly little chat with you has quite perked me up."

Stirianus glanced at Philadini. Both rolled their eyes again.

Soon they set out and made good progress across more flat, hard terrain. Strinku seemed fast to Finn and was in the lead most of the time, making the pace, but, actually, he was moving relatively slow for a mangsnake. Again the sun was fierce.

In the early afternoon Maggie saw, still some way off, a large green patch that looked like a big untidy lawn, "What's that?" She called out, pointing.

Stirianus held his hand high indicating they should halt.

"I know *exactly* what that is." Philadini said.

"So do I." Stirianus said. "Take a look Strinku, I think we might have a chance of some fun."

The mangsnake raised his head high into the air. "Well, a haw, hic, haw—it looks like it's my turn to be the hunter."

Whilst they waited and watched, Strinku slithered and sashayed, silently gaining ground on the green patch. He paused now and again and raised his head a smidgen to take a peek. Finn shifted in his seat and strained to see. When Strinku got close he put on a spurt, shot right into the green patch and hissed like a hundred witches. Gronks flew every which way screaming their heads off as they fled a slight depression in the ground. Strinku picked out a particular one, darted after him, and snared him in his coils. Both magicians guffawed.

Maggie felt tears welling up, "You have to stop Strinku! Please!" But she just caused them to laugh louder, "Loopy!" Maggie demanded. "Quickly—go save that gronk." But Loopy was doing the muckleback equivalent of laughing too. He turned his head to Maggie and waggled his ears, "Oh—you horrible muckleback!"

Finn frowned and scratched his head, "Somethings wrong, I don't think Strinku would kill him."

When they rode to the gronks Finn saw that it was Houni and Mindal's tribe. Their mucklebacks became surrounded by gaggles of them, all pleading for the life of the gronk. Many had small snakes hanging from their belts.

"That's my Himso that mangsnake has caught!" Mindal shrieked at Stirianus. "You put that him up to that!"

"I don't think he appreciates you hunting his cousins." Stirianus said.

Houni and Mindal were beside themselves, "He's our only son!" Houni exclaimed. "And you know we're petrified of mangsnakes!"

Strinku was running his forked tongue through Himso's hair. Himso grimaced but could do little else as his arms were bound up. His forehead was bubbling with sweat and he was blinking fast. He yelled for his mother.

"Please stop the mangsnake!" Mindal pleaded. "Please Stirianus, don't let it eat Himso."

"But he's hungry—Strinku's my pet and he hasn't eaten for weeks."

"No—please—not our Himso!"

"He's all yours Strinku!" Stirianus shouted.

Mindal clasped her hands to her head, Houni hugged her tight and Maggie watched horrified as Strinku squeezed Himso ever tighter in his coils until his face turned beetroot red. Strinku's big diamond shaped pupils peered right into Himso's bulging eyes and he flicked his tongue over his face. The mass of gronks were appalled, some clasped their hands to the sides of their heads or tugged at their hair, others bunched their fists and yelled at Strinku, still others sobbed and moaned. Then Mindal broke free from Houni and ran to her son.

Strinku couldn't hold it in any longer, "A haw, haw, haw—hic, a haw, haw, haw—hic." He collapsed into a pile of shaking tubes, and a haw, haw, hiccupped over and over.

Mindal had a face like thunder. She dragged Himso a safe distance away then chased Stirianus about, attempting to slap the chortling magician. Houni mopped his brow.

"That was so cruel!" Maggie said. "*Stop laughing, Stirianus!*" She yelled.

"You've got to make your own fun around here, Maggie." Philadini said between hoots.

She opened her mouth to scold him but no words came out. A tear trickled down from her eyes and fell off her nose.

"So, Houni," Stirianus said, once Mindal was out of puff and all the gronks saw the threat to Himso was past, "you'll be after a piece of our adventure?"

Houni had one eye on the magician and the other on Strinku. He wrung his hands and glanced at Mindal who was holding her stomach and breathing deeply.

"There must be something we can do to help." Houni said.

Strinku raised his head high and peered down at him, "You could eat vegetables."

Houni gazed up. The sky was half blotted out by Strinku's jaws whose fangs dripped green droplets.

"I get your point." The gronk said.

"You'll get my bite!"

Stirianus stepped in, "Houni, we might need some bait."

Houni shook his head, then dropped his gaze, he had been almost lost in Strinku's hypnotic eyes, "Bait? What do you mean, bait?"

Finn's ears pricked up.

Stirianus smiled inscrutably, "There's a strange beast guarding a maze that lies deep within Uderzandu Prison and we need some live bait to distract it . . ."

Uh oh, Finn thought as he watched Strinku acquiring an evil smile. He grabbed Tom and Maggie, distancing them from the others so they could talk. "We can't let them make the gronks do that." He said, once they were out of earshot.

Maggie stamped her foot, "That Stirianus is a mean, horrible man —*magician*—and that's worse! He's not even *fit* to be a man. He ought to be made to go into that maze all by himself!"

Tom shrugged, "Well, it keeps on turning out that the magicians always know what they're up to."

Finn glanced from one to the other. Tom is usually right, he thought, "Philadini is watching us." He said. "He's got wicked ears."

"So what?" Maggie said. "I don't care whether he can hear me or not. In fact I'm going to demand those bloody magicians explain properly to Houni." She marched off. Tom stared after her.

"You can't stop her when she gets like that." He said

"Come on," Finn said, "let's go do the right thing."

"You guys . . . " Tom breezed out, whilst shaking his head, but he fell in behind Finn.

"Philadini, what is going on!" Maggie demanded. "Why are you treating the gronks so! Isn't it too dangerous for them to go into that maze alone?"

Philadini pressed his lips together. He seemed to be trying not to laugh, "Maggie, it'll be tricky for whoever goes into that maze. The thing is, you've not seen a pack of gronks on the hunt. Believe me, they are nasty. I'm not sure if even I would—"

"You're being horrible!"

"Listen, you can't see the funny side because you don't know gronks, that's all. Beneath their timid, put on exterior those little people are fiends—vicious, barbaric fiends. And—"

"I don't believe you!"

"*Maggie*—gronks will *kill* just for entertainment, as well as food. The thing is, the only creature that gronks fear in the whole of the Atta Desert is a mangsnake."

Finn shook his head, "But when I saw my first gronk with you it was too scared to even come out of its hole and say hello."

"Ah, but that was a young gronk and on its own, too. They change personality once they're out hunting in a pack."

"Guys," Tom said, "let's just wait and see,"

Maggie glared at him them lowered her gaze, "Okay, but I think I'll go and check what lies Stirianus is telling to Houni."

When she approached, Stirianus waved Houni to be quiet. "Don't you ever feel sorry for a gronk, Maggie." Stirianus said in a strong tone.

"*I am not impressed!*" Maggie declared, her brow was so knotted that her eyebrows were touching.

But this time it was Stirianus who stared her down. "We need to press on." He said, when she finally dropped her gaze.

Maggie looked for help from Houni and Mindal but they just smiled sweetly at her as if gazing at a favourite niece. She gave up and everyone went and sat in the depression where the gronks had been. A small pool of rippling water bubbled up there. Strinku coiled up turban-like, keeping one eye on proceedings and one on Himso who had discreetly removed the snakes hanging from his belt. Once all had refreshed themselves and the mucklebacks had drank their fill too, Strinku unravelled himself again and everyone moved on. The gronks fell behind a little but they could run surprisingly fast in the desert heat and soon caught up at the evening camp. At supper they were mindful not to eat any snake. Afterward Stirianus spoke to them.

"Ok, Houni, Strinku here, my *best* friend in the whole of the Atta desert, will elucidate you on your task."

Houni drew in a breath and stared at Strinku. Mindal lowered her eyes then gave Houni a little nudge, "You wanted to come, dear."

Houni looked grim when Strinku puffed himself out and wore a cheeky smile, "Ok," Houni said, "let's get on with it."

Once the gronks had gathered around Strinku redrew a plan of Uderzandu Prison for them, and, by firelight, graciously went over all the details. When his description of the maze included his fear of whatever lurked there the gronks actually seemed to like their part in it even more and Finn relaxed a bit. Maggie saw Tom's smirk, she closed her eyes briefly, shook her head slowly and exhaled.

"This is going to be the best hunt ever!" Houni exclaimed.

But Mindal didn't look best pleased, "You be careful, Houni gronk, playing the big hero at your age."

But now it was Houni's turn to puff his chest out and he grinned at his clan. When he raised his arms high all his gronks thrust their fists into the air, saluting him. Mindal's shoulders slumped, "Don't you worry," Houni said to her, "that thing in the maze will be no match for a couple of hundred of us gronks."

Stirianus and Strinku grinned at each other.

"Tomorrow," the magician said to Houni, "we will reach the meeting point where Goodhook and Grindlebrook, the Attuks, await us. Let's all get some sleep. Who wants to take first watch?"

At least a hundred gronks put their hands up.

Finn slept straight through and awoke soon after dawn but the gronks had already left, having set off at first light.

"It's Grindly day!" Was the first thing Maggie said to him.

They had breakfast then resumed their journey. As the day wore on the sun became vicious, and, had there been any moisture, the desert would have been steaming. Finn guessed they were close to the rendezvous when desert vultures put in an appearance, all making beelines on the same course, more and more flying by as the day wore on. A line of hills came into view. With Strinku in the lead, they traversed them. Beyond, their route led to a deep and dry valley which

THE BOY WHO FELL THROUGH THE SKY

they descended into by following a zigzag track. The mucklebacks plodded down the steep incline in single file then followed the valley to its head where it was scooped out like a huge amphitheatre. It was glittering, splattered by flock after flock of shimmering desert vultures. Finn needed to squint just to look at them. Unusually, not a single bird uttered a single caw. They dismounted.

"We must be very close to Uderzandu Prison." Finn whispered.

"Why are you whispering?" Maggie said.

"So's no drunes hear me." He said and looked behind to make sure.

Tom laughed, "Drunes?" He said. "Seeing all these vultures, I pity them."

Amongst all the glitter were splashes of green, where the gronks had gravitated into smaller family groups.

Maggie searched around, "Where's Grindly and Goodhook?"

Finn ran his gaze about the amphitheatre. There were lots of caves, "In a cave, maybe?"

Tom shook his head with lips pursed, "One of them would be on watch. They'd come out for sure."

They were distracted when an argument broke out. Stirianus and Houni were at each other. The magician towered over him but the little gronk had his hands on his hips and glared right back. Their words echoed around the amphitheatre.

"Now listen here, Houni gronk," Stirianus said, imitating Mindal's tone of voice, "we might have an abundance of desert vultures but all you gronks are still going down that manghole with Strinku!"

Many gronks left their families to see what the fuss was about. When they all demanded to join in the fight for the prison entrance, Stirianus had to quell a rebellion. Strinku meanwhile, had coiled himself up into his usual turban shape, but, rather than just leaving one eye and his tongue poking out, his whole head was extended forwards. He had a mad grin on his face whilst his head was jerking this way and that like a spectator at a tennis match as he followed the argument.

Just then, Grindlebrook whooped out, "Tom! Maggie! Finn!" She was waving frantically to them from a cave, The trio rushed up a slope to her. "Where have you been?" She squealed. "I've been beside myself with worry—you were supposed to be here ages before us! And where did all the gronks come from? Woah—*is that a mangsnake!*"

235

They all hugged madly.

"You have no idea how much we missed you!" Maggie exclaimed. "How was your journey? Did you get lost? Did you meet any drunes or other nasties?"

Tom just stood there grinning with his hands in his pockets. He's trying to look cool, Finn thought, but it's not working.

Yawning, Goodhook stumbled out of the dark. He was bleary eyed and ran his big hands through his uncontrollable white hair. "Don't you know it's rude to wake an Attuk up?" He said, grinning. "We've been expecting to hear a munkhorn calling us to come and rescue you." He became aware of the great gaggle of gronks and Stirianus and Houni's bickering. "Ah, now I see why you got delayed—hello—there's a mangsnake down there!"

"It's Strinku." Finn said. "He's Stirianus's friend."

"He was dying!" Maggie said. "Finn helped to save his life with the ring."

"So you're getting the hang of it?" Goodhook said.

"Not really," Finn said, "it seems to know what to do all by itself."

"Well, in my experience that means it knows what *you* want it to do."

"Really?" Finn gawped at his ring. "It's so—erm clever and—"

"Have you got the telescope?" Grindlebrook said. Tom nodded. "Great, there's a lookout point up there beyond the desert vultures. You can see Uderzandu Prison from there! I've been dying to see it properly with the telescope." She pointed up to the head of the amphitheatre and grabbed Tom's hand. "If we keep to the shade I'll be safe." She almost dragged him out of the cave, then they dashed for the shady side of the valley.

"Come on." Finn said and grabbed Maggie's hand.

"Wait!" Goodhook called. "Take the chameleon cloaks."

Maggie clutched them under one arm and reached up with her other. Goodhook bent down so that she could plonk a kiss on his cheek, "I can't tell you how pleased I am to see you!" She said, then shot off with Finn.

"Keep your heads down!" Goodhook shouted after them.

Many gronks saw Maggie and Finn pelting up the hill at the head of the amphitheatre, chasing Grindlebrook and Tom through flock after flock of glittering desert vultures. The gronks quickly guessed what they were up to and hoards of them sprinted after them.

"*GRONKS!* Stirianus virtually screamed at them. *Get! — Back! — Here! All of you! You unruly bunches of pestering, feral, midgets!*"

Finn and Maggie broke out into raucous laughter and stumbled. They pulled themselves into sitting positions and, gazing back over the amphitheatre, guffawed at the sight of Stirianus flailing his arms about and the gronks shaking their fists at him. In that moment, they finally got the irritating irrepressibility that constantly burst out of the gronks and they forgave the magicians and Strinku. Finn turned to Maggie.

"I get it." He said.

"So do I."

They sat there for a while, lost in their mirth and drinking in the myriad of events unfolding around them. Eventually, Finn made a move to get up and join Tom and Grindlebrook at the vantage point.

"Wait a second." Maggie said. She reached out and ran her fingers through his hair. Finn's heart thumped as he held her gaze. Then Maggie pulled their heads closer together and now her breath caressed his face. Everyone in the whole amphitheatre was watching them as she gently brushed her lips across his and lay her head cheek to cheek with him, her breath now blowing in his ear.

"Oh to be alone with you in England." She whispered so quietly that he wondered if he had imagined it.

To be continued in Book Two.

Afterword

A letter to you written by the author from deep within the misty and mysterious estuarine marshes, Essex, England, 31st January 2018, the night of the 'Super Blue Blood Moon'.

Dear Reader,

Oh, I do hope you have enjoyed this, my first attempt at writing a story. It certainly was a thrilling experience for me throughout the composing of it because I had absolutely no idea where it was leading. I simply kept on writing with trust and blind faith that it was taking me on a worthwhile journey; a journey that I've loved every minute of.

The sequel is now finished and currently going through rigorous editing. It will be available later this year.

If you feel moved to, I invite you, dear reader, to leave a fair review on Amazon. Many thanks.

Yours,

Peter North

About the Author

This is Peter's first book. He has no previous writing history. Currently, he works full time in an Adult Acute NHS Mental Hospital, as a Senior Health Care Assistant.
Essex
February 2018

Proof

Made in the USA
Columbia, SC
12 February 2018